MW00623978

ABOUT LAST NIGHT

AIMEE NICOLE WALKER

About Last Night
Copyright © 2022 Aimee Nicole Walker

aimeenicolewalker@blogspot.com

This is a work of fiction. Names, characters, places, and incidents either are the product of the author's imagination or are used fictitiously, and any resemblance to the actual person, living or dead, business establishments, events, or locales is entirely coincidental.

Cover photo © Wander Aguiar, www.wanderaguiar.com

Cover design © Jay Aheer, www.simplydefinedart.com

Interior design and formatting provided by Stacey Ryan Blake of Champagne Book Design, www.champagnebookdesign.com

Editing provided by Susie Selva, www.susieselva.com

Proofreading provided by Lori Parks, lp.nerdproblems@gmail.com

All rights reserved. This book is licensed to the original publisher only.

This book is intended for adult readers only.

Copyright and Trademark Acknowledgments

The author acknowledges the copyrights and trademarked status and trademark owners of the trademarks and copyrights mentioned in this work of fiction.

ABOUT LAST
NIGHT

CHAPTER ONE

Julian

I didn't arrive in Savannah on a wing and a prayer. It was more like a Prius and a song. I had my windows down, my radio cranked up, and Kelly Clarkson and I belted out "Since U Been Gone." Queen Kelly was perfectly on pitch, of course, while I sounded more like a cat in heat as I rolled to a stop at an intersection. The latter didn't matter because the song resonated deeply with me. I knew all too well what it felt like to rediscover yourself after a breakup, so whatever I lacked in musical talent, I more than made up for with feeling.

A cute brunette in cut-off shorts and a pale pink tank top clapped her hands. "Yeah, baby! Sing it!" she yelled. And I knew my decision to move to Savannah had definitely been the right call. It wasn't like I'd thrown a dart at a map and moved to wherever it landed. I'd spent my summers as a kid in Savannah at my great-aunt Tallulah's house. Lulu had taught me the most important life lessons, and though she'd sold her house years ago to move in with my parents in Atlanta, Savannah still felt like the perfect haven for my bruised heart and battered reputation. The grand dame of the South didn't just tolerate eclectic people; she drew us in and cradled us against her bosom, whispering, "You're safe here."

The gorgeous brunette danced around and sang the following lines with me until the driver behind me honked their horn in annoyance. I blew the pretty lady a kiss, which she caught and held to her chest as I drove away. The impromptu duet put a smile on my face, which lingered until I took an unplanned detour down Seiler Avenue. Lulu's white craftsman bungalow looked the same yet different. The current owner hadn't made many changes, but it looked like an entirely different house. No wind chimes hung from the porch nor birdfeeders from the trees. The flowerbeds were overgrown with weeds, and the grass was a good three weeks past due for a mow. The little house had always felt alive to me, buzzing with vitality, but it now seemed hollowed out and stunted.

Tears flooded my eyes when I drove past Lulu's house, which was probably why I didn't see the stop sign at the next intersection. However, I didn't miss the flashing lights in my rearview mirror or the cop with thighs as thick as tree trunks sauntering up to my car once I pulled over. I just knew the view would be as good going as it was coming until the officer stopped at my window, putting his crotch at eye level. Oh yeah, that view would be hard to beat. Lord almighty, it was a crime to frame something that fine in polyester pants. Then the cop leaned down and peered into my vehicle, and I forgot to breathe. He had hair the color of a tawny lion and golden amber eyes rimmed with ridiculously long eyelashes. I expected someone as beautiful and built as him to radiate cockiness, but there was something different about this guy, though I couldn't put a finger on it. Of course, I would've happily put all ten digits on him if he'd let me.

"You ran the stop sign back there," the officer said. He narrowed his eyes and studied my face. "Are you okay?"

"Okay?" I asked, then became aware of my wet face. I quickly wiped away the tears. "Yeah, I'm fine."

The officer leaned over to look into my back seat before meeting my gaze. "Did you get into an argument with someone?"

"Nah, I dumped his dumb ass a few months ago."

I didn't see a flicker of reaction in his golden gaze, but his mouth curved into a wry smile. "Ouch," he said. "Pretty sure more than a few of my girlfriends have said the same about me."

I clasped my imaginary pearls. "Say it ain't so."

The officer chuckled and crossed his heart. "What upset you so much that you ran the stop sign?"

"Oh, I just drove by my aunt's old place and was sad to see the new owners don't love it as much as she did. It's no excuse, and I'm sorry."

Officer Hottie nodded and said, "I'll need to see your license, registration, and proof of insurance."

"You don't want to frisk me for weapons?" One of these days, my mouth would get me into a lot of trouble.

The cop blinked a few times, and then a slow smile spread across his face until twin dimples peeked out from his cheeks. "Pretty sure you've shown me your weapons already."

I knew he was talking about my sharp tongue and quick wit, but I couldn't let him off the hook. "Oh, darling," I cooed, "there'd be no doubt if I had."

A series of beeps emitted from the radio hooked to his vest, followed by a tinny voice calling out codes and unit numbers. The sexy officer stood up straight and turned toward his patrol car. I glanced up in the rearview mirror and saw his partner, a super sexy Hispanic man, signaling for my new fantasy boyfriend to hurry up.

"You're in luck," the tawny cop said, startling me.

I clutched my nonexistent pearls again and said, "You sure move quickly and quietly for such a big guy," I said.

"Like a lion," he replied with a wink. "You won't see me coming until I'm on you."

"Promises, promises."

Another flash of those dimples. "I have to answer another call, so I'm letting you off with a verbal warning."

"Oh, good," I purred. "Oral is my favorite."

He shook his head and straightened to his full height, putting me at eye level with his big dick again. "Drive safely," he called out as he retreated to his cruiser.

I shamefully stared at his ass in the side mirror and wiggled my fingers at them as they drove by with their lights flashing and sirens blaring a few seconds later. I released a sigh, relegated the handsome man to my fantasies, and drove to the store to grab a few staples before heading to my new apartment. My belongings wouldn't arrive until the following day, so I'd brought a sleeping bag and a pillow to tide me over. All I needed to survive was something quick to eat for dinner and breakfast.

Afterward, I tucked my sleeping bag and pillow under one arm and carried the meager groceries I'd purchased in the other. I'd feel more motivated to fill the cabinets and refrigerator once I had my familiar things around me, but this would do for a night. I shifted a few things in my hand to open the lobby door.

"Wait!" a lady called out. "I got you."

I turned and stared in disbelief as my pretty brunette duet partner walked up with a broad smile on her face. I felt an inexplicable draw to the woman as if she were the missing puzzle piece I'd been searching for. She eased the groceries out of my hand and opened the door for us.

"Where have you been all my life?" I asked.

She looped her arm around my shoulders and leaned her head against mine. "Right here, waiting for you."

I didn't spend my first night back in Savannah on my apartment floor; I spent it getting to know the greatest gift I'd ever received—Harper Frances Carnegie. We cuddled on her couch and ordered takeout, then talked and laughed until the sun rose. She helped me set up my apartment, which happened to be directly across the hall from hers, and took me home for Sunday family dinner. I'd been hesitant to intrude, but she simply said, "Nonsense. You're my family now."

I was still nervous when we pulled up in front of the two-story home, but Harper hooked her arm through mine and led me into her parents' house. I met her two older sisters, Emma and Shelby, first. They were every bit as gorgeous as Harper, and I wasn't surprised to learn they were also former beauty queens. Their parents, Denver and Audrey, were warm, welcoming, and eager to learn more about me.

"Is Topher going to make it tonight?" Harper asked.

"He said he would, but police officers don't exactly keep office hours," Audrey replied. "He's hoping to make detective soon, so he's volunteering for overtime and extra duties." She set down a charcuterie board on the table. It was overflowing with deli meats, cheeses, veggies, fruits, and other yummies to nosh on before dinner. The sisters all reached for the board, but Audrey cleared her throat. "Guests first."

"He's no guest," Harper replied. "He's family."

Denver chuckled and said, "Well, let's dig in."

The mention of a police officer momentarily derailed my thoughts. I pictured tawny good looks, thick thighs, a tight ass, and a big dick stuffed into snug, unyielding fabric. I blinked and brought the room into focus just as the patio door opened and closed behind me. I blinked again because the Carnegie girls and their dad had already cleared half the board. How long had I been daydreaming about the cop?

I helped myself to some crisp veggies and cheese while the Carnegies launched into a spirited debate over the song lineup for an upcoming show. Harper had told me about their band and described how they performed at local festivals and events. Every Carnegie played an instrument and provided their vocal talents, though Denver and Shelby were the ones who usually sang lead. It was plain to see how much this family loved one another because each of them suggested a song that would highlight someone else's talents. Shelby wanted a song where Emma could have a violin solo. Harper suggested one that would let Christopher's drumming skills shine. Emma wanted a song to showcase Harper on bass guitar. Audrey wanted to do an acoustic version of one of their favorites so Denver's vocal would be the main focal point. And Denver suggested "Landslide" by Fleetwood Mac because it was the song Audrey had sung when they first met.

I was so completely charmed by them, that I didn't hear the sliding glass door open behind me until a familiar voice said, "Hey, Mama. Sorry I'm late."

I turned in my chair and smiled up at the tawny lion cop, who somehow looked even sexier in a simple T-shirt and a pair of jeans than in his uniform. "Hello again." They called him Topher, which I learned was short for Christopher.

"Hello again?" Harper asked. "You two know each other?"

"This ought to be good," Shelby said before *crunch*ing into a carrot.

Christopher took the empty seat next to me and grinned. "Do you want to do the honors or should I?" he asked.

I recounted the tale of our encounter with a few embellishments here and there because the Carnegies were hanging on to my every word. "Christopher let me off with a warning after I ran a stop sign, and I asked him to marry me. I'm still awaiting his response."

Christopher turned his head and met my gaze. "And I told him it was rude to propose without at least buying me a steak dinner first."

I fell so freaking hard for him right then. Forgetting my manners, I plopped my elbow on the table and dropped my chin onto my palm. I peeked at him through my lashes and said, "We can go now."

"I'm sure Hillary might have a thing or two to say about the steak dinner and marriage proposal," Emma said. Of course Christopher had a girlfriend. Dammit.

Harper mumbled something under her breath, but I couldn't tear my eyes away from Christopher. Surprisingly, he held my gaze until Emma knocked into him while reaching for something on the board.

Christopher turned toward his sister and said, "Take it easy there, killer."

"She's started a new diet," Harper said.

"Ahhhh," everyone but me said.

"Where is Hillary?" Audrey asked. "I thought she was joining us."

Christopher shook his head as he snagged a red grape off the board in front of him.

"She's not joining us tonight?" his father asked. "Or ever again?"

A wry smile tugged at the corner of Christopher's mouth. I had no idea what it meant, but his family sure did. They immediately launched into a conversation about why the relationship went south. One of them would say Christopher was trying too hard to settle down, another would claim he wasn't trying hard enough, but Audrey would always smile indulgently and say, "You just haven't met the right person yet. Everything will click into place when you do."

Fast forward three years, and the dynamic was the same. Harper remained the greatest gift I'd ever received, the Carnegies continued to treat me as family, and I passionately loved my adoptive city. My unrequited crush on Christopher persisted, and his family continued the same postmortem discussion after each ensuing breakup. When Audrey would say, "You just haven't met the right person yet," my soul would cry out, "Yes, you have! It's me! I'm right here!"

Wise gay men in love with obviously straight men would keep their mouths shut but not me. I wasn't brave enough to announce I was the one Christopher was looking for, but I eventually added my two cents to their postmortem discussions with, "Or maybe you're just not playing for the right team."

Christopher's reaction to my suggestion varied weekly, monthly, and yearly. Mostly, he'd snortle. Sometimes he'd shake his head.

The last dissection of Christopher's love life occurred a few months back. Abigail had lasted the longest, and they'd even moved in together, so his family was especially perplexed when their relationship fizzled. But me? I was thrilled. Not only had that been a close call, but Christopher moved in with Harper temporarily until he found his own place. He was in my orbit more often since they lived across the hall, and I spent more time in Harper's apartment than I did in my own. Christopher had joined us for takeout and movie or reality television nights on the couch, although he bitched about our chosen content until Harper let him pick what we watched on Sunday evenings. He preferred movies with action and chaos, but I sat there and soaked up every second of just being with him. I was a lovesick fool with no hope of fulfilling my heart's biggest desire. I was a bonified, or boneheaded, glutton for punishment.

"So, Toph," Shelby said, "how was your blind date last night?"

My heart fell. Christopher hadn't mentioned a date to me, but he wouldn't. He was as kind as he was beautiful. Dread built inside me like a noxious gas as I waited for his response. Was this the lady who'd steal my man for good?

Beside me, Christopher set his fork down and sighed heavily. I recognized his reaction, and relief flooded through me like a giant antacid tablet. The date had not gone well. His family recognized the signs too and immediately ran through their Goldilocks routine without Christopher uttering a single word. Too little. Too much. Not the right person. I, of course, chimed in with my suggestion that Christopher just wasn't playing for the right team. I got a little bolder this time and rested my hand on his shoulder and batted my eyelashes at him.

Christopher didn't snortle or shake his head. He set his fork down, looked me straight in the eyes, and said, "Maybe." Oh, how that one word packed a wallop.

He looked at me expectantly, as if he anticipated a comeback, but I'd frozen. I was too afraid to hope the glimmer in his golden gaze meant something more profound, and I didn't want to blow my chance with a flippant response. I quickly regained a handle on my riotous emotions. Christopher wasn't into me or any guy. He was just giving me a dose of my own medicine, and I deserved it.

But what if? I still couldn't speak, but luckily, Audrey came to the rescue by changing the subject. I tuned in to hear about Shelby's pregnancy, Emma's promotion, and Harper's nerves over emceeing her first charity event since hanging up her tiara and sash for good. I knew she didn't want to do it, but the proceeds benefited children's cancer research, so I offered to design a custom dress for the occasion.

"Are you excited to teach your first college course, Julian?" Denver asked. "Environmental ethics in fashion design, right?"

Oh shit. It was my turn to speak. My brain was still stuck on Christopher's answer, so I took a quick sip of water before smiling at Denver. "Yes, sir, but excited might be a stretch," I replied. When imagining my future, instructing at an art college had never been on my bucket list.

Christopher nudged me. "You'll do great. I bet you become everyone's favorite instructor in no time."

Warmth spread through my chest and up my neck. Christopher searched my eyes, then dropped his gaze as if captivated by the blush his compliment incited. He shifted his attention upward, lingering on my mouth for several moments. *What was happening?* "Thank you," I managed to say, breaking the spell. Christopher met my gaze again, and I found it hard to breathe. "So, are you ready for your *CrimeStoppers* interview on Channel Eleven?" I asked.

He shook his head. "No, but I hope it brings in new tips. Solving all cases is important, but this one hit me here." He *thumped* his fist against his chest. "I do have something exciting to share. I found an adorable house to rent." Everyone erupted into congratulations, no one louder than Harper. Three months of cohabitation with Christopher probably felt like an eternity to her, but my heart was breaking in two.

"When do you move out?" Emma asked.

"The house is going through some remodeling, so probably not until the first of October."

Six weeks. That was all I had left with Christopher. Once he moved out, I'd only see him at Sunday dinner, holidays, or when the Carnegies' family band performed at local functions. No more midweek movies, game nights, or shared dinners. There'd be a giant, Christopher-sized hole in my life that no one else could fill.

The conversation continued around me, but I checked out until Audrey offered dessert. I'd lost my appetite and politely declined. Harper and Christopher did too, so Audrey packed an entire pie in the leftovers she sent home with us. We'd ridden together in Christopher's truck, and I sat in contemplative silence during the trip back to our complex and the elevator ride up to our apartments.

"At least we'll have delicious dessert for *Jaws*," Harper said.

My nerves were as tangled as a ball of Christmas lights, and the idea of sitting close to Christopher on a couch for a few hours was more than I could handle. "All the talk about my first class made me want to review my lecture notes again. I think I'll take a rain check on the movie and pie."

Harper searched my eyes for several seconds before kissing my cheek. "Try not to overthink it."

"Me? No way," I teased.

Harper unlocked the door and stepped inside, but Christopher remained in the hallway. Our eyes met and held. My skin tingled as something shifted and sparked between us. Christopher's eyes burned with intensity and something else. Curiosity, perhaps?

"See you later," Christopher finally said.

And because I desperately needed to regain the upper hand in our dynamic, I plastered my flirtiest smile on my face and said, "Yes, in my dreams."

I felt his scrutiny as I turned and stuck my key into the lock. I glanced over my shoulder and caught him staring at my ass. Sensing he was busted, Christopher jerked his gaze upward. I winked, and he smiled until his dimples emerged. I entered my apartment, closed the door, and leaned against it.

What was happening?

CHAPTER TWO

Topher

MY BRAIN WAS SCRAMBLED, AND MY SKIN FELT LIKE IT NO LONGER fit when I stepped inside Harper's apartment. I hadn't experienced the sensation since the summer I'd gone camping with my cousins and skipped sunblock because it wasn't cool. Julian's adoration typically had a soothing effect, but our most recent interaction left me feeling scorched. Something inside me recognized that getting tangled up with Julian would be worth any discomfort.

Harper stood inside the door with her arms crossed over her chest, and the scowl on her face warned me of imminent danger. "What the hell?" she growled.

My brain still wasn't functioning at full capacity. I'd recognized the peril but wasn't cognizant of how to navigate around it. "Huh?" I asked.

She took two steps forward and stared at me with burning dark eyes. "Don't play coy with me and sure as hell don't play games with Julian's feelings."

The accusation was like a cold shower for my sluggish brain, and I was suddenly firing on all cylinders again. "I would never."

Harper took a deep breath and calmed down a little. "You flirted with Julian over dinner."

"I didn't flirt." Her scowl deepened again. "I mean, I wasn't trying to flirt." It just happened naturally, and it felt right. "I was just bantering with Julian. You know I wouldn't hurt him."

She sighed and uncrossed her arms. "Maybe not on purpose, but accidents hurt just as bad."

I'd seen firsthand the damage accidents could cause, and I wouldn't want Julian to be a casualty of my curiosity. The new attraction sparking in my soul was more than curiosity, though. But since I didn't understand when or how I'd arrived at this point, I struggled to put my feelings into words. If I couldn't talk about the attraction, I had no business acting on it. Especially not with someone as wonderful as Julian.

"I'm not going to do or say anything to hurt him." No matter what it took, I would keep my promise.

Harper held my gaze for a few minutes before asking if I wanted pie. I'd forgotten I had carried in the bag of leftovers and dessert.

"Nah. You and Julian seem to be able to eat anything without repercussions, but I've gained at least ten pounds since I moved in with you. My six-pack is down to two, and my pants are getting tight."

"Still want to watch a movie?" Harper asked.

It wouldn't feel right without Julian, but I didn't dare say that to her. "I'm bushed after helping Diego and Levi move into their new house." The mental gymnastics had been more taxing than the actual heavy lifting. I was happy for my friend and his new husband but also conflicted about why I couldn't land a healthy relationship like theirs. "I think I'll just take a shower and hit the sack," I told Harper.

She didn't bother hiding her glee. "Woohoo! I get the television to myself."

I snickered and said goodnight before heading to my bedroom. Instead of grabbing a pair of shorts to change into after I showered,

I flopped down onto the bed and stared at the ceiling. Ignoring my growing feelings for Julian wasn't getting me anywhere, but I hadn't figured out how to safely explore this new side of me beyond watching porn and jerking off. I got up and ensured I'd locked the door, changed into a comfortable pair of shorts, and grabbed my earbuds and laptop. When I pulled up my browser, a frozen image of Julian appeared on the screen from where I'd paused his latest YouTube episode. He sat on a stool with his back to the camera, wearing nothing but a pair of leather pants. I hit Play, and the steady sound of the sewing machine needle working up and down filtered through the earbuds. I stared at his perfectly sculpted shoulders and arms as he fed the fabric through the machine. He was demonstrating how to make his latest corset creation while all I could think about was the amount of time he must've spent at the gym. Julian's toned back tapered to a lean waist, accentuating how perfectly round and tight his ass was.

The camera angle changed so viewers could see exactly what was happening as he pieced two fabric sections together. Julian's fingers were long and nimble like a pianist's, and he made sewing look graceful and seductive. I tried not to read all the thirsty comments people made but often failed. Sometimes I was outraged by his subscribers' audacity, but other times, I learned valuable lessons, such as the term power bottom when two subscribers got into a debate about what Julian would be like in bed. I'd looked up the definition and had gotten so turned on that I immediately searched for porn to get a visual of the dynamic. I could see Julian as the sexual aggressor while bottoming whether he was beneath his lover or, like in the porn clip, had his partner pinned to the bed while he rode him like a bronco.

After I watched the scene and understood the dynamic better, I realized what was missing in my past sexual encounters. People saw a man my size and expected me to be the dominant, in-charge partner. But what I wanted was someone who'd take complete control in bed. Julian had never responded to the comments on his video, so I didn't know if he was a power bottom or not, but I couldn't stop imagining him in that role.

I closed my eyes and pictured Julian lying beneath me in bed, guiding my dick into his ass. He'd whisper encouraging words while kissing my neck or lips. I slid my right hand beneath my waistband and gripped my dick. Julian seemed fascinated by my size. When he and Harper had discussed their health and fitness goals recently, Julian had responded, "Having Christopher on top of me would be my ideal weight." He'd waggled his eyebrows, Harper had gagged, and I'd just shaken my head. But now, I couldn't stop thinking about it. I stroked my dick while imagining Julian's kickass body moving against mine, yielding to me while he instructed me how best to please him.

"Nice and slow," Julian said on the video. "That's it. There's no need to rush. Everyone is in a hurry to reach the end, but building anticipation makes for a more satisfying finish."

His voice in my ear just made me hornier, so I listened to him, pretending he was in the room with me. He'd somehow made sewing sound erotic, and it didn't take me long to come, even though I'd tried to take it nice and slow. I lay there panting with my softening dick still in my hand and spunk splattered all over my chest.

"Would you look at that?" Julian said in my ear. I kept my eyes closed and pretended he was talking about me. "Absolutely beautiful."

The combination of my orgasm and the steady whir of his sewing machine made me sleepy. I should've gotten up and taken a shower, but I used my discarded shirt to clean up instead. I closed my eyes and vowed to get up in a few more minutes, but the next thing I knew, I jerked awake to the sound of Julian's voice the following morning. I looked around my room in confusion until my gaze landed on my laptop. His videos had continued to play while I slept. I checked the time and saw that I had to be up in an hour, so I put on my workout clothes and headed to the gym on the first floor.

I spied Julian jogging shirtless on the treadmill and would've turned right around if he hadn't seen me in the mirrored wall in front of him. My gaze drifted down his back to land on his taut ass. Those had to be the shortest and tightest shorts I'd ever seen on a man. Julian's pace slowed to a brisk walk, and I glanced back up and met his gaze in the mirror again. He crooked his finger at me, and I headed over to him. Julian slowed his pace again to cool down when I stopped by his treadmill.

"Are we okay?" Julian asked.

"What?"

"You and I?" he said, gesturing back and forth between us. "Are we okay?"

I scrunched up my face. "Why wouldn't we be?"

Julian stopped the treadmill and turned to face me. Rivulets of sweat ran down his perfectly toned chest and ripped abdomen. Julian was completely smooth where I was hairy. I trimmed my chest hair and often shaved my stomach because my girlfriends had preferred it that way, but maybe I should consider buzzing it all off. Julian didn't show the front of his chest on his videos much. He saved that for the moments when he put on his creations. And lord, he looked sexier putting clothes on than most people looked taking them off.

"You were about to bolt," Julian said, jerking my gaze back to his face. He had the prettiest green eyes I'd ever seen—a hunter-green rim with pale green irises and yellow striations around his pupils. His dark, curly hair was wet from sweating and plastered to his forehead. I knew if I brushed the locks away, there'd be a frown line to match the down-turn of his full lips.

"Was not," I replied childishly.

"Were too." He took a deep breath. "There's this new...*tension* between us. It's never been there before, so I can't help wondering if I said too much or took my flirting too far."

"No."

"Then what's wrong?" Julian pressed.

Wrong wasn't the right word, but my thoughts and feelings were jumbled, leaving me tongue-tied. I wanted to tell Julian he was beautiful and that I thought about touching him a lot. I yearned to confess my fascination with his skin and the desire to know if it felt as soft as it looked. And would his mouth be as wicked as he promised? What would Julian say if I told him the fantasy version of him makes me come harder than any actual encounter I've had?

I wouldn't say or do any of those things, though, because, even without the promise I'd made to Harper, I'd never do or say anything to hurt Julian. But I did step a little closer and inhale a little deeper, breathing in the scent of his sweat and soap. "I guess I'm just figuring some things out."

"Oh," Julian said breathlessly. That spark of awareness arced between us again. "Let me know if I can help in any way."

"You'll be the first to know," I said with a wink, then left him staring after me with his lips parted and cheeks flushed.

I moved over to the rack of free weights and began moving through my routine to get a full-body workout with as little fuss as possible. I'd spent a ridiculous number of hours in a weight room while playing football in high school and college. Now I focused on maintenance workouts instead of trying to get bigger or stronger. Julian was nowhere in sight after I finished and headed upstairs to shower and get dressed for work.

I ate a massive slice of peach pie—breakfast of champions—and enjoyed a cup of coffee before heading to the precinct. I'd just pulled into my usual spot when I saw a tall blond guy striding toward the entrance. Coy fucking Beaufort, my nemesis for as long as I could remember. We'd always competed for the same football and baseball positions and even girlfriends. Every avenue I pursued, he followed with the intent to do it better. I broke away from Coy in college when he signed to play for Alabama instead of becoming a Georgia Bulldog like me. My luck ended when I entered the police academy after obtaining my bachelor's degree in criminal justice because his dumb ass reappeared again. I made detective first and was promoted to the Major Crimes Unit a full year before he landed there. I'd only had to work with Coy for a few months before transferring to the Cold Case Unit. Thank goodness there were no open positions in CCU, or I had no doubt he'd be clamoring to drive me nuts there too.

I waited five minutes after Coy disappeared inside before exiting my truck. Even though I'd eaten an enormous slice of pie, I took out my emotions on two donuts that my sergeant, Sawyer Key, had brought in for our meeting.

Sawyer quirked a brow as he sipped coffee from his "Hot for Teacher" mug. The teacher in question was his husband, Royce Locke, who oversaw the department's Explorer program for high school students seeking a future in law enforcement. I had mad respect for the two men and had recently stayed at their house to take care of their cat while they honeymooned. Royce was the only person I'd talked to about my shifting feelings for Julian because he'd come out as bisexual in his midthirties. I'd asked how he knew it was right to act on his attraction to Sawyer, and he'd told me it had felt like he'd been struck by lightning when they met. My fondness for Julian had been instantaneous, but my sexual attraction to him had developed slowly over time. Unlike Royce, I couldn't name the moment I realized I wanted something more from the existing relationship I shared with Julian. Had he been anyone else, I probably would've acted on my feelings without hesitation. I was afraid of hurting someone my family loved so much but also terrified of ignoring the way he made me feel. Royce had listened without judgment and encouraged me to be open and honest with Julian, but so far, I hadn't taken his advice.

"Everything okay, Toph?" Sawyer asked. "Or are you just really angry at that glazed donut?"

I forced myself to chew slower and settle down. "Just stressing about my *CrimeStoppers* interview this morning." That wasn't a complete lie.

"I have a feeling the camera and viewers are going to love you," he replied.

Holly Locke, Sawyer's sister-in-law, patted me on the back. "I suspect you'll have quite a fan club after the segment airs."

"God, I hope not." I groaned and looked longingly at the pastry box before deciding against it.

"Sworn off dating, huh?" Holly teased.

"Something like that."

"All right," Sawyer said, "let's call this meeting to order."

Our Cold Case Unit, while newly established, had solved an impressive number of cases, including a high-profile serial killer investigation. Lately, the win streak had cooled off a little, and each of us was eager to add a few more wins to our columns, hence trying new methods such as pleading our case directly to the viewing audience. We achieved this by working with a local true crime podcast called

Sinister in Savannah and with Channel Eleven's crime reporter, Jude Arrow, who was also married to a *Sinister* podcaster.

We kicked off our meetings by recapping our current investigations. Holly was working on an old art theft case that had gotten hot again when a stolen piece had shown up in a recent auction. I was going to plead with the public to help me solve Yolanda Purky's murder because without new tips, it wouldn't get solved. I was also working on unsolved forgery and counterfeit cases I thought might be connected. Sawyer was working on a double homicide from the late seventies. The victims were two carnival workers attached to a traveling circus that had passed through Savannah.

After our meeting ended, I headed to Channel Eleven to film my segment. Jude was a pleasant guy who put me at ease. I'd worked with his husband numerous times on the podcast, so it felt like two friends chatting about an unsolved case.

"Forgive me for saying this," Jude said, "but this investigation feels like it might be a little personal to you. Is it?"

"The truth is, I shouldn't have allowed it to become personal, but it is. Mrs. Purky was the kind of person we all should strive to be. She was generous of spirit, good to her core, and never turned away anyone who needed her. Mrs. Purky was a retired music teacher who continued instructing children in her home because she loved it so much. While her crime looks like a random home invasion, I'm not convinced. I think someone took advantage of her kindness in the most heinous of ways." I paused and rubbed my aching chest. "Mrs. Purky reminds me of my mama and meemaw, who both taught music—in school and in their homes. We can't live in a society where these crimes go unpunished. I'm asking anyone who might have information to please come forward. You can make an anonymous tip to the *CrimeStoppers* number, and no one has to know your identity. But you will know you did your best to help bring Mrs. Purky's killer to justice."

"The toll-free tip line is on the bottom of the screen, and it's also on the station's website," Jude said. He reached over and shook my hand. "Thanks so much for your time, Detective Carnegie. I hope you'll come back again."

"I'd love to."

Someone came over to remove the microphone clipped to my suit jacket while Jude and I chatted off camera for a few more minutes. Afterward, I ran potential leads in my counterfeit and forgery cases for the rest of the day. I received a text from Harper around five, instructing me to pick up takeout for three because she and Julian planned to watch my televised interview at six and *Jaws* right after. When I'd asked what kind of takeout, she'd responded that I should surprise them.

So I headed to Rascal's. It was the best barbeque in the city, and they used biodegradable containers and bamboo utensils wrapped in recycled paper. Julian had changed how I looked at the world in more ways than one, and I enjoyed the light in his eyes when I did nice things for the environment. Luckily, the barbecue pit wasn't too busy, and I made it in time for the news.

Julian saw the name on the paper bag and smiled at me. Yep. So worth it.

"I'm starving," Harper said. "The vet clinic was so busy today that I barely had time to eat a peanut butter sandwich. I might shove my face in the peach pie after I devour this."

Julian ate like he wanted to savor every bite or avoid overeating from consuming his food too fast. I fell into the latter category but tried to match his tempo. Not Harper. She whirled through it like a hurricane. My segment was halfway through the hour, so we had plenty of time to eat.

When it was over, Julian placed both hands over his heart. "Absolutely precious."

Harper snorted and said, "Bet that ends your dry spell."

Julian batted his eyelashes. "I'll fight them all."

"You have nothing to worry about." I raised my arm, and Julian cuddled up against my chest. This interaction wasn't new for us, which should've clued me in a long time ago. Harper narrowed her eyes at me, but it was easy to ignore her indignation when Julian's body heat seeped into me and his soft curls tickled my chin. I picked up the remote and cued up the movie.

Julian burrowed deeper into my side, curled his legs up on the sofa, and laid his hand against my stomach. If he felt my muscles quiver beneath his hand, he didn't say. It took all my mental energy to focus on the movie and not the things I wanted to explore with the man who'd fallen asleep in my arms almost as soon as the movie started.

CHAPTER THREE

Julian

I PICKED AT MY CHICKEN PECAN SALAD AT LUNCH ON TUESDAY while scrolling through comments on the TikTok video some thirsty user had made about Christopher. They'd even given him a nickname—the Darling Detective. I didn't even want to know what the private messages looked like on his social media accounts. I grew more sullen after reading each comment, knowing it was just a matter of time before one of these ardent fans found someone who knew Christopher and would wrangle an introduction. And just when it seemed like something was blooming between us too. Snuggling into Christopher while watching television wasn't new, but him holding me while I slept for two hours was.

I woke when the credits started rolling, surprised I was still at Harper's and even more shocked to find myself in Christopher's arms.

I'd bolted up quickly, and that's when I noticed the wet spot on his shirt. "I'm so embarrassed."

"Nah," Christopher said with a twinkle in his eye. "You've been drooling *over* me for three years, and now you're drooling *on* me."

I grinned at him as my usual sass surged to the surface. "Excellent point."

Harper let out an exaggerated yawn and aimed a death glare at Christopher. "I think it's time for you fellas to go to bed. Julian teaches his first class tomorrow, and Topher will need his energy to run from all the single ladies."

"So, your bed or mine?" I teased huskily. "Harper told us to go to bed, but she said nothing about going to separate ones."

That earned a flash of dimples from Christopher. He opened his mouth to say something, but he glanced over my shoulder, and the humor slid from his face. I turned to see what Harper was doing, but she just smiled innocently. So I kissed her cheek, blew Christopher a kiss too, and shuffled home only to discover Harper's prediction had come true the next morning. It was like my girl had summoned a hoard of horny demons. Then again, it didn't take clairvoyant vision or other paranormal persuasions to deduce Christopher would become an overnight sensation. He was the real deal—looks, intelligence, and a kind heart. And some lucky girl was going to get to enjoy all of it.

Reed Davies, my fifty-year-old fairy godfather, tailor extraordinaire, and employer at A Cut Above, sailed into the break room just as I released a heavy sigh that was dramatic even for me.

He stopped and placed a hand on his hip. Reed was tall, debonair, and always impeccably dressed. Today's dove-gray suit featured a deep purple waistcoat and a top hat to match. The color combo accentuated his gray hair and made his light blue eyes pop. "Why so glum, sugarplum?" Reed asked. "If you tell me, I can help you fix it."

I wasn't ready to admit how out of hand my crush on Topher had gotten. I'd never allowed myself to fall for a straight guy, but one look at him and I'd been a goner. My infatuation only intensified over the years when I learned his character was even greater than his looks.

"You could teach my environmental ethics class," I suggested.

"No way, darling."

"You'd be great," I countered.

"Of course. I'm fabulous at everything, but that wasn't what I meant." Reed placed a finger on his chin and studied me. "I know full well you're not intimidated by the students. Hell, it's only been a few years since you were one of them."

"A lot has changed since I graduated from college six years ago," I replied.

I'd worked in Milan, Paris, New York City, and Atlanta as an intern, an associate designer, and a fashion buyer. I'd even appeared on *The Next Face in Fashion*, a reality television show intended to boost the career of a bright new designer. Each opportunity had left me feeling more jaded and alienated in the toxic fashion industry. I'd had my ideas stolen by one fashion house, been verbally abused by another, and Greer Spalding, my last employer in Atlanta, had ensured no other designers would work with me. What crime had I committed to get blackballed? I'd dared to dream. Greer had made her feelings about the reality show crystal clear: join the cast and lose my job. I already knew I didn't have a future with her, so I rolled the dice, finishing runner-up on the show. I hadn't crawled back to Greer on my hands and knees as she'd claimed, but I had tried to find a position with other fashion houses, only to have the doors slammed in my face.

Professional disappointments had spilled over to my personal life until I felt suffocated, fractured, and untethered. Then I'd moved to Savannah. I loved working for Reed and appreciated the freedom he afforded me to pursue other ventures. It was through his connection at the Savannah College of Art and Design that I landed the teaching gig. I'd obtained my MFA through SCAD's Atlanta campus, but that alone wasn't enough to get me an interview.

Reed crossed his arms over his chest. "Spill the tea."

"Things between Christopher and I are…strange." I tilted my head and tasted the word on my tongue, and it wasn't right. "Not strange. They're different."

His mouth curved into a wry smile. "Now we're getting somewhere, baby. Different how?" Reed didn't need to ask who I was talking about because he was thoroughly versed in all things Christopher Carnegie.

"Well," I said, still shocked by the words about to come out of my mouth, "he's been flirting back, and I've caught him staring at my mouth and ass. He's always let me invade his personal space, but he's never held me while I slept for two hours."

Reed arched an impeccably shaped eyebrow. "Interesting. And what do you make of these changes?"

I grimaced. "That's part of the problem. It seems like maybe Christopher feels something for me other than friendship. But now? After three years? He's never dated men in all that time, and I'm pretty sure I would've heard if he'd dated them before my arrival."

Reed sighed and shook his head. "We both know sexuality is a fluid thing and operates on its own timeline. Men and women older than him have opened their minds and bodies to exploration. How old is Christopher?"

"Thirty-six," I replied.

Reed nodded sagely. "Still so young in the grand scheme of things. He might be eight years older than you, but you're probably lightyears ahead of him in this arena. You're crazy about this guy. Why aren't you happy?"

"It can't be real."

"Why? Because you're afraid the man you've been mooning over for three years might return your feelings? Listen, kid, you've been teasing the guy mercilessly."

"Never when he was involved with someone," I clarified. "I've always been respectful of the women he's dated."

"Because you're a doll. But stop and think for a minute. Christopher would've shut you down long ago if he didn't like the attention you've showered on him. I think there's been something between you all along. Don't let fear run the show."

"He's found a house to rent and will be moving out of Harper's apartment in October."

"No time like the present to make your move, doll," Reed said.

My phone pinged because I'd foolishly set up an alert for posts about Christopher. Several other notifications followed the first. I'd have to turn it off, or I'd lose my mind.

"What's that all about?" Reed asked, pointing to my phone.

I told him about the interview Christopher had filmed for Channel Eleven and the hysteria it had created. Reed snatched up my phone and played the video. When he finished, he held my phone against his chest and looked at me with heart eyes.

"Are you just going to roll over and let these ladies snag your man?" Reed asked.

"I'd like to roll over, grab my knees, and pin them against my chest for him."

"Scamp," Reed said, sounding shocked by my lewd comment, even though he encouraged it every chance he got. "Listen, don't live a life full of regret. If he tells you he's not interested in you like that, at least you'll know where you stand and won't be asking *what if* for the rest of your life." Shadows crossed over his eyes as they often did whenever we discussed matters of the heart. I wondered who or what had scarred him. "Trust me when I tell you it's miserable."

"Yeah," I said. "I know you're right."

The bells over the front door chimed. "I'm up," Reed said. "Put down your phone and eat your lunch. See you out on the floor in a bit."

I deleted the alert I'd set, tucked my phone away, and finished my salad. I'd need the fuel to get through the rest of my workday and power me through my first lecture. Luckily, there were no tailor emergencies at the shop, so the day went by fast, which put me in front of college kids quicker than I was ready for.

I'd received a text from Topher right before I entered the classroom. *You've got this!* It was short, sweet, and endearing. I wanted to reply with a flirty response but went with a simple thank you and kissy lips instead. I always ended my texts to him like that, and he'd be suspicious if I didn't.

The class was already full when I walked in, and several students greeted me with friendly smiles. None looked bored or pissed, which I thought was a huge win. Then again, environmental ethics in fashion was an elective class for the BFA program, and there were plenty of other electives available if a student didn't have interest in this topic. No one had forced these students to take the course.

I'd put together a PowerPoint presentation for my introduction, and I'd included some witty graphics and silly jokes, which seemed to land well with the group. Their positive feedback made me a little bolder, and I allowed my personality to shine through. As I moved through my goals for them, I talked about my roles in the industry and how I drew from my experiences to *tailor* their class.

"That brings me to your semester project," I said. "Everything I'm about to tell you is in your syllabus, but I like to hear myself talk. Lucky you." I advanced to my next slide, a side-by-side comparison of Vivien Leigh as Scarlett O'Hara in her green dress made from repurposed draperies and the Carol Burnett skit where she'd also worn repurposed drapes but with the rod still in them. It was doubtful these kids had ever heard of either woman, but the image received a lot of laughter.

"Your challenge, if you choose to accept it, and you will unless you want a third of your semester grade to be an F, is to create an original design made from entirely eco-friendly materials or completely repurposed materials such as my friend Scarlett in the photo. A list of acceptable materials and due dates are in the syllabus, so I strongly suggest you read it thoroughly. The first deadline is in two weeks when you will submit your concept to me for approval *before* you start the actual design. Concepts include color sketches and a list of items you will use and where you plan to source them. Every detail must be eco-friendly, and I mean down to the thread and the enclosures. It can be men's or women's fashion, but it must be an original piece. No replicas of existing gowns or costumes made from repurposed materials. I want to see what you're capable of creating. Any questions so far?"

A few hands went up, and I noticed the other students remained engaged while I answered questions. Afterward, I went around the room and asked what they hoped to gain from the class. By the time I finished the round, I was thoroughly impressed and happy I had taken a leap in teaching the class.

After the last student left, I turned off the light and headed to my car. I'd already told Harper I'd pick up pizza for the three of us.

Christopher wasn't there when I arrived, and Harper informed me he'd be late. I tucked his pizza inside the refrigerator and joined her on the sofa. She wanted to hear about the class and squealed with delight when I told her everything. By the time I finished eating, I'd worked up the courage to ask what had been on my mind since I'd arrived, even though dread tied my stomach in knots.

"So, did Christopher strike gold with the plethora of ladies vying to be Mrs. Carnegie?"

Harper snorted. "Hell no. He's so annoyed." My nerves eased when Harper threw her head back and cackled. "He said if he wanted this kind of attention, he would've tried out for *The Bachelor*. Topher's checking out the tips that have come in through the hotline. He sounded optimistic about them."

I let go of all the tension and swirling thoughts that had pervaded my mind lately and just enjoyed time with my best girl. I went home at nine to start planning content for my YouTube channel. I received a text about an hour later from Topher, thanking me for the pizza. He ended his message with the same kissy face emoji I always sent him. I stared at the brief message for a long time. He rarely used emojis in our text exchanges and never blew me kisses.

Hope, dangerous and intoxicating, unfurled in my heart.

CHAPTER FOUR

Topher

I DRUMMED MY FINGERS AGAINST THE DASHBOARD TO THE LED Zeppelin song playing in my head. I'd struggled with the drum solo in "Moby Dick" during the last family jam session, and it was still bugging me a month later. While I'd never match the talents of John Bonham, I knew I could do better. Rhythmically tapping my fingers against the nearest surface was about more than perfecting a drum track. It was a trick I'd learned at an early age to manage my nervous energy when I couldn't physically expend it. The habit came in handy while keeping my eyes trained on the house we had under surveillance. According to an anonymous tipster, the person who'd brutally murdered Yolanda Purky was squatting in a vacant house on the corner of Stevens and Forty-Sixth. Even in the dark, I could tell the structure had been abandoned for a long time. The house was dark and derelict, and the yard had been surrendered to Mother Nature a long time ago. The grass and weeds were nearly as tall as the chain-link fence surrounding the property. There was no telling what dangerous hazards awaited the unlucky person who ventured back there. *Please don't let it be me.*

"What's that drumming sound?" Diego asked through our comms.

I stilled my hands and placed them in my lap. "Oops. My bad."

"Why?" Coy asked. "Is it a hoard of your eager fans running toward you?"

I rolled my eyes and would've ignored him if not for the others listening through our comms. "I was drumming my fingers on the dashboard."

Diego chuckled. "I should've remembered that from our early days on the job."

"You're still doing that?" Coy asked. "I thought you would've outgrown that habit by now. It drove our teachers nuts."

Not just teachers either. My family, friends, and my girlfriends all wanted to strangle me over the habit. The only one who didn't seem to mind was Julian. He always tried to place the song based on the beat I tapped out. It was our version of *Name that Tune.* A stakeout wasn't the time to dwell on my shortcomings, failed relationships, or my growing obsession with my sister's best friend.

"Look alive, everyone," I said into the mic. "If the tipster is correct, our perp will be here soon." My comment received several affirmative responses from the task force, but Diego wasn't going to pass up an opportunity to tease me again.

"How sure are you about this tipster?" Diego asked. "What if it's just another enamored lady hoping to get you alone?"

Several chuckles filtered through my earpiece, and I rolled my eyes. "The joke would be on her." She'd figure out the most exciting thing about me was my job and maybe my part-time gig in the family band. She'd find me boring and dull just like the rest of my exes.

"You've probably got the next ex-girlfriend lined up already," Sergeant Chen said. Kyomo Chen was the new leader of the Major Crimes Unit, who had supplied backup to the smaller CCU and was the reason Coy Beaufort had joined the mission. He sure as hell hadn't tagged along at my request. I'd pulled Diego aside after our debriefing and made him promise that Coy wouldn't be the one to take down the suspect no matter what.

"Leave Carnegie alone," Sawyer said.

"Yeah," Holly added. "You're all just jealous because Topher has collected more hearts in three days than you knuckleheads could gather in a lifetime."

"Okay, okay," Diego said. "I'll lay off." I shook my head because the reprieve wouldn't last long. "But seriously, you think this is a solid tip, Toph?"

I knew most of the calls into the hotline over the past three days were dead ends, but I'd still followed up on them. One particular tip had stood out among them and made my blood zing. Some would call it a Spidey sense, but I wasn't under the delusion I possessed super-hero powers, though I'd lost track of the number of people who'd said my square jaw belonged in comics.

I couldn't fly. I didn't have X-ray vision. I couldn't heal quickly. I was just an ordinary man with an extraordinarily diligent streak that wouldn't let me give up until I got justice for the seventy-five-year-old widowed mother of two, grandmother of five, and teacher who'd molded thousands of children's lives through music. My soft spot for music teachers had shone through during my interview with Jude. I'd let my guard down, hoping my relatability would result in informa-tion on who was behind the homicide that took Yolanda's life. My plea hadn't been a gimmick, and though I'd taken a lot of ribbing from my fellow officers, I'd do it all over again if given the chance because the approach had resulted in hundreds of tips. I just ignored the dozen or so marriage proposals.

"Toph?" Diego prodded. "You there?"

"I'm here," I replied. "The tipster knew details of the case that SPD never revealed to the public or press. They provided the connection between Mrs. Purky and our suspect, Terrence Ramone. The suspect wasn't known to her children or neighbors, so he's flown under the radar all these years. According to the tip, Terrence had moved to Savannah a few months before Mrs. Purky's death. He'd fallen on hard times, and the kind woman had hired him to do some odd jobs around the house. That's how he'd stumbled onto the nest egg she had stashed in her bedroom. Granted, the tipster could just as likely be our killer and be setting up this Terrence guy to take the fall, but we won't know until we take him in."

My phone vibrated in my pocket, momentarily diverting my attention. I pulled it out to ensure there wasn't a family emergency. The text was from Harper, reminding me that *The Next Face in Fashion* would be on in a few hours. Definitely not an emergency. She probably just wanted to rile me up because I loathed reality television, but the joke was on her. I'd take any excuse to be near Julian, especially when he was giving lively commentary on the reality show he'd once appeared on.

Stakeout, I tapped out. *Be home as soon as possible.*

"Yo," Diego said. "Heads up. There's a dude approaching at two o'clock."

I fumbled the phone and nearly dropped it to the floorboard before sliding it back into my pocket. After a deep breath to steady my nerves, I turned my head to look for our target. The sidewalk was clear, so I checked the other direction but still didn't see anyone.

"I got nada," Sawyer said.

"Same," Holly replied.

"My bad," Diego said. "My two o'clock. Your ten."

I squinted into the darkness but still didn't see anything. The streetlamps closest to the abandoned house were out, which likely wasn't a coincidence.

"Be patient," Diego urged. "He's probably just too far down the street yet. See that old rusty Buick?"

"Which one?" the rest of us asked.

"The faded green one parked in the middle of the block. Our guy is fast approaching that section of the sidewalk, so we'll be able to get a strong visual."

My heart thundered in my chest as the seconds ticked by. Then a tall, skinny white guy stepped into the circle of light, pushing a grocery cart. The tipster had said Terrence Ramone spent his days panhandling at various spots throughout the city but returned to the abandoned

31

house at night. The target wore a ball cap, shadowing his face so I couldn't tell if he wore glasses and had a beard, but the straggly, long dark hair matched the tipster's description, as did the man's unusual gait.

"The dude really does walk like a sasquatch," Chen said. "This is your op, Topher. How do you want to play it?"

I was parked nearest to the house but on the opposite side of the street from where Terrence Ramone approached. "I'm going to ease out of the passenger door and crouch down at the back of the vehicle. It's dark, but I'll still be able to see him approach the house. My goal is to take him down before he reaches the porch. We don't know what we'll get into if forced to pursue him inside the residence. This could be an ambush."

"I want everyone else to merge on foot," Chen said. "Stick to the shadows, crouch low, and stay on the grass to avoid spooking our guy. We'll be in position to cover you, Toph."

I took one last steadying breath and slid across the back seat to open the rear passenger door. The interior lights didn't come on when I pulled the handle because they'd been disabled when the motor pool converted the older Cadillac to a stakeout vehicle. Ignoring my pounding heart, I crouched down and tuned my senses to the sidewalk across the street. I eased my gun from its holster and slid the safety off. Terrence's footsteps and the squeaky wheels on his grocery cart grew louder as he drew nearer, but my target wasn't close enough for me to make my move. I risked a quick peek over the trunk of the Caddy. Terrence was still a few houses away from the intersection, so I eased along the side of the long vehicle until I came up even with its rear corner. I'd just started to make my approach when I heard a car heading in my direction.

"Everyone, take cover," I whispered.

"Roger," they all responded.

The car slowly drove by my location before turning at the next intersection farther down the street. By the time it was safe for me to ease out from behind the Caddy, Terrence Ramone had reached the sidewalk in front of the dilapidated structure and had turned toward the porch. *Shit.*

I burst from my hiding spot with my gun trained in front of me.

"Yo, Terrence!" I called out, aiming for a laid-back vibe to get his attention without spooking him. The suspect jerked and spun around. "Savannah PD! Freeze and get those hands where I can see them!" I heard the team moving in through my earpiece and was about to tell Terrence we had him surrounded, but the startled suspect recovered quicker than I would've liked. He abandoned his cart and darted right for the overgrown backyard.

Fuck me!

I didn't have time to ponder the types of creepy crawlies or slithering snakes hiding in the tall blades. I launched myself after Terrence, and suddenly the pursuit felt like a throwback to my linebacker days on the gridiron. Gripping the top of the metal fence, I whispered a silent prayer and used my momentum to vault into the overgrown backyard.

"Stop!" I yelled when my feet landed on the other side of the fence. I immediately sprinted after the suspect, noting the grass and weeds were nearly up to my waist. "I just want to talk to you," I tried.

"Yeah, that's why you have your gun out," Terrence yelled.

Through the comms, I heard the rest of the team moving to intercept Terrence once he cleared the fence on the opposite side of the yard.

"Toph, you okay?" Diego asked.

"In pursuit," I replied tersely. "Target in sight."

I once again tried to get Terrence to stop, but the skinny man turned on his jets instead. By some miracle, we'd nearly reached the other side of the backyard without either of us stumbling over tree roots or detritus left behind by a previous owner. I'd almost caught Terrence by the time he reached the other fence. With a good vault, I'd easily catch the suspect within a few strides. If not me, someone on my team would. I placed my hand on the top metal rail and got decent height, but a jagged metal section of fencing at the top snagged my jeans midthigh. Instead of the denim tearing free, the imprisoned fabric caused me to pitch forward. The next thing I knew, I was falling face-first toward the ground. A few seconds before impact, my jeans ripped, and I twisted my upper body so my left shoulder took the brunt of the collision instead of my head. Unfortunately, it was the same shoulder I'd had surgically repaired after playing college football. The pain was so severe that I nearly blacked out. Stars danced before my eyes, and I feared I'd undone all Dr. Chu's good work.

I yanked my leg until the fabric ripped free, and I felt a little woozy when I pushed myself into a sitting position and looked for Terrence Ramone. I just needed a moment to gather myself before I resumed the pursuit. My head swiveled in the direction of the running and shouting sounds coming from a dozen feet away. The cone of light cast by the streetlamp acted as a spotlight, allowing me to watch as Coy fucking Beaufort closed in on my suspect with Diego quickly gaining on both of them. *Come on, Diego. Don't let me down.* As if he heard me, my friend sprinted past Coy, then performed a beautiful flying tackle to take Terrence Ramone down. Chen and Holly ran up to assist Diego while Coy scowled down at him.

Sawyer dropped to the ground beside me. "You okay, Toph?"

"Yeah, Sarge. Just rattled my cage a bit."

Sawyer shined his cell phone flashlight in my face. "Do you need medical attention?"

"I might now," I said grumpily, throwing up an arm to shield my eyes from the blinding light.

Sawyer chuckled and extended his hand to help me up.

The dizziness and disorientation faded as adrenaline dulled my discomfort and heightened my senses. "We've got him!" I cheered euphorically when Diego pulled a cuffed Terrence Ramone to his feet, even though it was just the beginning. We'd have to interrogate the man, and it wasn't likely he'd voluntarily confess. We had forty-eight hours to hold Ramone and get a subpoena for a DNA sample. It would be months before we would get the results back, but if Terrence's fingerprints matched the bloody ones at the crime scene, it would be enough to formally charge him with Yolanda's murder. The DNA evidence would just be the nail in his coffin—figuratively and maybe even literally.

Porchlights came on up and down the street as the team exchanged high fives. A couple of neighbors called out to see what was going on. Chen, Sawyer, and Coy decided to chat with the neighbors, both to assure them everything was okay and to find out what they knew about the man who'd been squatting in the abandoned house. Holly, Diego, and I headed back to the precinct with Terrence.

As predicted, our suspect claimed not to know anyone named Yolanda Purky and denied killing her or anyone else. Terrence was pretty convincing and acted as cool as a cucumber until I fingerprinted him, and Holly asked him to voluntarily submit his DNA for testing. His entire tune changed from patient and helpful to stubbornly mute in moments.

"You should do everyone a favor and confess," Diego told him. "I think the DA will go easier on you if you save the taxpayers a ton of money. I bet she'll at least take the death penalty off the table."

"Death penalty?" Terrence asked with a slight quiver in his voice.

Holly stood opposite him and crossed her arms over her chest. "It never fails to amaze me how *brave* these assholes are when they enter the home of a defenseless woman, bludgeon her to death, and steal the money she'd been tucking away all her life. You killed Yolanda Purky and stayed in the house with her dead body for hours, tearing out drywall and looking for hidden stashes of money."

"Then you fixed yourself a nice breakfast," Diego added before looking over at me. "What was it again?"

I'd never forget the Purky crime scene photos and police reports for as long as I lived. "Poached eggs, bacon, fried potatoes, and toast," I replied with a snarl. We already knew the DNA on the fork belonged to a male, so it was just a matter of comparing the previous test to Terrence's sample.

Holly shook her head. "And you have the audacity to get a quivering lip when we mention you'll face the death penalty for your crimes. Un-fucking-believable, you coward." She pushed back from the table. "He doesn't deserve a deal. I say we let Gillian Babineaux have her way with him in court." Holly walked over, yanked the interrogation room door open, and gestured for a uniformed officer to take Terrence away.

Sawyer and Chen entered the room a few minutes later. They'd made it back to the station in time to observe the interrogation.

"Nice touch, Hols," Chen said, bumping his fist against hers.

"We'll have results on the fingerprints soon," Sawyer said. "I hope we can get a judge to sign off on the subpoena for a DNA sample."

"The bloody fingerprints will be enough to convict," I said. "But proving Terrence casually made breakfast after he killed Yolanda and ransacked her house will guarantee he never knows what freedom feels like again." And that wasn't conjecture on our part. The ME's official time of death was between nine and midnight on Saturday night. Mrs. Purky's oldest daughter had swung by to pick her up for church on Sunday morning. The house had been ransacked, the walls were demolished, and she'd discovered her slain mother in her bedroom. When the daughter ran into the kitchen to call for help, she'd notice the breakfast remnants on the table and noticed the stove was still warm. If she'd arrived earlier, she might've been a victim too.

"Damn straight," Chen said.

After a few celebratory hugs and high fives, the group parted ways.

"Wait up," Diego called out, halting my progress. He jogged to catch up and then slapped me on the shoulder. Thankfully it was my good one. "Where you headed so fast? Come over to my place for a few beers and some baseball."

"Oh man, that sounds great, but I already made other plans."

Diego narrowed his eyes. "With whom?"

"It's not a date, D. Let it go." I could tell Diego anything, but I was still struggling to put my feelings for Julian into words, another habit I'd carried over from my childhood. I tended to communicate through music, but I didn't think Diego would welcome me bursting into song in the precinct parking lot. That would surely get the tongues wagging.

My friend quirked a brow. "That's exactly what I'd say if I were trying to hide something."

"I promise nothing hinky is going on. Go home to your handsome husband."

"What about something kinky?" Diego pressed.

I snorted. "Sadly, no." I nearly gave in and went to Diego's house just to shut him up, but I couldn't. Check that. I definitely *could* change my mind and share a few beers and catch a few innings of baseball, but I didn't want to back out of my commitment. "Rain check?" I asked.

Diego started walking to his car. "I'm holding you to it," he called over his shoulder.

"I'll bring the beer. You grill the burgers."

"You got it," Diego said, then turned around.

I noted the time on the dashboard when I pulled into the apartment complex parking lot. I took the stairs to the fourth floor to burn off the excess energy buzzing through me instead of using the elevator, but my decision only seemed to amp me up even more. Harper was in the kitchen making popcorn when I walked through the door.

"How's my favorite brother?" she asked.

I could point out that I was her only brother, but I rubbed my knuckles over her dark hair instead.

"Jerk," Harper said as she hastily straightened her ponytail. She placed an overflowing bowl of popcorn in my hands and pointed to the living room. My three sisters inherited our mom's dark hair, chocolate brown eyes, elfin features, and petite stature. I got my tawny hair, amber eyes, brawny lumberjack body, and square jaw from our dad. "How'd the stakeout go?" Harper asked as she followed me with a smaller bowl of popcorn in one hand and three drinks tucked into the crook of her opposite elbow. We had our viewing routine down to an art. Julian and I liked our popcorn lightly buttered and salted, so we shared a bowl. Harper preferred to drown her kernels in fat, cholesterol, and sodium and made a separate bowl for herself.

My gaze landed on Julian. His damp brown hair curled around his face, and his piercing green eyes were glued to his phone.

"Another Grindr notification?" Harper asked.

Julian nodded without looking up. "I had no idea there were so many gay and bisexual men in Savannah."

"Or you might've moved here sooner?" Harper prompted.

Julian smiled, but I couldn't tell if it was a response to Harper's question or because the Grinder app had matched him with someone good. What if I'd waited too long to make a move? The last thought knocked the wind out of my sails.

"This guy is a pompous son of a bitch," Julian grumbled. "Hard pass."

Harper snorted. "Um, don't most of them fit into that category on Grindr?"

"Yeah," Julian said, "but I have high standards even for my hookups. I must at least like the man if I'm going to bend over and—"

Julian's words died when he looked up and saw me crossing the room. He narrowed his eyes and raked his gaze from my work boots to the roots of my hair. My skin tingled as if Julian had physically caressed me, and then our eyes met. He cocked his head to the side.

"Something's wrong," Julian stated, his gaze darkening with concern.

I shook my head. "Nope. In fact, everything is right." Unless you counted the jealousy burning a hole in my gut like battery acid.

"Are we still talking about the stakeout, or did one of those marriage proposals land?" Harper teased.

Julian stiffened and shifted his gaze back to the television. Harper, unaware she'd hurt Julian's feelings, set the drinks and her bowl of popcorn on the coffee table and plopped down beside him on the couch.

"I was referring to the stakeout." I placed the big bowl of popcorn on the coffee table and sat on Julian's other side. I fought the urge to lean closer and inhale his intoxicating scent, a sexy combination of a masculine woodsy smell with a hint of something softer and fragile. "We got a helpful tip, which resulted in us finding the right person."

Julian turned and looked at me with the kindest eyes I'd ever seen. He patted my leg but left his hand on my thigh instead of removing it. I stared at his long fingers, willing them to move higher until his voice cut through my fantasy. I tuned in long enough to hear him acknowledge how difficult this investigation had been for me.

"Yeah," I said. "All homicides are horrible, but some just get deeper under my skin."

I gave them a quick rundown of how the stakeout had ended, glossing over the part where I'd ripped my pants and playing up the part where Diego bested Coy and tackled the perp to the ground.

Julian narrowed his eyes. "Why does Coy's name sound familiar? I don't think I've met him."

Harper coughed like she'd choked on a popcorn kernel.

"You okay?" I asked.

She nodded, then took a sip. "I'm just shocked Julian doesn't remember Coy Beaufort is your lifelong nemesis." She *tsk*ed and shook her head. "And you call yourself Topher's number one fan."

Julian and Harper exchanged a look I couldn't decipher. Annoyance? Warning maybe? The two had never been at odds in three years, so I had to be misreading the situation.

Julian looked at me and smiled. "Congratulations on the big takedown." He raked his gaze over me again, and I swear it was hotter than the first time. "Clearly, you've changed pants."

"I had extra clothes in my locker."

"Where are the ripped ones?" he asked. "I can probably fix them."

I reached for a handful of popcorn and smiled at him. "This is rich." When Julian quirked a brow, I said, "You're usually trying to get my pants off, not put them on."

Harper choked on her popcorn again and stared daggers at me, but Julian's grin lit up the room. He leaned forward, and I thought he was going to kiss me, but instead he said, "I'd settle for getting *in* them."

I squeezed my fist around the popcorn so tight the kernels exploded out of my hand and landed on my lap and the floor. I picked up the mess off the carpet first before cleaning off my lap. Julian, the little imp, grabbed the piece of popcorn closest to my crotch and popped it into his mouth. I couldn't tear my eyes away from his lips as he chewed. Once they stopped moving, I forced myself to meet his gaze.

"So you're not going to swipe right on the pompous ass?" I managed to ask.

"Swiping right is Tinder, not Grindr," Julian said.

"What's the difference?"

"One is for dating and the other is for fucking," Harper replied. She gyrated her hips in a grind that made me grimace. "I'll let you figure out which is which."

I'd reintroduced the topic and didn't want to let it drop, so I said, "You're not interested in dating?"

Julian tilted his head to the side and slowly licked his bottom lip as he contemplated how to respond. I could see the debate in his eyes, but what exactly was he deciding? How far to push me? Whether I could handle the truth? After a brief pause, he straightened his head and lobbed a grenade at me in the form of a flirty smile. "Tinder is for people looking to find a mate. I've found mine," Julian said with a wink. "I use Grindr to work out the kinks until you come to your senses. I mean, you haven't exactly been celibate these past three years."

A wave of heat engulfed my body, and I reached for my drink before I could respond. Julian's lips curled into a knowing smile as he watched me gulp down half my beverage before setting my glass back on the table. I cleared my throat and said, "When you say kinks, do you mean maintenance to prevent your skills from getting rusty or are you referring to kinky sex?"

Julian opened his mouth to respond, but Harper loudly announced the show had started. "To be continued," he said with a wink.

I forced my attention to the television where the people on-screen were talking about things I didn't understand. My knowledge about designing and crafting clothes was nada, but Julian and Harper had strong opinions about the reality show and the newest fashion designers competing for a big win. I was entertained by their reactions to the drama unfolding on the screen.

Julian had competed on the show before moving to Savannah and had finished as the runner-up. He interjected with his firsthand experiences and shared production secrets. I had covertly watched every episode Julian had appeared in at least three times and was convinced Bren with no last name had made a deal with a demon because there was no way he would've beaten Julian otherwise. Just Bren had no business making it to the finals at all. Again, if I could see that, how had he survived one panel of judges let alone all of them? According to the many online forums I read, art was subjective, not objective. I'd said similar things about music over the years, so the logic wasn't new to me. It just felt more personal because I knew firsthand how badly Julian had wanted to win and was aware of some of the backlash he'd faced afterward. Greer Spalding Designs had shot to the top of my family's do-not-support list after Julian told us she'd blackballed him.

The longer I sat on the sofa, the more my adrenaline rush faded, and my body stiffened with discomfort from my impact with the ground.

I tried subtly rotating my left shoulder because I didn't want Harper to fuss. She and Julian seemed too focused on the show to notice me. The camera panned to an up-close shot of Bren, distracting me from my growing aches. I snorted and said, "He's had some work done."

I felt two sets of eyes swivel in my direction and quickly searched for something to say that wouldn't divulge my little secret. I had no reason to know what Bren looked like since this was only the second season we'd watched together, and the asshat hadn't appeared in the previous season. I hadn't confessed to anyone that I'd watched Julian's season and didn't want to do so now. It would just prompt questions I wasn't prepared to answer.

Julian tilted his head to the side and studied me. "Yes, Bren has had some surgical work done, but how would you know that?"

"A promo I saw," I replied dismissively. "It included footage from Bren's season. He looks a lot different in this episode."

I moved to grab a fistful of popcorn, and Julian must have had the same idea because he leaned forward at the same time. Our fingers bumped and lingered amid the buttery kernels, then Julian looked over at me and smiled. A frizzle of heat bloomed in my gut.

Holy shit. If Harper hadn't been sitting there, I would've pulled him onto my lap and kissed him senseless.

CHAPTER
FIVE

Julian

T HE ATTRACTION SPARKING IN CHRISTOPHER'S AMBER EYES HIT
me like a bolt of lightning straight to the groin. If I hadn't shaved
my pubes, I'd give a whole new meaning to a burning bush. I took
Reed's advice and ignored my inner scaredy cat to really pay attention
to Christopher's body language. It would tell me so much more than
his words ever would.

I ghosted my fingers over Christopher's thick forearm, noting
the way his nostrils flared and his eyes darkened. Lust was a wildfire
burning through my body, urging me to be bolder.

"If you wanted to hold my hand, sugar, you should've just said
so," I teased.

I traced his veins, and of course, my mind wondered about
the veins I'd find on a different thick appendage. Christopher's lips

parted, allowing a shaky breath to slide between them. His eyes darted to my hand. It was sliding slowly back toward his wrist, but I kept my attention anchored on his face, gauging his every reaction to my touch. Christopher swallowed hard before licking his bottom lip. He lifted his head, and his gaze immediately zeroed in on my mouth. My pulse rocketed when I recognized the signs. Christopher wanted to kiss me.

I should've said something flirty or sexy, but the moment called for action. Leaning toward him was as natural as taking my next breath. Christopher tilted forward, his gaze volleying between my eyes and mouth. Was this really happening? My heart pounded against my chest like a caged beast dying to escape.

"Son of a bitch!" Harper shouted.

Christopher and I lurched apart like naughty little kids and turned our heads back to the television. It took me several seconds to clear my thoughts and focus my attention on the unfolding scene. Bren was brutally criticizing a contestant's design and was utterly oblivious to the devastation he was inflicting.

Harper turned and looked at me. "Hasn't Bren ever heard of constructive criticism?"

I shook my head. "Nope. And he's not alone. Fashion is a brutal business, and many in the field want to weed out anyone who isn't tough enough to handle it. It's disgustingly toxic. And to think I once thought I could take the industry by the balls and make them see a better way."

Christopher made a strangled noise before gulping down the rest of his drink. Was it my reference to ball grabbing that shook him up? He reached for my glass, and I thought he was going to knock it back also, but he extended it to me instead. "Thirsty?"

I raked my gaze over his broad chest and down to his groin. Heat suffused my cheeks when I saw his state of arousal. Meeting his eyes again, I accepted the drink and said, "Very."

I forced my attention to the television, but I felt him watching me as I ate popcorn and sipped water. If I let my brain fixate on his erection, I'd forget all about Harper sitting there and embarrass us all.

I held out for half of a minute before allowing my gaze to drift over that delicious body again. God, those thighs. The thrusting power—

"Oh, come on!" Harper yelled at something Bren had said or done. She snapped her head around and glared at me. "Why aren't you angrier? This is the kind of snarky thing he'd say to you during your season on the show."

"I have no words," I finally said.

Harper quirked a dark brow. "You? Speechless?"

"Bren's not only rude," Christopher said. "He has no taste. He just suggested the designer pair plaid and paisley together. It's like he's trying to sabotage her chances."

Harper and I both looked at him. "What? I pay attention."

I would've taken him more seriously if not for the smear of butter on the right side of his mouth. My fingers itched to swipe it from his skin, so I balled my hands into fists.

"Except for how to properly put things in your mouth," Harper said. "I've seen toddlers with cleaner faces."

Christopher scowled and darted his tongue to the left. I gave in to my urge and swiped the butter from his face. I had planned to wipe it on a napkin, but we hadn't brought any over from the kitchen. So I licked the butter off my finger and returned my focus to the show.

"Gross," Harper said. "Might as well have licked his face."

I looked over at Christopher and winked. "If he plays his cards right, I just might."

A telltale blush crept up his neck, and Christopher hooked a finger in the collar of his shirt and fanned his skin.

Oh yeah. It's getting hot in here.

A laconic remark from Bren snagged my attention. He was eviscerating a contestant during the Off the Cuff challenge. The results wouldn't send anyone home, but the winning contestant would gain an advantage in the final round. "I've never seen anything as ugly in all my life," Bren said on the screen.

Christopher snorted so loud it made me jump. "It's still better than that hideous dress you designed in your finale, Just Bren," he said to the television.

I snapped my head in his direction once more. *Just Bren?* It was the second time he'd remarked on Bren's performance or appearance, and to the best of my knowledge, Christopher had never watched my season. Or had he?

"How do you know about Bren's finale design?" Harper asked.

Christopher huffed a frustrated sigh and rolled his eyes. "It was in the promo I mentioned. Bren was standing on the stage next to a model wearing the most hideous dress I'd ever seen. Confetti was falling all around them, and the lead judge guy—"

"Hudson," Harper and I both said.

"Yeah, him," Christopher quipped. "Hudson was handing him a big shiny trophy." He mimicked the presentation and winced.

I bolted upright. "Are you hurt?"

"Nah," he said, waving me off. "I just had an incident with the ground tonight, and my shoulder is stiff."

I scooted back deeper on the couch, spread my legs, and patted my thighs. "Let me see if I can ease some tension for you."

Christopher gave me a tentative smile and shook his head slightly. "I'm okay."

"Take him up on his offer if you're hurting, Toph," Harper said as she returned her attention to the drama on the TV. "He has magic hands."

"Words I never want to hear my sister say again," Christopher said.

I lifted my hands and studied them as if seeing them for the first time. "They look pretty average to me," I said.

Harper snorted. "Magic. Capital *M*."

I waggled my brows at Christopher, then patted my thighs once more. He smiled and shook his head, even as he eased off the couch and scooted over to sit between my feet. Christ, his shoulders were broad. I had to spread a little wider to make room for him.

I looked at my ordinary hands once more. *Please don't fail me now.* I gently placed them on Christopher's shoulders and noted the tension tightening his body. Was it from being so close to me, or was he in more pain than he was letting on? I carefully pushed my fingers into the meaty part of his shoulder. "Tell me where you need me most," I said, moving my thumbs around to probe the areas.

"Warmer," he said when I moved lower. "Maybe both hands on my left shoulder since that's where I hurt most."

I moved my right hand over and used both thumbs to dig into each new knot I discovered.

"Oh!" Christopher said, his entire body stiffening.

I stilled. "Oh or ow?"

"Maybe both," he said. "I want to pull away and lean into your touch at the same time."

Harper snorted. "I'm getting grossed out."

"Yeah," Christopher said, "and I didn't like hearing your headboard banging against my wall when you had a visitor on Saturday night."

Harper's face flushed red, and she narrowed her eyes. "You were supposed to be on a date."

Trying to head off a fight, I adjusted my pressure and said, "How's this?"

Christopher let out the sluttiest moan I'd ever heard. "Holy fuck, that feels good. God, give me more." I pushed a little deeper into the knot and worked it until the muscle relaxed. "Magic hands, indeed. Not just a capital *M*. All caps and bold print."

I leaned closer to his ear. "But not underlined?"

Christopher's head fell back onto the couch cushion between my legs, and he stared up into my eyes. "Double underline," he said huskily, then closed his eyes. "Please don't stop."

"Seriously, should I go to my room?" Harper asked.

"Yes," Christopher replied while I said, "No."

She giggled and returned her attention to the show while I watched a blissful expression wash over Christopher's face. His eyelashes fluttered a few times, but he didn't reopen his eyes. A few moments later, Christopher's lips slackened, and his breathing changed to a slow, steady rhythm. Instead of pulling my hands free,

I continued to rub his left shoulder and neck. And if my fingers slid through the silky hair at his nape just once, well, who did it hurt?

"I saw that," Harper teased and bumped her shoulder against mine.

We continued watching the rest of the show in silence, but I couldn't have said who won the weekly challenge and whose dream got cut short. I only recalled the feel of Christopher's warmth seeping through his shirt and into my skin.

"What do we do about Sleeping Beauty?" I asked once the show ended.

"I'll wake him up and help him to his room if he needs it," Harper said.

I reluctantly pushed off the couch and rose to my feet. A chill permeated the places that had been toasty warm just moments prior. Harper stood up too and hugged me.

"Should I thank you for having your wicked way with my brother?" she teased.

I glanced over at Christopher, who looked like an oversized boy in his sleep. I smiled wickedly at Harper and said, "Baby girl, if I'd had my way with him, you'd know it. Hell, the whole building would know it."

She scrunched up her face and swatted at me. "Sweet dreams." I started to say something naughty, but she covered both ears. "I can only take so much in one night."

I nearly got bowled over by Bruno, our neighbor's exuberant dog, when I stepped into the hallway. He was just a big fluffy baby boy, which I told him when I leaned over and scratched his ears.

"So sorry," Sally, Bruno's owner, said. "We're working on obedience at his school."

"No worries. He didn't manage to take me down this time, so I'd say it's an improvement."

Sally apologized again and took the lumbering puppy out for his final walk of the night. I unlocked the door directly across from Harper's and let myself in. I should go to bed, but I was far too keyed up. I went into the spare bedroom that I'd converted to a sewing room to work on Harper's dress for the charity gala. The fuchsia silk would look amazing against her fair skin. I just had a few more finishing touches before I revealed the creation.

After a few hours of sewing, the yearnings Christopher stirred within me still hadn't subsided. I lovingly set the dress aside and headed to the shower, where I could let my what-if fantasies play out. For the first time since I'd met Christopher Carnegie, those far-fetched imaginings felt a little closer to reality.

CHAPTER SIX

Topher

I WAS WIDE AWAKE LONG BEFORE MY ALARM WENT OFF, THANKS TO the excruciating pain in my left shoulder. I phoned my orthopedic surgeon's office as soon as it opened and was relieved to snag an afternoon appointment with Dr. Chu. Even though I wasn't hungry, I fixed myself a light breakfast so I wouldn't take Aleve on an empty stomach. I'd made that mistake more than once and had no desire to add painful stomach cramps to the mix of discomfort.

I should've washed my laundry days ago, so I had a limited wardrobe to choose from. My instincts told me the case was going to break wide open this morning, which meant I had to be camera ready if the chief decided to hold a press conference. With the attention Mrs. Purky's case had garnered, I figured a press conference would be the least of my obligations. My SPD polo shirts were all dirty, so a dress shirt and tie were my only options. Unfortunately, Harper had already left for the day, which meant I needed to seek someone else's help with the tiny buttons and tie. Julian was the smartest choice, even though I'd spent too much time thinking about his hands all over my body. I just needed to keep my head out of the gutter when he was standing so close to me.

I pulled a pale blue shirt off a hanger and eased my left arm into the sleeve before taking care of my pain-free side. My shoulder surgery had been fourteen years ago, but I still recalled the tips my physical therapist had given me on how to dress. I pulled on a pair of navy slacks and could zip and button them without assistance, thank goodness. Luckily, I had a nice pair of loafers I could slide my socked feet into because asking Julian to tie my shoes would derail my commitment to clean thoughts.

Julian didn't answer on the first knock, the second, or even the third. Just as I decided to dig around my hamper for a polo that didn't smell too bad, Julian swung open his apartment door. He rendered me speechless when the reason for his delay became apparent. I swept my gaze over his wet hair, damp skin, and the towel wrapped around his waist. I fervently wished for gravity to take hold of the teal terry cloth and give it a good yank.

"Is everything okay?" Julian asked breathlessly.

My mouth had gone dry, and the only sensible remedy would be for me to lick the drops of water cascading down Julian's torso. I didn't reach for him or put my mouth anywhere near his body. I just stood mutely and watched the droplets get absorbed by the towel.

"Eyes up here, handsome," Julian teased.

I snapped my gaze up to his. Heat spread throughout my body, but most of it was centered in my upper chest and neck. "We both know I've dreamed of this moment for a long time," Julian said in a silky voice. "Having you at my door in a partial state of undress with desperation etched on your face is so much better than my wildest fantasies." He sighed dramatically. "I think the reality of what happens next is drastically different, though."

"I need your help." My voice sounded as dry as my mouth felt. I cleared my throat but doubted it would help much. "My shoulder—"

Julian's playfulness died in an instant. Sympathy and guilt flooded his beautiful eyes. "Of course," he said, stepping aside so I could enter. "Forgive my awful behavior. Let me put on some clothes, and I'll help with your shirt and tie."

I wanted to snag his hand and pull him back, but I let him go, using the time to look around his apartment instead. Julian's home was immaculately clean but not so fussy that it made my skin itch. He changed up the décor every year or so, and right now, the space was filled with comfortable-looking furniture in cool neutral fabrics, jewel-toned accent pieces, and bold artwork. My favorite piece was a ginormous peacock painting centered over the couch. The teal feathers matched the towel wrapped around Julian's waist. I looked around and found the color in other places, like the stand mixer and coffee maker in the kitchen and the vase with white flowers on a table near the front door. Clearly, teal was a preferred color.

"I'm back," Julian said breezily. He'd pulled on a white tank top and loose navy sleep pants with thin white stripes. Had Julian worn these clothes to bed, or did he sleep naked?

Keep your thoughts clean, jackass, or you'll get a boner again.

"How bad is it?" Julian asked as he approached me.

Bad. I had it really bad. "I'm not sure," I replied instead. "I have an appointment with my doctor this afternoon. I'm sure she'll run tests and recommend physical therapy."

Julian cocked his head to the side as he reached for the bottom shirt button. "Sounds like you have a lot of experience with this kind of injury."

Just as I started to respond, Julian's fingertips brushed against my bare abdomen as he moved up to the next button. The air whooshed out of me in a little gasp instead. My stomach muscles tensed and quivered beneath his touch. Julian smirked as he slid the next button through the loop.

"Ticklish?" he guessed.

"Looks that way," I lied.

"So you've injured this shoulder before?" Julian asked.

"Yeah. I nursed it along during my senior year of college because I didn't want to miss a football game. I had surgery to repair the shoulder as soon as the season ended and spent months afterward in physical therapy to restrengthen it. I'm afraid I might've ruined Dr. Chu's hand-iwork last night."

Julian's nimble fingers stilled, and he looked up at me. Damn, he had the prettiest eyes I'd ever seen. Julian's full lips pursed into a pout, and he gripped my shirt tighter. "You could've been hurt."

"I was," I replied dryly.

"Much worse than this," he countered. "What if he'd had a gun?"

"Mine is bigger."

Julian snorted and continued buttoning my shirt. Just how many of the little fuckers were there anyway? "Please don't be flippant about your safety."

I had the strongest urge to lean forward and kiss his forehead until the furrow there smoothed. "I wasn't," I replied. "I'd bet on my aim over his any day."

"At least you caught your man."

I balled my fists to keep from gripping Julian's narrow waist and pulling him closer. "I did." My voice sounded much huskier than usual, but he didn't seem to notice. I needed to change the topic to distract my brain. Julian's nearness kept me from dwelling on the discomfort in my shoulder, but this diversion had its own set of perils—namely, my blood rapidly heading south. So I latched onto the first boner-reducing topic that came to mind.

"Do you know who Harper is seeing?" I asked,

Julian chuckled as he finished the last button and reached for my tie. "You know I wouldn't say if I did. She's my best girl, and I'd never be-tray her confidence." He looked into my eyes and said, "Unless I thought she was in danger."

"I just want to be sure she's safe and not involved in a toxic thing."

Julian shook his head. "No concerns on that front."

I narrowed my eyes. The last I'd heard, Harper was hardcore crush-ing on a young vet at the clinic. I'd heard her say several times the guy was out of her league, which I thought was complete bullshit. "It's that vet, right?" I asked. Julian didn't reply, but he lowered his gaze. "Workplace romances are a bad idea," I said. "There are just some relationships or situations you know to avoid."

Julian finished with my tie but didn't step back. He met my gaze once more and said, "Like refusing to give up on impossible crushes?" I knew he was talking about me, and discouraging him would be the right thing to do, but I couldn't form the words. "And speaking of impossible crushes or misbehaving, I have a confession."

The brevity of his tone made me smile. "Okay. To whom?"

Julian straightened his shoulders. "You."

"Me? I don't—"

"I felt you up a little while you slept against me last night."

I choked on what little saliva I had. Julian walked to his refrigerator, removed a water bottle, and brought it to me. He waited patiently while I downed half of it.

"You were saying something about fondling me while I slept," I said.

Julian snorted. "As if you would be so lucky. I just needed to know if your hair felt as soft as it looked. I slid my fingers into the strands at the base of your neck. Just once and only for a few seconds, but I'm sorry. It won't happen again."

I felt a devilish smile creep across my face. "That's too bad," I said. Julian's eyes widened, and his beautiful lips parted. I loved that I had stunned him for once. "So is that one of your kinks?" Julian blinked and looked confused, so I expanded. "The ones you work out on your sex hookup app." A delicate pink flush bloomed over his cheeks. "Last night, you mentioned we'd continue our conversation about Grindr. I'd asked for clarification: kinky sex acts or maintenance sex to keep everything in proper working order?"

Julian's mouth opened and shut, then opened again. He shook his head. "We'll have that discussion when you can explain to me why you care about my Grindr activity so much."

It was my turn to stumble over a response. Everything I wanted to say to him felt too big to fit through my mouth, so I winked playfully. "Thanks for your help, Julian. I owe you one."

Usually, he would jest about the kind of favors I could return, but I'd shocked him, and he had no sassy reply. I whistled on my way out of his apartment and out to my truck. Maybe the Aleve was kicking in, or perhaps the encounter with Julian had boosted my spirits, but I'd nearly forgotten about my bum shoulder by the time I walked into the precinct. I headed straight for my unit to check for updates on Terrence Ramone. Holly wasn't in yet, but Royce Locke stepped out of his husband's office with a cup of coffee in one hand and a bear claw pastry in the other.

"Congratulations on the bust," Royce said.

"Thanks, Ro." I didn't let my eyes linger on his pastry because the man was territorial when it came to his husband and his bear claws. "Are there any updates?"

"That's what I was about to ask you," Royce said, then took a sip of coffee.

"Me?"

"On the relationship front," Royce prodded. "Have you told the guy you have feelings for him?"

"Not in so many words, but I'm working on it."

"Attaboy, Toph," he said before he headed for the Explorer academy down the hall.

I wasn't sure my feeble attempts to show Julian how I felt were worthy of celebration, but there was no denying I'd grown bolder every day.

Sawyer came out of his office with sheets of paper in both hands. "I thought I heard your voice," he said. "We got him, Toph!" Sawyer showed me the fingerprint analysis results in one hand and the signed subpoena for Terrence Ramone's DNA in the other.

"That's fantastic news." Relief flooded my system as I thought about the phone call I'd get to make to Yolanda's family.

"I'm having Ramone brought up to an interrogation room in a few minutes. I hope he'll confess when faced with the positive fingerprint match and signed subpoena. Either way, Chief Mendoza has instructed us to formally charge him with Yolanda Purky's murder based on the fingerprint evidence alone. He will hold a press conference later and wants you to attend." Sawyer took in my attire and smirked. "Looks like you already planned for the possibility."

"Nah," I said. "I just ran out of clean clothes."

Sawyer laughed. "God, you sound like my husband."

"Thanks."

"Not sure it was a compliment," Sawyer replied on the way to his office.

Holly and I headed up to the interrogation room when she arrived a few minutes later. Ramone looked in far worse shape than the night before. The dark circles under his eyes gave them a concave, hollow appearance. His skin was sallow and waxy, and his dark, greasy hair hung lank over his slumped shoulders. Ramone looked pitiful and frail, but I couldn't work up an ounce of sympathy for him.

I read him his Miranda rights again. Ramone acknowledged them without making eye contact and waived his right to an attorney. "Do you know why we wanted to see you this morning?" The man mumbled something inaudible, and I slapped my hand on the table. The loud bang in the small room resembled a shotgun blast, and Ramone jumped a few inches. "Look at me when I'm talking to you." Ramone slowly lifted his head as if it had taken great effort. "Do you know why we wanted to see you this morning?" I repeated.

"To ask me more questions, I guess," Ramone replied.

"No," Holly said. "Fingerprint analysis is back. Those were your bloody fingerprints all over Mrs. Purky's house."

"And we have a signed subpoena to collect your DNA," I added. "We're going to formally charge you with Yolanda Purky's murder and turn your sorry ass over to the DA."

"Wait," Ramone said quickly. "If I confess, will she take the death penalty off the table?"

This weak-ass bitch had some nerve to ask for mercy when he'd shown none to an elderly woman, but I had to keep a tight handle on my emotions. "I can't make that decision," I replied calmly, "but I can call her office and see if she's available to meet with us."

"Please," he said, then leaned over and rested his forehead on the table.

Holly and I stepped out of the room. She placed a quick call to the DA's office while I observed Ramone on the monitor from the room next door.

It took Gillian Babineaux thirty minutes to arrive, but it only took her two minutes to get a full confession from Ramone after he agreed to life in prison without the possibility of parole. Chief Mendoza came down soon afterward to congratulate me on solving the case and asked me to attend his press conference.

"I'd like an opportunity to speak with Yolanda's family first, sir."

"Of course," Mendoza replied. "Let me know once you talk to them, and I'll have my assistant set up the press conference."

"Yes, sir."

"Oh, and Topher," Mendoza said, "you have an interview with the *Sinister in Savannah* podcast team tonight at six."

I bit back a groan. The appearance on Channel Eleven might've been responsible for the tip that led to Terrence Ramone's arrest, but it had also stirred up a lot of trouble for me. No one told Mendoza no, though. "Sure thing, sir."

As soon as Mendoza left, I called Yolanda's daughter, who still lived in Savannah. Chantelle Sebastian answered on the second ring.

"We got him, Chantelle," I said.

"Praise Jesus," she replied, then burst into tears.

By lunch, the adrenaline from Ramone's confession began to wear off, and I started favoring my arm.

"What kind of pain are you in right now?" Sawyer asked.

"On a scale of one to ten?" I asked.

"Sure."

"About a fifteen," I admitted. "I have an appointment to see my doctor later."

"Keep me posted."

"Yes, sir."

The news conference wasn't as bad as I'd anticipated since Mendoza fielded most of the questions. I did appreciate the opportunity to thank the tipster who made the arrest possible and encouraged other citizens to step up when necessary to make our city as safe as we could.

"Well, well, well," Dr. Chu said when she entered the exam room. "It's been a long time, Christopher. I'd ask how you are, but I'm guessing not great if you're here to see me." Dr. Chu listened as I described the collision, then she examined my shoulder thoroughly. "We'll start with X-rays for now. If I don't see anything, we'll move on to an MRI."

The X-rays were clear, so she ordered additional testing at the hospital, put me in a sling, and prescribed muscle relaxers.

"I don't want to start you on physical therapy until I know what I'm working with," she said.

"Sounds fair."

"Unfortunately," Dr. Chu said, "You will have to restrict your work activities, which most likely means desk duty."

I sighed. "I understand, ma'am."

I showed my doctor's note to Sawyer, who referred me to HR.

Most of my time investigating cold cases was spent at a desk, so I'd still find plenty to do. I'd hoped my injury would get me out of the *Sinister in Savannah* interview, but no such luck.

Jonah, Felix, and Rocky, who made up the podcast trio, shook my good hand while commiserating over my injury and congratulating me on my collar. They led me through a series of questions about the investigation and resulting arrest. Felix playfully fanned his face when I spoke about my interview with his husband on Channel Eleven, which had led to the tip. I wasn't the type to put on false airs, so I was honest about my run-in with the fence. The guys and I shared a good laugh, and Rocky told me about one of his private investigations that had resulted in a dog chasing him through a neighborhood.

"His name was Snickerdoodle, and he ripped off a section of my jeans," Rocky said.

After another shared laugh, Felix narrowed his eyes and assessed me. *Oh shit, here it comes.*

"Did you really hurt yourself running after a fugitive, or was it from fighting off the ladies? A little birdy told us you've received several proposals from Savannah's single women. Is that so?"

My face heated with embarrassment, but before I could respond, Rocky joined in.

"Where can the ladies send their resumés?" he asked.

I cocked my head to the side and said, "I think it's very narrow-minded of you to think only the ladies should apply."

"Touché," Felix said and toasted me with a coffee mug.

The conversation returned to my job, and I got to talk about why

I loved working cold cases. I was starving and exhausted by the time we wrapped up the interview. I couldn't say what I wanted more—food or my bed. When I walked into Harper's apartment fifteen minutes later and interrupted her yoga session with Julian, I had to reassess my cravings and priorities. I was no yoga expert, but I could name the triangular pose they were in because it put Julian's sweet ass on perfect display. Downward dog. It definitely made me want to throw back my head and howl. I'd never forget the first time I saw Julian strike the pose. I'd been living with Harper for only a few days when I came home to a similar scene. I'd been completely thunderstruck by his grace, strength, and beauty. Maybe that had been the lightning bolt moment Royce had mentioned. Lust surged through my body as I continued to stare at his sleek muscles and taut ass. It was a damn good thing my dominant arm wasn't injured because I would need my right hand later.

CHAPTER SEVEN

Julian

H ARPER WAS TOO BUSY CURSING ME UNDER HER BREATH TO notice her brother had entered the apartment. I was pretty sure sweet Christopher was an ass man, but I chose our next pose to show off the strength of my legs. If he was as curious as I suspected, I wanted him to wonder about all the things I could do with them.

"Walk your hands back toward your feet and slowly rise to a standing position," I said, hoping my voice sounded as soothing as my previous instructors'. "We're going to do the firefly pose." Harper's exhale was more like an angry hiss than a cleansing breath. I had to bite my lip to keep from laughing at her silent outrage.

"Why do you hate me so much?" she whined.

Ignoring her, I said, "Your feet should be slightly wider than your hips. Slowly fold forward from the hips and reach through your legs to grab your right calf with your right hand. Use that as leverage to work your right shoulder behind your right calf." I glanced over at Harper to ensure she was in position before we repeated the same step on the left side.

"I hate you," she repeated.

I chuckled and added a bit of camp to my yoga instructor's voice. "This pose is great at toning your arms and wrists, but I especially love what it does for my groin and hips. It really opens them up and helps me achieve optimal flexibility."

"Yeah, I bet you're jonesing to flex those hips," Harper snarled.

Ignoring her, I said, "Breathe through the frustrations and repeat this move on the left side, tucking the left shoulder behind the left calf."

Harper huffed out one last indignant breath and followed my lead.

"With the top of your head toward the ground, wrap your forearms around the sides of your shins and place your palms on top of your feet," I said. "Mmm, feel that beautiful stretch in your hips and groin." A slight hitch of breath came from the vicinity of the kitchen, and I knew for certain I had a captive audience. Again, Harper was too furious with me to notice Christopher's presence.

She looked over at me. "Sounds like you're enjoying this way too much. Do you need a moment with yourself? I'll happily leave the room."

"We can't stop now," I said. "We're almost there."

Harper snorted. "Yeah, I bet."

"Squeeze your torso firmly with your inner thighs and keep your head heavy," I said. "Shift your palms on the ground behind your feet and bend your knees deeply as you lower your pert ass and lift your feet."

"I really hate you," Harper hissed.

"Firm your upper arms and extend your gaze in front of you to maintain your balance." I glanced over and made sure Harper was with me. For all her bitching, she had mastered this pose beautifully so far. "Let's finish up strong."

"You can't see it, but I'm flipping you off with my middle toe."

I snorted, which caused me to wobble slightly. I firmed my upper arms once more and said, "Straighten your legs, reaching out through the balls of your feet. Keep your sternum lifted and shoulder blades moving back to prevent tension in your neck. Lift the gaze and smile."

"I will not," Harper said adamantly, but I caught the ghost of a smile tugging at her mouth.

"Think of how toned your arms will look in your dress for the gala."

"How could I when I don't even know what my dress will look like?" she countered.

"I love that you trust me enough to design a dress without input," I said, then guided us back out of the firefly pose.

Once our feet were firmly planted on the ground, Harper turned to me with her hands on her hips. "I trust you enough to bend me like a human pretzel, so why wouldn't I—" Her gaze drifted past me, and I knew the source of her distraction. Harper's eyes widened in alarm, and she made a beeline for the kitchen. "What happened to you?" she asked.

I spun around and saw Christopher's left arm was in a sling. Any euphoria I'd felt from giving the man a peep show wilted like a thirsty flower beneath the hot Savannah sun. That is until I noticed Christopher hadn't taken his half-lidded gaze off me.

"I'm fine, Harper," he said as he raked his golden eyes over my body.

I resisted the urge to reach out and brush a wayward strand of sandy blond hair off Christopher's forehead. "How'd your appointment go?" I asked instead.

"What appointment, and why does Julian know before me?" Harper asked.

I forced myself to look at her then and noticed the worried expression in her pretty dark eyes. "Christopher needed some assistance this morning, and you'd already left for work."

"Because you're aiming for employee of the month, right?" Christopher asked. "I can't imagine another reason you'd want to arrive forty-five minutes early."

Harper rolled her eyes. "Coffee and pastry run."

"Uh-huh," Christopher said.

"And I'd like to point out that we're not talking about me," Harper replied. "Though you get extra points for the nice deflection."

"Luckily, Dr. Chu had a cancellation this afternoon," Christopher said.

He hadn't worn the sling during the press conference about his big bust, so either his appointment had been afterward, or he'd removed the sling before it. I didn't share my musings out loud or reveal that I'd watched the conference. Chief Mendoza is hotter than sin, but he couldn't hold a candle to my Christopher. *My Christopher?* Someone needed to get a grip.

"What did Dr. Chu say?" Harper asked.

Christopher shrugged his good shoulder. "Not much. X-rays came back clear, but

she's waiting for my MRI results before deciding how to proceed."

"When is your MRI?" I asked.

"Tomorrow afternoon, and I follow up with Dr. Chu the day after. I have a good feeling, though. It's sore, but this injury feels different from the last one."

"Whew," Harper said theatrically.

I turned to my friend and quirked a brow. "What's with the melodrama?"

Harper snorted and shook her head. "You have no idea what a whiny cry baby he was during the first surgery."

"Was not," Christopher bit back.

Harper rolled her eyes. "Were too."

"Okay, okay," I said, moving to stand between them as I'd seen Audrey do dozens of times since I'd known them. "Instead of fighting, let's focus on a different word starting with *F*."

Harper held her hands up and took two steps back. "I'm out."

Christopher smiled wolfishly. "But I'm listening."

"You dirty, dirty birds. I'm talking about *food*," I said. "I'm famished. Also a word that starts with *F*."

"What is this? An episode of *Sesame Street*?" Harper asked.

The intensity in Christopher's eyes made me think of activities best performed without an audience, especially not children or his sister.

"I want to shower and change before I eat," Topher said. "I'll try not to take long."

"Need help?" I called after him.

He spun around and walked backward. "With which part?" Instead of waiting for me to answer, he pivoted and continued down the hallway.

And just like that morning, Christopher's remark left me speechless, a rare feat he'd managed twice in a single day. I had to be dreaming, right? I pinched my arm but didn't wake up. I was still standing in Harper's kitchen, and Christopher was still striding toward his bedroom. He hadn't said no to my offer to help. What would happen if I simply followed him to his room? How far was Christopher willing to take his curiosity? Reed's advice echoed in my head, and though he made a valid point, I couldn't wrap my head around the possibility that Christopher could really want me. I continued to stare in a trancelike state until Harper pushed a cold bottle of water against my stomach. The chill of the plastic permeated my shirt and my exhausting internal dialogue.

"What's happening?" Harper asked dryly.

"I'm about to whip up some cornbread to go with the Brunswick stew I made." I knew it was Christopher's favorite, and it felt like the perfect situation to dust off Aunt Lulu's recipe. I edged around Harper and headed into the kitchen, but she followed on my heels.

"Nice try," Harper said. "We both know that isn't what I meant, but just in case, I'll be clearer this time." She set her water down and placed both hands on her lean hips. "What is going on between you and my brother?"

I snorted and got busy gathering ingredients to avoid looking her in the eye while I lied or at least hemmed around the truth. "Do you hear yourself right now? It's just my typical shameless flirting. I've been doing it since the day I met him. I'd think you'd be used to it by now."

"Huh-uh," Harper said. "This isn't the same thing, and we both know it. I noticed a different vibe between you guys at Sunday supper, and it's only intensified since. Topher isn't just soaking up your adoration like a sponge. He's flirting back. And you!"

I affixed an innocent expression on my face and placed a hand over my heart. "Me?"

Harper swatted my question away like a pesky gnat. "Save it

for someone who doesn't know you better. You got flustered with Christopher just now. You *never* get flustered. And don't think I missed the little arm pinch. This isn't a dream, but I'm starting to suspect it's a nightmare for me." Despite our pseudo confrontation, I couldn't help but grin at her. I wanted to assure her that everything would be fine, but I didn't know what *everything* entailed. "So I'll ask again," Harper said. "What is happening?"

I turned to face her, placed both hands on my hips, and stared into her eyes. "Are you seriously asking what my intentions are toward your brother?"

Harper made a retching sound. "Hell no. I know damn well what you'd like to do to my brother. Until now, it's never bothered me."

"Why until now?"

"Because Toph has never shown the slightest inkling he'd welcome the wicked things you'd like to do to him."

Hope was a dangerous thing. It could rise out of nowhere and send a person soaring into the clouds, then disappear just as quickly, hurtling them toward the ground. I'd crashed and burned more times than I wanted to acknowledge, but it would hurt so much more with Christopher.

"And I just can't get behind it." Harper's woeful tone was the pin to my balloon, and my stomach dropped because I'd soared higher than I'd realized.

"You don't think I'm good enough for your brother?" *Ground, meet face.* Fuck, this was going to hurt. Harper was the sunshine on my cloudiest days and losing her friendship would leave me in a perpetual state of darkness.

Harper's worried expression morphed into regret. "No, sweetie. How could you think such a silly thing?" She crossed the space and hugged me tightly. Harper pulled back, cupped my face, and sighed. "I'd have to kill my own brother if he hurt you. That's my dilemma."

And just like that, the sun shone brightly again. "It's a good thing you have nothing to worry about because prison orange isn't your color. It was just some innocent flirting. Maybe Christopher was just trying to turn the tables on me for once."

Harper shook her head. "I know what I saw."

"And that was…"

"A smoldering gaze," Harper said. "I'm surprised your yoga clothes didn't burst into flames." She narrowed her dark eyes. "Wait a minute. Did you choose that torturous pose for Christopher's benefit?"

"Maybe," I teased. "I think Christopher could be a little curious, and maybe I'm pushing the limits to see how far he's willing to take it." I sighed. "But I won't jeopardize our friendship. If it bothers you this much, I'll back off."

I held my breath while Harper worried her bottom lip between her teeth. "No, don't," she finally said. "I think Christopher is more than curious when it comes to you, and I'm convinced no one could possibly love him the way you do. So even though the naughty banter makes me cringe, you have my blessing."

I refrained from squealing when we hugged again, but I held her longer and squeezed her tighter. "I suppose it's no more awkward than Christopher overhearing your bedroom gymnastics."

Harper stepped back and swatted my chest. "We're not talking about that."

"I think we should," I replied. "Topher thinks you're banging your boss. That's what he meant by his employee of the month remark."

Harper's eyes widened, and her bow mouth parted on a gasp. "Really?"

"Uh-huh."

"What did you say?" Harper asked.

"I didn't tell him anything." Informing Christopher that his sister was shagging Coy Beaufort was the last thing I wanted to do. I felt terrible about withholding the information from him, but Harper was my best girl.

She sighed with relief. "Because you're my ride or die."

"Always," I said and kissed her cheek. "By the way, I might have tormented you just to get a rise out of your brother, but you nailed that pose."

"Does that mean I get a sneak peek at my dress?"

"Hell no, but you can help me make this cornbread."

We worked in companionable silence for a bit before Harper nudged me. "Am I to believe it's a coincidence you made Topher's favorite comfort food after learning he reinjured his shoulder?"

I placed the cornbread in the oven, shut the door, and turned to her with a smile. "Believe what you wish."

"Mmm," Christopher said. "Smells like Brunswick stew."

Harper and I jumped because we hadn't heard him coming down the hallway, which was unbelievable considering his size. He truly had the prowess of a lion, and I was dying to have him on me.

I turned and smiled at Christopher. "Yep. It's my aunt Lulu's recipe. Would you like to be my taste tester? It's been a while since I made it."

"God yes." Christopher stepped beside me, tipped his head back, and inhaled deeply. "I can't believe I didn't notice the enticing aroma sooner."

I dipped a spoon into the stew and held it up to my mouth, then proceeded to blow on the soup so it wouldn't burn him. Christopher's attention fell to my lips and remained there as I blew a second time.

"Can't imagine why either," Harper said dryly.

I was aware of her presence but couldn't acknowledge the remark because Christopher had chosen that moment to look into my eyes. Hell, I forgot all about the spoonful of stew I'd promised him.

"You can probably stop blowing now," Christopher said.

I adopted the flirty smile and heart eyes he'd come to expect from me. "Said no man ever."

I held the spoon to his smiling lips, and he opened them for me. The look of pure delight washing over his face made my heart sing with joy, but the sexy little growl he emitted made other parts of me stand up and take notice.

"Christ," Harper snarled. "I'm leaving."

Christopher shifted his gaze in her direction. "Got a hot date?"

"No," she replied, drawing out the word to showcase her annoyance. "I thought maybe the two of you would prefer to eat your stew privately."

Christopher's brow furrowed, and I longed to trace the groove with my fingers. "Bye, Felicia."

The movie quote made me laugh but Harper only scowled at him.

It was getting way too hot in the kitchen, so I changed the subject to find out how their days went. Mine had been thankfully uneventful, which wouldn't last long because homecoming season was almost upon us. Harper's and Christopher's days had been much more exciting than mine. I dished out stew as soon as the cornbread finished baking, and we gathered around the small table in the kitchen nook. Christopher took great delight in my stew, but his pain became more evident as the night wore on.

"Did Dr. Chu give you muscle relaxers or pain meds?" Harper asked.

"Yeah, but I don't want to take them yet. They'll knock me out, and I'll end up wide awake at three in the morning." He ate his final spoonful of stew, then shoved the bowl away. "I had two bowls and can't do anymore."

"I'll put the leftovers in your refrigerator," I said. "You can munch on it for days."

Christopher smiled and sighed happily. "Thank you."

After dinner, I moved to do the dishes, but Christopher insisted on doing them.

I pulled the dirty bowl from his hand and stacked it in the dishwasher. "Your shoulder hurts."

"Doesn't give me an excuse to be lazy," he replied.

"Since when?" Harper asked.

"Why don't you do something productive instead of busting my balls," Christopher tossed over his shoulder.

"Such as?"

"Pick a movie for the three of us to watch," Christopher said. "I've stomached all the reality TV I can take this week."

"Does that include baseball?" I asked.

Christopher snorted. "Of course not."

We worked side by side for several moments until Harper started calling out movie options. Christopher and I vetoed each one until she mentioned *Miss Congeniality*, a rare film we all liked.

Midway through the movie, Christopher leaned closer to me and whispered. "I have a favor to ask."

I turned my head and found his face much closer than I expected. His lips were right there. All I had to do was lean forward a few inches. "Yes," I said without hesitation.

Christopher smiled and shook his head. "You might want to find out what it is first."

"Doesn't matter."

He slid onto the floor and positioned himself at my feet like he'd done the previous night. "You don't have to wait until I fall asleep to play with my hair."

Harper snapped her head in my direction. "You told him?"

Christopher laughed and repeated our conversation from when he'd come over for help with his shirt and tie. While he talked, I massaged his shoulder and flirted with the idea of playing with his hair. Christopher sometimes moaned a little or expressed his appreciation in other ways. Each noise elicited a look of disgust from Harper.

"Hey, at least we're not making my headboard rattle up against your wall," Christopher reminded her.

She opened her mouth, and I knew she was about to spew something like "Not yet," so I cut her off with a quick head shake. Harper rolled her eyes and turned her attention back to the movie.

Christopher tilted his head back and looked up at me. "Go ahead. You know you want to."

I moved my hands into his hair. The cool, silky strands slid through my fingers as I massaged his scalp. Christopher sighed and leaned his head to rest against my leg. He was asleep in minutes, but I kept massaging him to ensure he stayed that way. When my touch lingered long enough to be considered creepy, I eased my hands free and rested them on my thighs. I finished the movie with Harper before easing away from Christopher's warmth.

I kissed her cheek and looked at Christopher on my way to the door. My emotions were a jumbled mess when I walked into my apartment, so I retreated to my sewing room. My phone rang at nine thirty, and I saw it was my sister, Jorja, calling.

"Hey, sis. How are things?"

"Just now heading home from the office," she replied.

"Why so late on a Friday night? Being the daughter of the company's CEO should at least get you out the door by six."

Jorja snorted. "I've gotten myself in a horrible mess with our latest development project, Jules."

The dread in her voice made my stomach hurt. "What's going on?"

"Dad was against the project from the start, but he gave it a green light because he believes in me. It's been one disaster after another. I don't want to disappoint him and shatter his confidence in me."

"I'm sure that isn't the case. You're a genius, and if Dad has faith in you, it's because he knows you'll figure it out. Besides, I'm the one who insisted on forging my own path only to disappoint our parents and shatter their faith in me."

"Nonsense. How many times do I have to tell you that's not true?" Jorja replied. "They admire your independent streak, and Dad claims you got it from him."

I chuckled. "Well, he's not wrong about that. I also inherited a few of his less desirable attributes. I can be quite stubborn."

"Really?" Jorja teased. "I hadn't heard. But seriously, Jules. Your influence is felt all over our corporate office, even though you aren't physically here."

"Yeah? How?"

"Dad has implemented several green initiatives in your honor. We've reduced single use plastic materials by seventy percent, and he's set up recycling throughout the complex. But the changes don't stop there. They're spilling over to the actual construction projects too. He's so proud of you. He tells everyone he knows that his son is a professor."

Tears filled my eyes. "It's just one class, and it's a guest lecturing gig."

"For now," Jorja amended.

"Why has Dad never said anything to me?"

"Because, as you noted, you're both stubborn mules. But maybe you can find some time for a private chat when you come home for my wedding." She squealed. "I can't believe I'm getting married soon. The dress you made for my big day is the most beautiful creation ever, and I cannot wait to show it off to everyone."

"Thanks, sis, but you made my job incredibly easy. You'd make a potato sack look stunning."

She chuckled and said, "Now you're laying it on thick. Enough mushy talk. I can't wait to meet Topher."

"Um, what now?"

"Surely you plan on bringing your boyfriend as a date for my wedding."

"I never said Christopher was my boyfriend." But I may have implied it during my last trip home when my lackluster love life came up in front of Thad, my ex-boyfriend. To save face, I'd said I was seeing someone special. And I had seen Christopher nearly every day since he moved in with Harper. It wasn't a total lie. I'd foolishly thought that would be the end of the conversation, but instead, they pressed me until I'd at least given them his first name. Unfortunately, I used Christopher's nickname, which they'd recognized as Harper's brother.

"His *CrimeStoppers* interview has gone viral, you know," Jorja said. "Mom and Dad have told all their friends, including the Arisens, Christopher is your boyfriend."

Oh no. What have I done?

Completely unaware of my misery, Jorja continued chatting. "Christopher is so handsome. No wonder you want to keep him all to yourself. I can't wait to see the look on Thad Arisen's face when everyone fawns over your new man. He's been strutting around here like a proud peacock with his new boyfriend. Ugh. I hate that he's included in the wedding weekend festivities."

"There was no getting out of it," I said. "The Arisens and our parents go back a long way. I think Mom and Dad were much more upset over my breakup with Thad than I was." Just another way I thought I'd disappointed them. "Mom and Dad were excited about the prospect of me dating Christopher, huh?"

"Mom fanned herself, and Dad said, 'even I understand the fuss.'"

"Wow," I said.

"Yeah, you've got to bring him to the wedding."

This was when I should've come clean about the state of my

relationship with Christopher Carnegie. But when I opened my mouth to do just that, I said, "Okay. I'll ask if he's available."

Jorja squealed her delight and started chatting about everything she had planned leading up to her special day. After we hung up, I stared into space and said, "What have I done?"

CHAPTER EIGHT

Topher

THE CONVENTION CENTER WAS ALREADY PACKED WHEN I ARRIVED at the charity gala. I'd heard they sold a lot of tickets, but it seemed like a wall-to-wall sea of finely dressed people. One of them stuck out like a beacon of light, and I was drawn to him like the proverbial moth to a flame. I hadn't seen Julian in five freaking days, and my life had felt empty and dull in his absence.

With eyes locked on Julian, I crossed the ballroom to where he stood with Shelby and Emma. Shelby wore a knee-length dark green dress with a lacy overlay, and Emma rocked a long, strapless ice-blue dress. As beautiful as they were, I only had eyes for Julian. He'd made one of his corset vests from the same fuchsia material he'd used to make the bodice of Harper's gown. Julian had broken up the vibrant pink with a black lace overlay and alternated it with black leather panels.

He wore a pressed black shirt under the vest and—oh my god—black leather pants. The combination of leather and lace suited him perfectly.

Julian's head swiveled in my direction as if he felt my intense stare or heard my pounding heart from across the room. He'd used hair implements and goop to straighten his light brown hair for the occasion. It gave him a more polished look, but I missed the wild curls. I wanted to run my fingers through his hair and tug the strands and watch them bounce back when I let go. There were other activities I could think of to make his curls bounce, but I didn't want to go there in a crowded room. Julian's face lit up with pleasure at seeing me, and I was overcome with the urge to find out where he'd been all week.

Had I said or done something to chase him off? Was his flirting only good-natured teasing and not a sign of stronger feelings as I'd suspected? Julian's light dimmed and tiny frown lines formed on his forehead. Christ, had my obsessive thoughts and confusion manifested into an angry scowl? I took a deep breath and let my joy at seeing him shine through in a smile. The one he sent me back was so bright it temporarily blinded me, and I nearly staggered into a waiter carrying a tray of drinks. I apologized and continued toward my personal beacon.

My sisters must've followed Julian's gaze because they let out a squeal of happiness. They rushed forward and smothered me with gentle hugs in deference to my shoulder. My MRI results had been favorable. I hadn't torn anything, so I was looking at weeks of wearing a sling and going to physical therapy instead of having surgery.

"How's little Raylon?" I asked Shelby.

She rubbed her baby bump and smiled. "Growing. I can't believe he'll be here in a few more months."

"Uncle Topher can't wait to meet the little man."

Shelby looped her arm through my good one and led me toward Julian, where I wanted to be anyway. "I bet you can't wait for another male in the family." My sister expressed what everyone else had assumed about me.

I leaned toward her and whispered, "Honestly, I'd been hoping for a little girl to spoil. I even had my eye on a little pink fishing pole."

"My son can fish with a pink fishing pole if he wants to," Shelby said.

"I bet you end up having the little girls, Topher," Emma added.

I'd never given fatherhood much thought because all my attempts at relationships had failed miserably. I adored kids but raising them without a partner wouldn't be my first choice. "Maybe," I said.

By then, we had reached Julian, who looked at me quizzically. "What agreement are they trying to wrangle from you?"

Before I could respond, Emma said, "Shelby and I think Topher will be the Carnegie to have little girls."

Julian's smile faltered, and his brow lifted higher. "Does that mean one of the proposals landed?" His tone was light and carefree, but I knew it was a loaded question.

"Nope. Still single." I wanted to point out that he'd know that if he hadn't disappeared, but I didn't want to reveal my needy, confused feelings.

"Hey, is that Coy Beaufort?" Emma asked.

I turned and searched the crowd until my eyes landed on the tall blond dressed in a charcoal gray suit. My nemesis cleaned up well, though I'd rather eat glass than admit it out loud. "What's that asshole doing at a charity event?" I asked.

My sisters chuckled, but Julian sighed and shook his head.

"People can grow," Julian offered.

I looked back in Coy's direction and caught him fidgeting with his tie and shirt collar as he searched the crowd. He was clearly out of his comfort zone and looking for someone. Was he trying to impress a new lady friend? The guy I remembered from high school wouldn't have donned a suit and tie to please anyone, so whoever the lady was, she must've made one hell of an impression on him. Coy turned his head and locked gazes with me. His blue eyes widened briefly, but he held up his hand to offer an awkward wave. I wanted to flip him my middle finger, but I nodded instead.

"See? Growth," Julian said.

I still wanted to know what Beaufort was doing there but forced my thoughts back to something more pleasant such as the way Julian's vest molded to his sculpted torso.

"Now that's an asshole," Julian said, nodding to a dark-haired man across the ballroom.

Emma, Shelby, and I turned to see who'd caught his attention.

"Oh," Emma said. "Do tell."

"If he's an asshole, he's a handsome one," Shelby added.

I knew exactly who my sisters were drooling over. Thaddeus Arisen, Julian's ex-boyfriend, looked like a damn prince in his black suit, white shirt, and black tie. I'd overheard more than a few conversations between Harper and Julian about the man. Though their breakup had occurred before Julian moved to Savannah, the bond between their families meant Julian ran into him every time he went home to visit his parents and sister.

"That's Thad," Julian said.

"Ahhh," Emma and Shelby said, proving they'd heard his name mentioned before too.

I played dumb and acted like I didn't know who they were talking about since Julian wouldn't have expected the deep dive I'd performed on the guy. I'd googled him, checked his record, and stalked his social media to get an idea of the kind of man Julian liked.

Thaddeus Arisen was everything I wasn't—rich, powerful, and connected. I was willing to bet my dick was bigger than his, but that would only get me so far, especially since I was the king of Dullsville. Thad was the kind of guy Julian's family wanted him to date and marry. Thad, and guys of his ilk, could whisk Julian off to Italy for a lover's getaway on a whim. I could only take him to Olive Garden.

What the hell are you doing so far away from home, Thad? Had he and Julian rekindled their relationship? Is that why he'd pulled a disappearing act?

"Damn it," Julian hissed. "I hoped I had a few more weeks before I had to deal with that prick. But I should have realized he'd be here since he sits on the board of trustees for a national organization that raises funds for pediatric cancer research. I bet they've partnered with the Anderson Cancer Institute, which we're all here to support."

Okay, so they hadn't rekindled their relationship. Where had Julian been? Giving his Grindr app a workout? I had no right to be petty and jealous since I'd stayed silent about my growing affection for him, but petty and jealous I was.

"Wow," Emma said. "I bet he was hard to get over."

Julian snorted. "Surprisingly not."

His tone was as sincere as ever. Julian wasn't one to bullshit or beat around the bush. It was one of the things I admired most about him. I turned my attention to Julian, who immediately looked my way as if he were as tuned in to me as I was to him.

"He's not all that," I said. "I think you could do better."

Julian's beautiful eyes softened. They looked greener beneath the ballroom chandeliers. He eased closer to me until only a few inches separated our bodies. As cliché as it sounded, the world around us disappeared, fading to a fuzzy backdrop I no longer saw or heard. He reached up and straightened my tie. I'd used a doorknob to form the knot before looping it over my head and tightening it in place.

"You're too sweet," Julian said.

There were so many things I wanted to say. My thoughts must've knotted up in a ball and lodged in my throat because I suddenly couldn't speak. Julian watched me with a curious expression, so I swallowed hard and said, "I meant every word." But that wasn't good enough. It barely scratched the surface of my emotions. My instincts told me it was time to stop dancing around my feelings and take action. I reached out and placed my good hand on Julian's hip and guided him even closer. "I've missed you and your magic hands this week."

The light in Julian's eyes grew impossibly brighter, and he looked at me with unabashed desire. "I've missed you too."

This wasn't the playful, flirty banter I'd gotten used to and had started to crave. This was deeper and delicious. Someone cleared their throat behind me. *Ignore them*, I implored Julian with my eyes. He must've recognized the irritating voice because he broke eye contact to look beyond my shoulder. Annoyance replaced the longing in his gaze.

"Thad," Julian said tersely. "I'm surprised to see you here tonight."

I stiffened and turned to meet the interloper head-on and realized Emma and Shelby had wandered off at some point.

"Why? We attended dozens of these types of events all around the country when we dated." He turned and looked at me. "This must be Christopher, the boyfriend I've heard so much about," Thad said.

The remark caught me off guard, and Julian looked like he wanted a giant hole to open up in the floor so he could fall through it. What was going on?

"I never said Christopher was my boyfriend," Julian said.

"So you're not dating? Because I heard you were bringing him to your sister's wedding to meet your family." Thad raked his eyes over Julian and didn't bother to conceal his interest. Maybe Thad did have a professional reason for being there, but his heated gaze said the appearance was more personal. It took everything I had not to growl like a possessive beast.

"I, um…" Julian's discomfort was painful for me but an apparent source of delight for his ex, and that I just couldn't abide.

I looped my arm around Julian's lower back to rest my hand on his opposite hip and pulled him into my side. Julian was so surprised it took him a moment to reciprocate the gesture. The warmth of his body pressed against mine nearly made me forget my mission until Thad aimed a pitying look at his ex. I dug my fingers into Julian's hip to keep him in place and dropped a kiss on his head. Julian lifted his gaze to meet mine.

"Boyfriend seems like such an inane word to describe our relationship. It's a Britney Spears title when we're more suited to Van Morrison lyrics." As soon as the words left my mouth, the melody for "Crazy Love" played in my head.

"Who?" Thad asked. The dude was so unworthy of Julian's affection. Julian snorted and looked at his ex. "He means deep and insightful."

Thad didn't look convinced, so I turned Julian toward me, rested my forehead against his, and started singing the opening line to "Crazy Love," changing the pronouns to suit us. Julian sighed, looped his arms around my waist, and melted into me. My feet moved of their own volition, and Julian matched me step for step. We slowly swayed as I sang to him. Once again, I got lost in Julian's eyes, and the world around us faded into the background.

Julian darted a glance to the left and right as I finished the first verse, then he smiled up at me and said, "The coast is clear now."

But I didn't stop singing or swaying. It would've been easier to stop breathing.

Julian smiled up at me, then said, "Careful before I think you mean it."

I started to tell him that I meant it very much, but a guy with dark, slicked-back hair tapped him on the shoulder. Not even the interruption burst our bubble until the guy said, "Harper needs you." Then *poof!*

Julian retracted his arms from around my waist and stepped back. His smile was tentative and unsure, something I'd never associated with him. Julian always seemed so sure and confident with every decision, whether when designing fashion or flirting with me. "I, um, owe you an explanation, but duty calls first."

"You don't owe me anything of the sort," I said, though based on the conversation with his ex, perhaps he owed me a tiny one.

Julian rose on his tiptoes and kissed my cheek. The encounter was brief, but it zinged straight to my groin. It took everything I had to keep from reaching for him when he took two steps back. "Can we talk privately after the gala?"

"Of course."

Julian blew me a kiss before he walked away. I watched him until he was out of sight, then turned to look for my family's table. My parents were already sitting with Emma and her fiancé, Reno, and Shelby and her husband Dallas. There were two empty seats at the table, and I presumed one was for me and the other for Julian. All eyes shifted to me when I approached, and I could tell by their wide-eyed stares that Shelby and Emma had been filling them in about what they'd witnessed between Julian and me.

Mom stood up and leaned forward so I could kiss her cheek.

"You look amazing, Mama," I said, taking in her floor-length lavender gown. She'd swept her dark hair back in an up-do. Little wispy curls framed her face. She looked down the length of her body and met my gaze again. "Are you sure I don't look like I'm trying too hard?"

"Trying too hard to do what?" I asked.

"I think this strapless gown might be too young for me." She'd worn one of those super short lacy sweater things in the same color purple to cover her shoulders. She pulled it tighter around her as if it were a security blanket.

"You look incredible," I assured her.

"What about me?" Dad asked as he stood up and hugged me.

I slapped his back and said, "You look amazing too." We usually only saw Dad dress up for funerals and the occasional wedding, but everyone had stepped up to support Harper on her big night.

"So how is she?" I asked. By my somber tone, they all knew I was inquiring about Harper's mental state. I always thought pageants and public speaking came so easily to her until she confessed to experiencing high anxiety before each event.

"She's doing pretty good," Mom said. "Julian created the most beautiful dress for her, and he knows how to settle her nerves better than anyone."

"I think there's something about Julian that moves us all," Shelby said. "Don't you, Em?"

Emma, who'd just taken a sip of water, set her goblet down and smiled at me. Yep, these two brats had filled everyone in on the sparks they'd witnessed. "I think Julian inspires some of us a little more than others. Wouldn't you say, Toph?"

I darted a glance at my parents, who wore matching smirks.

"Is there something you'd like to tell us, son?" Dad asked casually.

I rubbed the back of my neck, unsure how to respond. There was no denying my attraction to Julian, but I wasn't sure how to word it. Up until recently, I'd considered myself straight. Sure, I noticed when guys were exceptionally handsome or well built, but I hadn't wanted to pull any of them close and kiss them until Julian came along. I knew there was something special when we first met, but even then, kissing him and…more hadn't been on my radar. My attraction to him had developed over time.

Of course I recognized Julian's physical attractiveness, but it was his personality that had sucker punched me. First, I admired the confidence Julian felt in his own skin and how he tried to help others achieve the same comfort. His quick wit and intelligence always kept me on my toes, but what moved me most was Julian's depth of love for those who'd won his loyalty. I'd witnessed it with Harper first, then with my parents and siblings. Since I'd moved in with Harper, I'd gotten to know Julian better, and my curiosity had grown into a strong desire to know him intimately.

"Son," Dad prompted, pulling me out of my reverie. "You must know we'd support a relationship between you and Julian."

My sisters leaned forward at the same time. If I hadn't felt panic rising inside me, I would've laughed at their reaction.

"I… We…" I took a deep breath, still unsure what to say. Maybe I'd know more after Julian and I had our private talk.

"Leave him alone," Mom chided gently, then winked at me. "This isn't the time or place for this conversation."

Dad lifted Mom's hand and kissed it. "Of course. You're right." He changed the subject to an upcoming music festival where we were scheduled to perform. With me out of commission for a while, he wanted to discuss rotating instruments and changing up the songs in each set. The topic bummed me out a little, but it didn't make my heart race or put me on the spot.

Soon after, the waitstaff came around with our entrées, but the seat next to me remained empty. My worry volleyed between Harper having a panic attack and Julian trying to avoid me after the encounter with Thad. I decided I'd investigate if the dessert arrived without any sign of Julian, but I suddenly felt his proximity without turning to look. The hair at the back of my neck stood up, and there seemed to be a charge in the air. Part of me insisted I was being ridiculous, but I told it to shut up when Julian pulled his chair back and sat down a moment later.

He smiled shyly at me, then laid his napkin over his lap. "At least I made it in time for dessert."

"Are you hungry?"

"Starved, but I don't want to cause a fuss," he said. "It's not the wait-staff's fault I'm so late."

"Is Harper okay?" Mom asked just as I flagged down a blonde server.

"She's just fine. Someone carelessly bumped into her backstage and sloshed a drink on her dress. It was nothing a little club soda and a fabric brush couldn't fix."

The server stopped at our table and asked how she could help. I quickly explained that Julian had been assisting the gala host backstage and had missed dinner.

"Oh, we have plenty leftover," she said sweetly. "Would you like chicken, fish, or steak?"

"I don't want to put you out," Julian said.

"It's no bother, sir," she said.

I could tell he was about to argue, so I placed my hand between his shoulders. "Please eat."

Julian huffed a frustrated sigh. "Fine. I'd love a steak, please."

"My pleasure," she replied. "Would you like me to bring out your dessert at the same time?"

Julian snagged my fork off my plate and speared a bite of chocolate cream pie. "I'll just eat his."

The server smiled at me. "Would you like a second helping?"

I'd been eyeing Reno's serving of banana pudding since they set it down in front of him. "We'll take a banana pudding too," I said.

She smiled warmly. "You've got it."

Julian helped himself to another bite of pie and let out a contented sigh. I should've removed my hand, but I kept it on his back until his meal and the banana pudding arrived.

"I want half of that," Julian said before I could take the first bite.

I drew a line in the whipped cream to separate the halves, then dug in. Moments later, the lights in the ballroom dimmed, and the festivities began. Harper looked like she was born to be onstage. Her strapless fuchsia bodice cinched tight around her torso and waist, and the tulle skirt fell in frilly layers to the ground, but a long slit showed a lot of leg when she moved around the stage. The color and style perfectly accentuated Harper's skin tone and figure.

I leaned toward Julian and said, "That's some dress."

Without taking his eyes off Harper, he said, "She's one amazing woman."

My sister had never shone so brightly, not even when she'd been crowned Magnolia Queen. She introduced the various entertainers and conducted the silent auction with humor, wit, and elegance. We waited around after the gala officially ended so we could congratulate Harper on a wonderful evening. She was thrilled the event had flowed so smoothly but was exhausted from having to be on for so long.

She fanned her face and said, "It's going to take me forever to decompress."

Mom, Emma, and Shelby offered suggestions to help her relax, and I took their distraction to get closer to Julian.

"Do you want to have a private chat now?" I asked.

A shadow of doubt crept across his expression, and I regretted bringing it up, especially if he was going to confess he wasn't that into me. "Sure. Walk me to my car?"

"Of course."

The late summer humidity held the city in her tight grip, not even loosening a little after dark. The air felt as heavy with moisture at ten o'clock as it had at six. Julian remained silent until his car was in sight.

"I owe you an apology," Julian said. "I'd made a misleading comment in my family's presence, and it led them to believe we were dating. It was a big dinner, and Thad and his family were there. The conversation turned to my love life, or lack thereof, and I was tired of the pitying glances from some and smug looks from others." I had no difficulty figuring out which camp Thad had been in. "I just blurted out that I didn't need anyone's matchmaking skills because I was already *seeing* someone special." Julian stopped by his car and pivoted to face me. "We'd shared a wonderful movie night before my trip, so I used your name when pressed for the identity of my new guy. It's a common name, and I didn't think much of it. I slipped and said Topher instead, though, which they recognized as belonging to Harper's brother. I should've cleared the air right then, but I didn't. I'm sorry."

I stepped closer, lifted my hand, and brushed the backs of my fingers over his flushed cheeks. Julian's skin was so warm, and even though it was already hotter than hell, I wanted to feel more of his heat.

"It's okay," I said. "I'm not mad."

"You haven't heard the worst part yet." He sounded so miserable, but a stupid smile tugged at my face.

"Lay it on me."

"Your *CrimeStoppers* appearance and post-apprehension press conference have gone viral on social media. Jorja told me my parents are smitten with you and are bragging to everyone that you're my boyfriend." Julian looked devastated, but my chest swelled with pride.

"You think I should be upset because your parents like me?"

Julian shook his head. "I wouldn't trust anyone who didn't like you. The problem is that now everyone expects you to attend my sister's wedding."

"I see. Well, there's only one solution."

Julian nodded vigorously. "I'll call my family tonight and explain everything."

"Nah," I said. "I've got a much better idea."

Julian tipped his head to the side. "You do?"

"I'll go to the wedding as your boyfriend."

Julian gasped and stared at me in utter shock. "You'll do what?" he asked once he recovered.

"You heard me. We'll convince your family we're dating. Later, you can tell them I'm a bore and that you broke things off with me."

Julian snorted. "Like anyone would believe me."

"Trust me. Every girl I've ever dated has told me I'm a drag."

"They're idiots," Julian said breathlessly. "And so are we if we think we can pull this off."

I leaned closer until my lips were nearly touching his. "I have faith in us."

Julian darted a glance behind me and stiffened. "Uh-oh."

Figuring the dickhead Thad was approaching, I closed the distance between us and kissed Julian. He stiffened at first, then melted against me. Julian's lips softened and parted, and I slipped my tongue inside his mouth. Fireworks ignited deep inside me, and I angled my head to deepen the kiss, wanting to get as close to him as possible. Julian moaned and fisted the back of my dress shirt, pressing himself tighter against me. Then he stood on his tiptoes, meeting my tongue stroke for stroke.

A sharp whistle and a catcall interrupted our intimate moment. *Shit.* I pulled back and stared into his dazed eyes.

"I was trying to tell you your family was approaching," he whispered.

Oops. I looked over my shoulder to see my entire family watching us with deliriously happy grins on their faces.

"Show's over," I told them.

"Damn it," Emma grumbled.

Shelby and Mom blew us kisses, but Harper formed a vee with her first and middle fingers. She pointed to her eyes, then to me in the classic *I'm watching you* sign, which I accepted with a nod. Julian groaned and buried his head in my chest as my family disbanded and headed for their vehicles.

"My family bought it," I said once they were all out of earshot.

Julian lifted his head and peered up at me. I smoothed the frown lines on his forehead. "These fake boyfriend plots don't work out so well in television shows and books."

I smiled down at him. "Afraid I'll fall in love with you?" The truth was, I was more than halfway there already.

Julian rolled his eyes. "Not hardly. I love your family so much, and I don't want to lose them when this all goes sideways."

"Our breakup doesn't have to be for heinous reasons. I'm a bore, remember?"

"I could never think that about you," Julian argued.

"Said every person I've dated until they learned the truth for themselves."

Julian shook his head. "No way."

I brushed my nose against his and relished his sudden intake of breath as he closed his eyes. "There's only one way to find out. Take me home to meet the family."

Julian slowly reopened his eyes and met my gaze. "I hope I don't live to regret this."

"It'll be fine. You'll see."

"Said every misguided movie or book character," Julian mumbled.

I placed my hand on his neck and felt his pulse racing beneath my thumb. "Just say yes, Julian."

"Yes," he whispered.

CHAPTER
NINE

Julian

"**W**HAT DO I NEED TO KNOW ABOUT YOUR FAMILY? I WANT TO make a good impression," Christopher said, sounding like an oversized puppy who was eager to please.

"You already have."

"Okay, a lasting impression, then."

"Why, so you can ruin my family for all other men?" I asked.

Christopher snorted, but I wasn't kidding. "Be serious. Tell me about your family. I'd planned to practice being boyfriends before our big debut, but I've barely seen you over the past two weeks. Where'd you run off to?"

I'd hoped Christopher was too busy fighting off his admirers to notice my absence, and since he didn't bring it up until we were three-quarters of the way into our drive to Atlanta, I thought I was literally home free. It turned out Christopher had been lulling me into a false sense of security with small talk and singing along with the radio.

Christopher's sexy singing voice had taken me right back to the moment at the gala where he'd stared into my eyes and sang "Crazy Love" to me. Oh, how I wished he'd meant it, but the song frequently appeared in the family's show. Denver always sang it to Audrey with the kids providing background vocals. I'd always loved watching Christopher performing with the band. So many emotions crossed over his handsome face as he got lost in the music they played. But my favorite part came when Christopher got hot during his performances and took off his shirt. Damn, what a body.

I felt Christopher's intense focus and realized I'd waited too long to respond to his question. I glanced over and noticed his right hand tapping out a beat on his thigh. Could he get any cuter? Christopher arched an impatient brow. Yep, he sure as hell could. The warmth in his gaze was the same as when he sang to me as we danced. And the kiss we shared in the parking lot? Holy hell. I nearly went up in flames. The intimacy had felt very real and was more potent than anything I'd ever felt with guys I'd actually dated. Christopher's wicked smile made him look like a plundering pirate. Was I the loot he sought? A horn sounded close beside me. I jerked my eyes back to the road and his truck into the proper lane.

"If you break it, you buy it," Christopher teased.

"You're the one who suggested I drive your truck."

He chuckled. "We both know I wouldn't fit in your Prius. Even if I scooted the seat back as far as it would go, my knees would still be jammed against my eye sockets. I'm not so good in cramped spaces."

I was ready to dispel his claims but kept my mouth shut.

"If you don't tell me why you disappeared, I'm going to assume you're bored with me too," Christopher said, and I remembered his claim that all his girlfriends had found him dull.

I risked a glance at him. "Are you serious right now?" He'd never struck me as someone with low self-esteem, but I was starting to wonder what the big man hid behind his affable smile.

"Why shouldn't my fake boyfriend find me boring too?"

I sighed and repressed the urge to roll my eyes. "Honestly, I was afraid you'd change your mind. My family is so excited to meet you, and I just couldn't face the idea of disappointing them *again*." Maybe one day I'd believe Jorja when she says I didn't let our parents down.

"I have a hard time believing you disappoint anyone, especially your family," Christopher said softly.

"When things didn't go my way in Atlanta, I gave up instead of digging in. My parents didn't understand my defeatist attitude. Dad would've kicked down any door that someone tried to shut in his face, and Mom would've charmed the hell out of them. Surrender was never an option for them, and they raised me to be the same way." I blew out a frustrated breath. "We're in a good place right now, and I'd like to keep it that way."

"I'd like to dispute a few points." Christopher sounded so serious, and it made me smile.

"Okay."

From my periphery I saw him raise a finger. "There is no one on the planet more charming than you."

"You don't have to lay it on so thick," I said. "My folks aren't around to hear it."

He ignored me and held up a second finger. "You didn't just run away from Atlanta. That Greer Spalding lady had you blackballed from every fashion house in the South when you tried out for *The Next Face in Fashion*."

"Wow. You really do pay attention."

Christopher chuckled. "You're important to me." Then he held up a third finger.

"Oh," I purred. "I really love three fingers. Keep that in mind if this weekend goes really well." God, I'd turned into a brazen hussy. My past flirtations had always been milder and a bit more generic. I'd expressed my interest in having Christopher's body over mine, but never went into great details about what we'd do once I had him there. I'd never wanted to push too far and run him off, but I couldn't seem to help myself. I wanted to test him to see how far his curiosity would take him—*us*. Christopher didn't say anything, and I worried I'd taken my flirting three fingers too far. Instead of apologizing or backtracking, I verbally nudged him instead. "What's the third thing?"

"Hell if I know. I forgot my own name." After a pause, he said, "Three fingers? Like at once?"

I glanced over and caught him staring at the three digits he held in front of his face. Was he picturing them buried in my asshole? I sure was. He turned his head, met my gaze and fascination shone in his golden eyes, encouraging me to be bolder. *Go deep or go home.* Okay, that wasn't the correct saying, but my brain wasn't running the show any longer. My pants suddenly felt tighter in the crotch, and I shifted for a more comfortable position.

"Are you wiggling in your seat because you're thinking about me and my three fingers?"

I somehow managed to keep the truck in the proper lane. "Yep," I said without shame or remorse. "I am. You'd start out with one finger to tease and tempt me. Then add a second finger to stretch me a little further. Honestly, with most men, two fingers would be enough to prep me for anal sex."

"I have big fingers," Christopher said.

"You have big everything, so that's why I'd want you to work up to three." I glanced over at him and winked, but he was still staring at his hand. "I'm a size queen, so I like that about you."

"Is that part included in your profile on Grindr?" he teased.

"What do you know about Grindr profiles?"

"Not much since you still haven't told me about your kinks, but I did a Google search."

Traffic slowed to a crawl due to an accident, and I looked over at him. He'd lowered his hand and now stared straight ahead and assessed the traffic situation. "What other kinds of things have you searched lately?" I asked.

Christopher's cheeks turned bright pink. "Quid pro quo. You answer my questions about your Grindr activities, and I'll tell you the other things I looked up."

"Fair enough. Working out the kinks is the same thing as letting off steam. Between the day job and my side hustles, I don't really have a lot of time to date." Well, I would if I didn't spend every spare moment hanging out at Harper's apartment with her and Christopher. "The truth is, my relationship with Thad was pretty toxic toward the end, and I'm not sure I trust my judgment anymore."

I hadn't wanted to date because the man beside me had ruined me for other guys before they could so much as bat an eyelash in my direction. I held every man to the impossibly high bar Christopher set, and they didn't measure up. My cute little tailor's pun nearly made me laugh.

"Tell me about the breakup."

"Tell me what you've been looking up on the internet," I said. "Quid pro quo, remember?"

"You want to hear about my late-night internet searches?" he asked huskily. I swallowed hard and nodded. "Last night, I looked—"

"Whoa. Whoa. Whoa. Set the stage. Were you in bed?"

"Oh yeah," Christopher purred. I wiggled in my seat again, and he chuckled. "And I was naked."

"Now we're getting somewhere. What did you look up?"

"Well, this is a little embarrassing," Christopher said. "I don't want you to think less of me."

"I promise that won't happen."

Christopher inhaled deeply, held his breath for a short count, then exhaled slowly. "I looked up proper silverware etiquette."

My mouth fell open, and I just stared out the windshield for several seconds. "You freaking tease. Boy, you played me like a cheap instrument, didn't you?"

Christopher laughed hard, and I fought a losing battle to hold on to my irritation. "I'm telling you the truth. It's not my fault you have a dirty mind and assumed I was looking up sex stuff."

"You used a sexy voice and claimed to research Grindr, so of course I made the next logical leap."

"The Grindr thing was the search before the silverware," Christopher said.

"Seriously?" He didn't sound like he was joking, but silverware etiquette?

"Yep. I would've asked you to show me, but you were MIA," he reminded me. "The Carnegie clan doesn't use formal settings as you know. I didn't want to embarrass you in front of your family by not knowing which fork, spoon, or knife to use."

And once again, I realized his easygoing nature hid his insecurities. I hated that he doubted himself for a single second, but I was incredibly charmed by how much he cared. He was so damn adorable.

"Nothing you could say or do would ever embarrass me, Toph." I wanted to pull his truck over, climb onto his lap, and kiss him until he believed me. "Is there anything else worrying you?"

"Not really," he said.

I glanced over and waggled my brows. "Care to tell me more about your search history?"

"Maybe after you tell me about your breakup with Thad."

I really wanted to know what made him curious, so I said, "Thad didn't believe in me or my dreams. He thought pursuing a career in fashion was selfish and frivolous. I can't be with someone who thinks so little of me. People thought my dad was crazy when he started his business, but my mom supported him every step of the way. That's the kind of partner I need in my life. Thad was too concerned about how my ambitions made him look."

"I don't like the guy," Christopher said, then heaved a weighted sigh. "But you could get him back with the snap of your fingers."

I snorted. "My sister says he can't stop bragging about his doctor boyfriend for more than two minutes. I doubt very much Thad is carrying a torch for me."

"I know what I saw," Christopher said. "Is there any part of you that still loves him?"

"No," I said without hesitation. "I don't think I ever loved Thad. I adored the idea of us. I loved how much my parents approved of our relationship. Our families have been best friends for decades, and they treated our relationship like we were joining two royal kingdoms. Having that kind of positive attention is addictive, but Thad and I didn't have the kind of relationship I crave. I don't long to hear his voice when I'm having a bad day. I don't reach for my phone to text him over the silliest things." *The way I do with you.* "Thad and I didn't have what my parents do and certainly nothing close to your parents' relationship. Denver and Audrey are relationship goals."

Christopher chuckled. "My folks haven't always had a storybook romance. They had some rocky years when we were younger. They even separated for a while."

Traffic had opened up again so I could only dart a glance in his direction. "Get out of here."

"No thanks," Christopher said. "I'd rather not jump from a moving vehicle." He was stone-cold serious, but I still didn't believe him. "Eyes on the road," he said when I looked at him again.

I kept my gaze focused out the windshield but reached over to pinch his leg. "Tell me more."

Christopher jolted in his seat, and his powerful thigh flexed under my hand. *Oops.* I'd been aiming for someplace around his knee but ended up closer to his crotch.

"You were either too high or too low. I'm not sure what you were aiming for," Christopher teased. I was not about to let his flirting distract me and told him so. "Fine, but I want to hear more about your family too."

"Deal," I replied. "How old were you when they split?"

"I was ten, and the girls were eight, six, and four. It took them a little over a year to work everything out. They just kept chipping away at the differences and building a bridge back to one another."

"I love them so much," I said.

"Me too. Now tell me the things a boyfriend would know about your parents," Christopher said.

"Uh, there's not much to tell," I hedged. "Graeme and Naomi were dirt poor when they met in college. They didn't have two nickels between them to rub together, but they were both driven to succeed. They worked hard to establish a construction company. One house became two, and two became five. Within ten years, my dad was the most successful builder in Atlanta. Eventually, he moved into commercial real estate development, and that's when their success soared. Jorja and I inherited their drive, work ethic, and independence. I couldn't wait to get a job when I was a teenager."

"Oh, let me guess," Christopher teased. "Gap at the mall?"

"Close. Old Navy. Their clothes were much cheaper to buy, cut apart, and reassemble into something I loved even more."

Christopher laughed. "Is that where your love of fashion began?"

"Oh no. It started when I stayed at Aunt Lulu's house in Savannah as a kid. She was one hell of a seamstress and taught me everything I know."

"When did you become interested in making the corset vests?" he asked. "I don't know much about fashion, but your designs are incredible."

His sweet praise sent a hot flush crawling up my neck. I couldn't imagine what would happen if his compliments became more carnal in nature. "Thank you," I said. "I've been fascinated by Victorian fashion for a long time. I decided to make one for myself, but I wanted to combine function and form with beauty and sensuality."

"I'd say you nailed it," Christopher said.

The blush crept higher as I smiled over at him. "Thank you. It took me several tries to get it right. And then the vests held a deeper meaning for me, especially after I moved to Savannah."

"How so?"

"I was so fractured when I left Atlanta, and it felt like the vests held me together until I got stronger. Some people say they struggle to breathe with them on, but I found it hard to breathe without them." Tears filled my eyes, and I silently willed them not to fall. "But I met Harper, and she brought me home to meet your family. You guys are the glue that pieced me back together. I'm crazy about all of you." I took a deep breath before confessing the next part. "And that's mostly why I stayed away this week. I can't lose you."

A rustling came from Topher's side of the truck, but I didn't dare look over at him. The next thing I knew, he'd freed himself from his sling and reached for my hand. He lifted it to his mouth and kissed the back of my knuckles. Instead of letting go, he rested our joined hands on his thigh.

"I won't let you get hurt," Christopher vowed. "If things go south—"

"*When*," I said firmly.

Topher laughed. "*If* things go south, I will take full responsibility. I assure you my family will have no difficulty believing I blew it with you."

"That doesn't make me feel better. I don't want anyone to get hurt."

Christopher squeezed my hand. "I have enough faith for both of us, so relax and let's have fun."

"Okay. Let's just have fun."

CHAPTER
TEN

Christopher

"**W**E'RE HERE," JULIAN SAID AS HE PULLED UP IN FRONT OF A gray, two-story, stone home in Buckhead. "Home sweet home."

The structure was L-shaped with a round tower in the center connecting the two wings. The high-pitched roof lines, second-story dormers, and towering chimneys were a gorgeous nod to French architecture. While it was the grandest house I'd ever seen, it wasn't the McMansion I'd been expecting. Then again, I had based my anticipation on clichéd assumptions.

"Huh-uh," I said.

Julian's brow furrowed. "You've changed your mind?"

I pivoted in my seat so I could cup his face with my right hand. "Savannah is your home now."

Julian's beautiful green eyes reminded me of a lush meadow I'd happily get lost in. His gaze softened, and he leaned into my touch. "You guys couldn't get rid of me if you tried. I'm yours forever."

My chest tightened again but this time with delighted anticipation. I had to remind myself Julian didn't mean me specifically but the Carnegie clan as a whole. Still, I unhooked the leash on my imagination and let it run wild. I stroked my thumb over his smooth cheek. "Yeah, you are."

Julian released a shaky breath-slash-laugh I found utterly endearing. He closed his eyes and whispered, "Hold on to your heart, Julian."

I arched a brow because I wasn't sure if he'd meant to speak the words out loud. The urge to lean across the console and kiss his soft lips was becoming impossible to ignore. Instead of closing the distance and kissing him, I said, "Or I could do it for you."

Julian snapped his eyes open and smiled. "Damn, you're good at this."

"Want me to prove just how comfortable I'll be if you invade my personal space?"

Julian leaned forward until his lips hovered near mine. "When," he whispered before closing the distance and kissing me. The impact was a fist to the gut and left me breathless and horny. I dropped my hand between us and unbuckled my seat belt so I could get closer and assume control of the kiss, sliding my tongue into his mouth. Julian released a guttural groan that didn't sound remotely fake, and I pressed my advantage further—sliding my hand up into his adorable curls I liked so much. The soft silkiness of his hair sifting through my fingers made me think of other instances where I might fist the strands and—

A knock sounded softly on the window behind me, and we jerked apart. Julian's eyes widened before narrowing into angry slits.

"Go away," he called out. "Can't you see I'm busy?"

Delightful giggles met his stern rebuke. Julian groaned and leaned forward to rest his head on my good shoulder. "They're incorrigible."

"Who?" I asked, though I had a good idea who stood outside my door.

"My mom and sister." Julian lifted his head suddenly. "We can still back down the driveway and peel out of here."

"No, you cannot," the two women said.

That made us both laugh. I tugged lightly at Julian's curls until he lifted his head and met my gaze. "Trust me?" I whispered.

"With my life."

I leaned forward and softly kissed his lips before easing back into my seat. I held my breath for a short count and released it slowly as I opened the truck door and stepped down onto the driveway.

"Hi, I'm—" I managed to get out before the ladies rushed me.

"Careful of his shoulder, you animals," Julian called out. His mother shushed him with a wave, but she and Jorja took a step back. I noticed they had green eyes like Julian, but they weren't nearly as pretty. The resemblance between Naomi and her children was uncanny. Same high cheekbones, patrician nose, bow mouth, and curly hair, though Naomi's was several shades darker than Jorja's and Julian's.

"Oh my," Naomi Fine said as she raked a curious gaze over my body. "You're even more handsome in person."

I chuckled nervously as Julian rounded the hood of my truck, then slipped an arm low around my waist. Damn, I loved it when he touched me.

"For crying out loud, back off, you cougar," Julian insisted.

"And you're bigger too," Jorja said breathlessly. She was six inches shorter than Julian's five-nine frame, so she had to tip her head back to look at my face. "So very handsome."

"This is pathetic," Julian said, but I heard the delighted pleasure in his voice.

Naomi giggled and walked toward him with open arms. "I've missed you so much."

Julian closed his eyes and returned his mother's hug. "I was just here a few weeks ago doing a final fitting for Jorja's dress."

"Feels like months instead of weeks," Naomi said. "The house isn't the same without you."

He leaned down and kissed Naomi's cheek. "I miss you too."

Jorja cleared her throat, muscled their mom out of the way, and launched herself into Julian's arms. He caught his sister and spun her around. "Can you believe I'm getting married?"

Julian pulled back, hooked his arm around her neck, and rubbed his knuckles against her head. It was such a brotherly thing to do.

"Off the hair," Jorja cried out, "or I'll get even."

Julian threw up his hands in surrender and backed away. "Where're Dad and Otto?"

Naomi and Jorja exchanged glances, then forced fake smiles on their lips.

"They hit the club for a round of golf this afternoon with a few other guys," Naomi said. "They'll be back soon. I have a very special dinner planned."

I suspected the identity of the "other guys" was the source of Naomi's and Jorja's discomfort, or at least one particular guy was responsible. Julian had stressed to me just how close the bond between the Fines and Arisens was, so it only made sense that they had joined Graeme and Otto at the club to celebrate the pending nuptials. I expected to spend most of the weekend with the Arisens. Studying Julian's tense frame, I vowed Thad wouldn't be a blip on his radar by Sunday night.

Naomi took Julian's weekender and garment bag while Jorja divested me of mine. I started to protest, but the little imp silenced me with a raised brow. Though she may be tiny, the woman was fierce.

Jorja smiled up at me. "Smart man."

I chuckled. "My mama didn't raise a fool."

"I'm dying to introduce Aunt Lulu to Christopher," Julian said.

"She's taking a nap right now," Naomi said. "She's been watching for your arrival for hours and tuckered herself out." She leaned into her son and put her head closer to Julian's. "You did warn him about her behavior, right?"

"Not really," Julian hemmed. "I was afraid of scaring him off."

I hadn't even met Aunt Tallulah and was already a big fan. Naomi glanced over her shoulder and winked at me before looking forward. "He looks like a big boy to me."

"Mom, I'm going to tell Dad you're acting like a shameless hussy," Jorja teased.

"Oh, you two killjoys never let me have any fun, but you're the ones who brought the most handsome men on the planet home to meet mama. How could I not fuss?"

Jorja giggled beside me. "Otto has gotten used to it, and you will too. I swear she's harmless."

"I'm not afraid," I quipped.

"Sexy and smart," Naomi said. "Better hang on to this one, Jules."

"Mom!" Julian and Jorja said at once.

The home's interior was just as elegant and lovely as the exterior. The décor was a mixture of modern, cream-colored fabric furniture and warm-brown, antique, French-country pieces, which conveyed a welcoming, homey vibe. I'd gone antiquing enough with my mom and grandma to realize the furnishings in the living room alone were worth more than my annual salary.

"That's a gorgeous French-country farmhouse armoire, Mrs. Fine," I said. I'd seen one in worse shape go for nine thousand dollars.

She released Julian and turned to face me. "Please call me Naomi."

"Okay."

"Shall we call you Christopher or Topher? I've heard you referred to as both."

I smiled at her. "Whatever you feel comfortable with."

She tipped her head to the side and studied me. "Christopher, I think," she said. "Do you enjoy antiques?"

"I appreciate their history," I replied, "but my interests run more to vintage guitars."

"Electric or acoustic?"

I smiled. "Both."

"Julian tells us your family has a band," Naomi said. "I would love to see a performance sometime."

"I have videos," Julian offered.

"Oh good," Naomi said. "I'm looking forward to watching them, but it can wait until you've had a chance to rest up and get a snack. I'm sure you're hungry after the long drive."

I patted my stomach. "I can always eat."

"Yes, I'm sure you require lots of fuel."

"Mom!" Julian and Jorja admonished again.

"What?" Naomi asked innocently. In case we didn't buy it, she batted her eyelashes. "I reserved the pool house for you guys. We'll have a houseful of guests shuffling in before the wedding, and I figured you might like the privacy away from prying eyes."

"You put us both in the pool house?" Julian asked.

Naomi rolled her eyes. "Son, I'm not that out of touch. I've never expected my children to stay chaste until their wedding days."

Jorja snorted. "Good thing."

Naomi ignored her daughter and furrowed her brow. "Do you think you'll be uncomfortable there, Julian? I could rearrange our guests."

I stepped up beside Julian, put my arm around his waist, and placed a kiss on his temple. "I think the pool house sounds great. And if furnished half as nicely as the main house, I have no doubt we'll be in heaven out there. Right, babe?"

Julian didn't answer right away. It was like he didn't realize I was talking to him. I glanced over and caught him staring off into space with a hint of a smile tugging at his lips. My ego hoped he was thinking of all the things we could get up to all alone in the pool house. I pressed my fingers into his hip. "Right, babe?" I asked again.

Julian shook himself out of his daydream. "Oh, right. We're going to love it out in the pool house, Mom. You always consider everything."

Naomi beamed beneath his praise. "Nothing but the best for my boy and his beau."

Jorja's phone rang, and she sighed dreamily after checking the caller ID. "It's my soon-to-be mister." She took a few steps back before looking up at us. "I'm so happy you're home, Julian." She smiled at me. "And I can't wait to get to know you better, Christopher." She turned and practically skipped out of the room before Julian or I could reply.

I looked over at Julian and caught him watching his sister's exit. A huge smile graced his handsome face and his eyes shimmered like emeralds. He met my gaze, and his smile grew even broader.

"I love seeing her so happy," he said.

Naomi chuckled. "Most brides are unbearable by this time, but your sister has stuck to her guns and kept the wedding an intimate affair." A wry smile graced her lips, and I had a feeling the two women might have clashed on more than a few occasions while planning the wedding. She looked at Julian and narrowed her eyes. "She still hasn't let me see the dress you designed for her. Most mamas get to go dress shopping with their daughters."

Julian held up his hands. "That was all her doing. She said it lessens the impact of seeing her in the dress on her big day."

Naomi sighed. "I guess." Then she made a shooing motion with her hands. "You two head on out to the pool house. I wasn't joking when I said the kitchen is fully stocked. I even baked your favorite cookies last night."

"Mmm. Peanut butter chocolate chip," I said.

Julian looked a little surprised that I knew his favorite cookie. He recovered quickly and pecked a quick kiss on Naomi's cheek. Then he tilted his head toward the rear of the house, and said, "Come on. You'll never have a better cookie." But Julian's eagerness faded as soon as we were out of earshot. "There's one tiny problem with staying in the pool house."

"Which is?"

"There's only one bed." Julian looked at me with dread in his eyes. "And it's not a very big one. Maybe a double."

"I can sleep on the couch if you're uncomfortable," I said.

Julian shook his head. "There's only a loveseat and a few club chairs. Nothing is big enough for you to sleep on, and I don't want you uncomfortable. I could probably fit on the loveseat."

"No way," I said. "I'm not running you out of your bed. We can share, right?"

Julian worked his bottom lip between his teeth. "I'm not sure it's a good idea."

I stepped closer to him and cupped his face. "Afraid you won't be able to keep your hands to yourself?" I teased.

"Actually, yes." Julian huffed a sigh. "I'm like a heat-seeking missile who doesn't know how to stay on his side of the bed." His cheeks turned adorably pink. "I could get handsy in my sleep without knowing it."

My heart pounded out a rhythm rivaling the beat of any heavy rock song. "I appreciate the warning, but I'll take my chances."

He sighed again. "Okay."

Julian opened a set of French doors that led out to the pool area, and I stopped to take it all in. The recreation area looked like something from a Caribbean resort. An outdoor living space with a bar and kitchen took up much of the patio, and a tidy row of loungers with navy-blue cushions lined the opposite side of the pool. Tropical plants and lush greenery were tucked into every space, adding bursts of color.

"Is that a brick pizza oven?" I asked.

"Yeah," Julian said. "Mom thought it was overkill until Dad perfected his pizza." Julian snorted. "His first few attempts were unrecognizable disasters."

The French doors opened again, and a guy stepped onto the patio carrying a book in one hand and a teacup in the other. He looked about Julian's age, and the similarities didn't stop there. In fact, they looked so much alike that I expected Julian to introduce him as a cousin. But there was no recognition on the stranger's face or in Julian's posture. Alarm bells went off in my brain. Was this Thad's new boyfriend? Had no one else noticed how much he resembled Julian? This guy's hair and eyes were slightly darker, but his build, posture, and height were uncannily similar.

"Oh, I'm sorry," the man said awkwardly. "Am I interrupting?"

"Um, no," Julian said. "We're just heading to the pool house to rest up after a long drive. Have we met? I feel like I know you." I wanted to point out the obvious but kept my mouth shut.

"I'm Tyler Tannehill," he replied. He started to extend his hand to Julian only to realize it held a teacup. He laughed nervously, and I figured he had guessed Julian's identity and recognized the same similarities I had. "I'm Thad's boyfriend."

"Ah," Julian said, then introduced us. "You decided to skip golf?"

"Every chance I get," Tyler replied. "Give me a quiet corner, a nice cup of tea, and a book."

Julian smiled. "You sound like my kind of people. I look forward to getting to know you better."

Tyler smiled. "Likewise. Don't let me hold you up."

Julian and I headed toward the pool house. I waited for him to remark on how much Tyler looked like him once we were out of earshot, but he either hadn't noticed or didn't care.

The single-story structure was built with the same gray stone as the main house but without the fancy roof, dormer, and tower. And though it was considerably smaller than the main residence, it looked larger than the apartment I shared with Harper. Julian punched a code into an electronic lock by the front door and let us inside, and I confirmed the pool house was twice the size of our apartment.

"Wow," I said as I looked around the open floor plan.

The same elegant tropical design carried over into the pool house too. Pale gray tile, polished to a high sheen, covered the floor. The kitchen cabinetry was a stark white, which contrasted nicely with the navy-blue furniture in the living room area.

"This is impressive," I said.

Julian snorted. "Until you see how small the bed is." He opened a set of double doors that led to the bedroom and bathroom.

The suite was small but beautifully appointed. The décor from the living room carried over, and the bedroom furniture looked like genuine French antiques instead of modern replicas. The ornately carved headboard was a gorgeous piece of art, but Julian hadn't been joking about the size of the bed. My feet would probably hang over the edge, but it would be worth it to have him beside me. I set my bags down and walked over to it. Leaning forward, I pressed my hand into the mattress. It was firm enough to support my weight but soft enough to make me feel like I would be sleeping on a cloud. "Just right."

"Mmmhmm," Julian said distractedly.

I glanced over my shoulder and caught him staring at my ass. The longing I saw in the green depths matched the pang in my heart. He wanted me, and I desperately needed him. So why the hell were we faking a relationship when we should be building a real one? The epiphany was a horse kick to my gut, and I sucked in a sharp breath. It sounded loud in the small space, and Julian jerked his head up to meet my gaze.

I crossed to where he stood, eased his luggage from his fingers, and set it beside mine on the ground. Cupping his face, I opened my mouth to say something profound and earth-shattering, but all that came out was, "I really like you, Julian." Feeling dumb, I moved to expand on such a banal remark. "And I mean *everything* about you."

He patted my good shoulder and rested his hand there after he finished. "I like everything about you too."

God, I was so horrible with this kind of thing. I wanted to convey every wonderful thing he made me feel, but I couldn't get the words to flow. It was as if my tongue wasn't receiving the signals my brain was sending out. I couldn't even find a song to represent the riotous emotions pulsing through my body. So I did the next best thing. I lowered my head, pressed my mouth to his, and showed him.

Julian immediately parted for me, and I slid my tongue inside his mouth, deepening the kiss. The taste of him combined with his soft whimpers drove me wild. I placed my hand at his waist and stepped backward until my legs bumped into the bed. I sat down on the edge and urged Julian to follow me. He sat on my lap, wrapped his legs around my waist, and slid both hands into my hair.

Since I only had one hand to hold him, I placed it on the small of his back and kept his lower body pressed firmly against mine. I angled my head, looking to deepen the kiss even more since I couldn't crawl inside his body and live there. Julian groaned and sucked my tongue. I couldn't stop thinking about his lips wrapped around something else, and my dick began to lengthen and throb with anticipation. My first instinct was to change the direction of my thoughts to cool things down, but I wanted Julian to feel how I reacted to him. Since I couldn't verbally express how much I wanted to explore these feelings between us, I would show him.

I slid my hand down to cup his ass and rocked his groin against mine. He was as erect as I was and responded with an adorable growl. Julian placed one hand on my good shoulder to anchor himself and started to grind against me. He fisted his other hand in my hair and devoured my mouth until I had to rip free to breathe. Julian tilted his head back, moaned low and long, and continued to rut against me. The friction was incredible, but the sight before me was the sexiest thing I'd ever seen. Julian had forgotten where we were and what our original purpose was. He was fueled by instinct and pleasure. I tilted my head and attached my mouth to his neck, sucking and licking a path toward his chin. I was desperate to reclaim those pretty lips for myself.

"Toph, maybe we should stop," Julian said before I reached my destination. "I'm about to…"

Knowing he was as turned on as I was only ratcheted up my pleasure. And that fucking slow, torturous grind of his dick against mine made my eyes roll back in my head. If we felt this good fully clothed, what would it be like if there was nothing between us? I worried I might not survive if given a chance to find out. I dug my fingers deeper into his ass cheek, fearing he'd pull away. He answered by tightening his grip on my shoulder.

"Please don't stop," I replied. "I'm right there with you."

I drove my hips upward to meet his thrusts, which knocked our rhythm off-kilter. Julian pushed me to my back but was still mindful of my sore shoulder. He braced his hands beside my head and stared into my eyes as he rode me.

"I'm going to make you come so hard," he said hungrily.

My eyelids felt heavy, but I willed them to stay open. I didn't want to miss one second of Julian flying apart in my embrace. "You already have," I told him. "Several times."

My confession caused Julian's eyes to widen and made his hips falter. He recovered quickly, and determination darkened his eyes. "Show me."

I pulled his ass up a little higher so his dick notched against that sensitive spot beneath my crown. "Oh yeah. Right there." He sped up his tempo, and the fireworks started in my groin and bloomed throughout my body. "Julian." My entire body tensed as I filled my underwear with hot cum.

Julian watched me unravel for him with a rapt, wonderous expression. The smell of my release drifted between us, and Julian closed his eyes and breathed deep. "Toph, I—" His words ended on a hitched breath, and he jerked against me, mouth and eyes open wide as he found his release. I dropped my gaze and watched the wet spot bloom across the front of his pants.

Julian remained leaning over me but closed his eyes until his breathing leveled out. I lifted my hand and brushed the curls away from his face. "Look at me." I needed to know he didn't regret what happened between us. I should've found a way to express my desire with words before anything physical happened between us. After what seemed like forever, Julian opened his beautiful eyes. No regret registered in his expression, and I breathed easier.

"What just..." Julian paused for a breath. "What just happened here?"

A chuckle rumbled out of me. "If I have to tell you, I'm even worse at sex than I thought."

Julian rolled his eyes and pushed off the bed to sit up. He made no move to climb fully off me, which made me deliriously happy. "Seriously, Toph."

A curl fell over his forehead, and I tugged it. "You made me come in my pants like a teenager," I said.

Julian shook his head like he still couldn't believe it. I reached up and tweaked his nipple to show he wasn't dreaming, then rested my hand over his heart. Julian gasped and wrapped his hand around my wrist but didn't pull it away from him. Another victory I'd gladly accept. "But how?" he asked. At my quirked brow, Julian rolled his eyes. "I know the biology behind you coming in your pants. What confuses me is that I...um...helped facilitate it." A shy, insecure expression bloomed across his face. "I would think it was just a physical reaction to our practicing intimacy, but you said..."

"I've been jerking off to fantasies of you for months." Smooth? No, but it was bluntly honest.

Julian looked neither happy nor distressed by my confession; he seemed utterly dumbstruck. "Are you..."

"Gay? Bi? Pan?" I said, trying to fill in the blanks for him. Julian simply nodded, and I chuckled. I cupped his face. "I honestly don't know what I am besides completely drawn to you. I'm not just talking about the physical stuff. You have to know you're incredibly gorgeous, but my attraction to you goes beyond the exterior. I feel like we connect on a deeper level. And if I'm honest, I can't claim the same about anyone else I've been involved with. Something about you draws me in and won't let me go." Where had my ability to converse been before we rutted ourselves to orgasm? The words would've been much more powerful then. "There was so much I wanted to say to you before we kissed and…"

"Frotted each other's brains out," Julian supplied.

"Yeah, that," I agreed. "I couldn't get the words out, so I decided to show you with a kiss. And things went quicker than I anticipated. I don't want you to feel used."

Julian swallowed hard and a wry smile formed on his face. I expected him to say something flirty or snarky, but instead, he said, "I'm honestly not sure what to think. I've wanted you—*this*—for so long, and I can't wrap my head around the idea that I could have you." He brushed the backs of his fingers over my cheek. I captured his wrist, brought his hand to my mouth, and kissed his palm. "Toph, you have the power to hurt me like no one else ever has. If we fuck this up, I don't just lose you. I lose your entire family."

"And you're not sure I'm worth the risk?"

Julian inhaled deeply, then slowly let the breath pass through his lips. "A short while ago, I would've said a chance with you was worth risking everything because the idea was pure fantasy. There were no repercussions. But faced with a real chance, I'm just not sure." Tears welled in his eyes. "But I'm terrified of wondering what it might be like to be loved by you for the rest of my life." A tear slid down his face, and I wiped it away. "You mean so much to me, and I don't want to lose you."

His honesty was the most beautiful thing I'd ever witnessed, more so than his orgasm. My thoughts and emotions knotted together until it felt like a bowling ball was stuck in my throat. I swallowed hard and managed to dislodge the tangled mess. "Let's get one thing straight," I said firmly. "You will not lose me, and you sure as hell won't lose my family. We're crazy about you, Julian, even if you decide not to explore the feelings between us. I don't need an answer right now. We can table the conversation, carry on with our original plan, and revisit the topic when we get back to Savannah."

Julian tilted his head to the side. "You mean it?"

I wasn't sure which part he was questioning, but it didn't matter. "Absolutely."

Julian released a soft sigh, then lay across my chest. I wrapped my good arm around him, placed a chaste kiss on the top of his forehead, and smiled up at the ceiling. We agreed to table the conversation for a few days, but I said nothing about suspending my campaign to prove just how right we were together. Neither of us mentioned anything about keeping our hands off each other either, but that wasn't the angle I was going for. My mission was to prove the affection I felt for Julian was real and not a flight of fancy. I closed my eyes and started planning out my strategy. When it came to Julian, I was playing for keeps.

CHAPTER ELEVEN

Julian

"**T**HERE HE IS!" AUNT LULU DECLARED LOUDLY AS WE STEPPED into the drawing room.

I turned to see what celebrity had walked up behind me, but the hallway was empty. I watched in horror as the gathering migrated toward Christopher and me, murmuring things like "It's about time" or "Now the party can start." How many predinner drinks had we missed out on, and since when did I warrant the rock-star treatment?

Then I recalled the stunning man standing beside me in a navy suit and crisp white shirt. I snorted internally. *Remembered?* Yeah, right. As if I could forget a single thing we'd shared or said since arriving at my parents' house. We'd crashed hard after our shared orgasm and slept well into the cocktail hour before I woke in a panic, which meant I hadn't processed the things we'd said or done in our rush to get cleaned up and walk to the main house. This fanfare wasn't for me; it was for my date. Unlike the attention Thad had garnered from my folks, I enjoyed watching my mom and sister fuss over Christopher until they both tried to hook their arms through his and lead him away. He'd left his sling at the pool house and assured me he was fine without it for a few hours, but he probably hadn't counted on Mom or Jorja latching onto his bad arm.

"Not so fast, you hussies," I called out. "I'll make the introductions." I looked over at my dad, who looked sun-kissed and very happy. He'd worn his favorite Hugo Boss suit, and like Christopher, he'd skipped the tie and wore his dress shirt open at the throat. He'd styled his light brown hair in the same quiff he'd always worn. Jorja and I used to tease him mercilessly about it until the style came back into fashion and we were forced to eat crow. Dad had texted a photo of himself next to a headshot of Eugene Levy taken during the height of *Schitt's Creek* fame. The caption read: Who Wore it Better? My sister had pleaded the fifth, but I reluctantly admitted that my old man rocked the look best. Dad's gaze met mine, and his eyes twinkled with humor. He seemed charmed by Mom and Jorja's antics.

"You better watch your wife," I warned him. "She's out of control."

Dad's smile turned wry, and he shook his head. He reached for my mom and pulled her into his arms. "I'm not worried about some young guy stealing my woman from under me."

Before I could point out Christopher wasn't the one who needed watching, Mom giggled and carded her fingers through the gray hair at Dad's temples. She pressed her lips to his for a quick kiss. And just like that, I suspected the rest of the room faded into oblivion for them. I'd shared a similar moment with Christopher a few times and recalled what an exhilarating and dizzying experience it was. My temperature soared as I remembered Christopher's face as he'd found release with me in the pool house. I would've fanned my face, but I didn't want to relinquish Christopher's hand. His solid presence kept me tethered and grounded when the memory made me want to float away like a feather in the wind.

"There's my boy!" Aunt Lulu called out seconds before she squeezed me in a shockingly tight hug. I released Christopher to return her embrace, albeit more gently. She smelled like Chanel and the peppermint candies she'd favored for as long as I could remember. The combination of fragrances reminded me of summers in Savannah, learning how to sew—first by hand and later on a machine—at Lulu's house. "Judging by your flushed cheeks," she said, "I can guess why the two of you are late."

"Aunt Lulu," I groaned as I pulled back. "Behave."

"Never," she vowed. "Introduce me to the man who's made you blush."

I sighed deeply and introduced two of my favorite people to one another. They launched into a harmonious conversation as if they'd been friends for a long time.

Lulu turned to face me suddenly with a broad smile on her face. "I like him."

Christopher chuckled. "And I adore her."

Lulu pursed her lips and patted her coiffed white hair. "If you were a few decades older…"

I hugged her once more and whispered, "I love you so much."

She laughed and patted my back. "I love you too."

I stepped back and studied her pink pantsuit. "Pretty sure Dorothy wore a similar outfit on *The Golden Girls*," I said.

"This is nothing like the satiny monstrosity Dorothy wore," Lulu said. "I know damn well I taught you how to recognize fabric better than that. I should take you over my knee. You're not too big, you know."

Christopher leaned forward and quietly said, "I told him the same thing recently, but he just told me not to threaten him with a good time."

Lulu placed a hand over her chest, and at first, I thought Christopher had triggered a heart attack. But she tilted her head back and emitted the most raucous laugh I'd ever heard. Every head in the room swiveled our way. I didn't need to look around to confirm my suspicion because I felt their attention. Once she stopped cackling, she cupped Christopher's face and kissed both of his cheeks. It was a move she reserved for those she held closest to her heart. Everyone in the room recognized the symbolic gesture for what it was—hearty approval. And if that wasn't enough, she glanced around the room and said, "*This one* is a keeper."

I looked around the gathering to gauge the reaction. Mom, Dad, Otto, and Jorja seemed deliriously happy. Tyler looked utterly charmed by my aunt, and I wondered about their prior interactions. Thad looked like he'd swallowed something sour, and his parents, Mark and Debbie, offered tense smiles. Aunt Tallulah had inadvertently, or possibly quite intentionally, insulted their son.

Christopher settled his left hand at the small of my back, and I leaned into his warmth.

Dad stepped forward, extended his hand, and said, "My turn to meet the man who's won the heart of everyone I hold near and dear."

"Christopher Carnegie," he said with a warm smile as he shook my father's hand. "It's a pleasure to meet you, sir. Julian speaks very highly of you."

Dad smiled warmly at me. "Well, I'm very proud of my son too."

He couldn't know just how much those words meant to me. My parents had looked so disappointed when I'd announced I was moving to Savannah. At the time, I'd thought they were frustrated that I'd broken up with Thad and had given up on my dream to become a fashion designer. I was starting to realize I'd misread the situation, as Jorja had always claimed, and that my parents had been disappointed *for* me, not *in* me. If the Carnegies were the glue that pieced me back together, this epiphany acted as a glossy glaze that made me shine again. The coating wouldn't erase the cracks from my previous damage; it would emphasize them and demonstrate that flawed things could be beautiful.

"Thanks, Dad," I said, my voice thick with emotion.

My father winked, then gestured for Jorja's fiancé, Otto Fortner, to join them. Dad met Otto, a financier, through a business venture and was so impressed he introduced the man to his only daughter. Jorja had been hell-bent on hating Otto on sight but fell madly in love with the dark-haired, dark-eyed man. He was brilliant, funny, kind, and head over heels for her. It was easy to see why my sister loved the man so much.

Otto and Christopher exchanged easy hellos, then Otto introduced his parents, Manuel and Zennie. They were as gregarious and charming as their son and greeted Christopher warmly.

Manuel narrowed his eyes and tapped a long, slender finger against his chin. "You look familiar to me."

"He's been on the news a lot because he solved a homicide cold case involving an elderly woman," Zennie said. She smiled at Christopher and added, "I think someone started a dashing detective hashtag in your honor."

"Darling detective," my mom called out.

"That's it," Zennie said.

Manuel shook his head. "No, that's not it."

"Honey," Zennie said softly, "you don't even know what a hashtag is."

Manuel chuckled. "You're right about that. I'm not disputing the darling or dashing thing. I know Christopher from someplace else. I just can't put my finger on it."

"Hope it wasn't one of his undercover assignments," I teased. "You'd have some serious explaining to do."

Manuel and Zennie laughed and moved on so the Arisens could meet Christopher. Manuel kept glancing over at him, and I could tell he was still trying to place where he recognized him from.

Mark and Debbie were both gracious when they shook Christopher's hand. Mark narrowed his eyes and said, "I agree with Manuel. I recognize you from somewhere besides the cop stuff."

Christopher chuckled. "Perhaps you do."

Manuel turned back around. "Thanks, Mark. Care to give us a hint, son?" he asked Christopher.

"Nope."

"Did it involve nudity?" Lulu asked.

"Nope," Christopher repeated.

Lulu snapped her fingers. "Damn."

"A reality show?" Mom guessed.

"Kind of," Topher replied.

"All right," Dad said. "Let him be. We don't want to scare him off."

"Yeah, that's not going to happen," Christopher said firmly. I noticed he was looking at Thad when he said it. My ex had just stepped up with Tyler after his parents stepped aside. Christopher greeted Thad with a nod, then shifted his gaze to the right. "It's good to see you again, Tyler."

"Again?" Thad asked snidely, looking between Christopher and Tyler. He settled his gaze on his boyfriend, who blushed. "How do you know each other?"

"I met Christopher and Julian this afternoon when they arrived."

"Why didn't you tell me?" Thad asked.

Tyler frowned. "Tell you what exactly? I encountered them when I went out to the pool to read a book and enjoy a cup of tea. I don't think it's unusual for me to run into them, considering this is Julian's home."

"Of course it's not," Thad said with an awkward chuckle. "I'm just surprised you didn't mention it."

Tyler narrowed his eyes. "Like you always account for every minute of your day while we're apart."

Thad stiffened and cupped Tyler's elbow before meeting my gaze. "I'll catch up with you in a bit, Julian," he said and guided Tyler out of the drawing room for what I guessed would be a very spirited argument in private.

A tense silence fell over the room once Thad and Tyler exited. Christopher's fingers flexed against my lower back, and I wanted to believe it was an act of possessiveness and not muscle spasms in his injured arm. Conversations resumed around the room, tentatively at first but loosened up the longer Thad and Tyler stayed gone. Debbie glanced toward the doorway a few times before returning her focus to the conversation. She didn't relax until Thad and Tyler came back.

At first glance, the couple looked no worse for wear, but a closer perusal showed tense body language, and I could almost feel a nip in the air. The few inches separating them might as well have been a gorge. I'd heard from Jorja that Debbie was pushing hard for Thad to propose to Tyler, but I didn't think their relationship was long for this world.

Luckily, Mom announced dinner was ready and led us to the formal dining room.

Once everyone had food, conversation resumed around the table with most of it centering on Christopher. Everyone seemed genuinely interested in hearing about his career and the cases that interested him most. Thad had tried to hijack the conversation a few times, but it always seemed to return to Christopher, who seemed unfazed by the attention. Then again, someone as humble as Christopher wouldn't let it go to his head. His humility and modesty were the things I admired most about him.

"Maybe we should let Christopher eat," I suggested. He'd asked about the silverware again during the walk to the main house, but he'd barely had time to put his knowledge to good use with all the chitchat.

"A body that big would need fuel," Lulu said. "You've got the shoulders of a linebacker."

I braced myself for her to make a bawdy remark about what those broad shoulders could be used for, but Manuel slapped his hand on the table at the same time Mark yelled, "Aha!"

"You played linebacker for the Georgia Bulldogs," Manuel said. "That's where I recognize you from."

"Yes, sir," Christopher said.

"But you didn't go by Christopher," Mark added. He narrowed his eyes. "I can't think of what it was, though. A middle name or something?"

"No, sir. I went by my nickname, Topher."

"That's it!" Manuel and Mark said.

"You were a beast on the field," Manuel said.

"Bet that's not the only place," Aunt Lulu added, then winked at me. I bit my lip to keep from laughing while Mom softly admonished her.

"You set the school record for sacks and tackles in that position," Manuel continued as if he hadn't heard Lulu's lewd comment.

"He still holds them," Mark added.

"Yeah, but Bix Miller is breathing down my neck. If he stays healthy next year, he'll catch me. He's a good kid, so I hope it happens for him."

Thad cast a suspicious look at Christopher. "You actually want someone else to break the school records you set?"

"Yeah, I do," Christopher replied.

Thad shook his head but left it alone.

"I never understood why you weren't drafted," Mark said. "Oh, wait. You had a bad shoulder injury, didn't you?"

"Yes, sir. I had surgery after my senior season, and I was still recovering during the scouting combines. But truthfully, I had different dreams in mind and didn't enter the draft."

"Do you mean your career in law enforcement?" Dad asked.

"Yes, sir," Christopher said. "After earning my criminal justice degree, I applied to the police academy. Served my time as a beat cop before getting promoted to detective."

"That's very admirable, Christopher," Dad said before looking at me. "Julian, how do you like instructing at SCAD?"

"It's only been a few weeks, but I love it. The students are great, and they've embraced their semester project with gusto."

"Tell me about the project," Dad said earnestly.

I gave him a quick rundown of the rules the students must follow before telling them about some of the individual projects the students chose. I was really pleased when the topic caught on and several guests joined the conversation. Christopher squeezed my knee then shifted his hand higher to rest on my thigh.

"And Dad," I said, "Jorja told me about the green initiatives you've implemented at the office. I'm really proud of you."

Dad smiled warmly. "Your passion for the environment is contagious, though I still have a lot to learn."

Going green was not only difficult but outrageously expensive, so we discussed other small ways the company could lessen their carbon footprint. I expected the guests to tune out, but I was surprised how many remained interested.

"My boy is passionate about climate change," Mom said.

"I think your boy is passionate about Christopher," Lulu countered.

Christopher lifted his glass of wine and toasted her. "He can multitask like no one's business."

When the conversation shifted once again, Topher inched his hand a little higher until the tip of his pinky rubbed against my balls. It was a damn good thing I wasn't eating or drinking, or I would've choked to death. I looked at him with an expression that hopefully conveyed the revenge I planned to eke out on his sexy body later. His smile said, "Bring it on."

CHAPTER TWELVE

Julian

I WOKE UP AT DAWN PLASTERED TO CHRISTOPHER'S SIDE FOR THE second morning in a row. The sun had filtered into the room through the tiniest gap in the blinds, laying thin stripes across our tangled legs. My morning wood was pressed against Christopher's lean hip and getting woodier with every breath. Topher's right hand strummed my lower back like a guitar, and his left hand played chords on my forearm resting across his abdomen.

I knew nothing about music, but this felt like the same song he'd silently serenaded me with the previous morning, so I asked again, "What song are you playing?"

His response was the same as it had been the day before and spoken just as huskily. "I'll sing it to you on our first date."

Topher's hand stilled on my lower back when I didn't react to his comment, and he pulled me even closer to his side. "What happened to the guy who practically proposed marriage to me at every turn? Not even a month ago, you texted me a picture of a fluffy kitten brought into Harper's office and said, and I quote, 'I want to adopt a sweet baby like this when we're married.'"

Embarrassment heated my cheeks, and I buried my face in Topher's neck. "I could say those things because I never believed they would happen." Christopher stiffened, and his hands fell away from my body. I realized I'd said the wrong thing. Fear seized my lungs, but my brain kicked into high gear. Before he could slide away, I moved my left leg up and over his abdomen to pin him down. His erection brushed against my inner thigh, and we both shivered.

"Don't go," I whispered against his neck. He trembled again and tightened his hold on me. "I've meant every word I've said to you, even if I never dreamed they'd land in a place where you'd take them seriously or return the sentiments." I took a deep breath. "I compare every man I meet to you, and they fail miserably. That's the real reason I've settled for Grindr hookups."

Christopher rolled onto his good side, and I stared into his eyes. Well, I did once I stopped ogling his bare torso and the erection straining his tight boxer briefs. I wanted to ease my hand under the waistband and teach him delicious things about his body. For two mornings in a row, I refused to act on my desires to preserve my sanity.

"What's holding you back now?" Christopher asked softly. "Is it because you don't believe my interest is genuine?"

I ghosted my fingers over his stubbly jaw. God, this man was too beautiful for words. "You're the most honest person I know, Toph." I started to accept his date, but my phone rang on the nightstand.

"I should probably get that," I said. "It's either my mom or sister."

Topher groaned but placed a chaste kiss on my lips before untangling his limbs from mine. I blindly reached for my phone so I wouldn't miss seeing Christopher's boxer-clad ass as he stretched his big, delicious body. A wicked voice inside my head reminded me I could pull his underwear down with my teeth if I played my cards right.

I found my phone and fumbled around with my thumb until I managed to accept the call. "Hello?"

"Julian!" my mom shrieked in my ear. I jackknifed into a sitting position and looked at the bedside clock, assuming I'd overslept. I breathed a little easier when I saw the time until the shower turned on in the bathroom. If I'd been brave, I could've joined him.

"*Your* sister won't let me see the dress." Mom's voice cut through my fantasy like a samurai sword.

A soft scuffle came through the connection before Jorja said, "I caught *your* mother sneaking into the room where my dress is to take a peek, even though I made my wishes very clear."

"Come on," Mom whined. "What's a few hours?"

"Give Mom the phone," I told Jorja.

"Most mothers get to go gown shopping with their daughters," Mom said when she came back on the phone. "I feel deprived."

"Mom," I said calmly, "Jorja doesn't mean to make you feel excluded. There's a special tribute to you and Dad on the dress, and it just won't be the same if you see it on a hanger. The wedding is only four hours away."

She took a deep breath. "You're right. I'm sorry." She repeated the apology to Jorja with a sniffle. "You and Christopher get over here for breakfast. There's enough food for an army, and the guys have already left for the golf course."

"Again?" I asked. Couldn't they go a single Saturday without hitting a little white ball at the country club?

"I don't get it either," Mom said. "They're only playing nine holes because your father knows I will kill him dead if they're late."

"Kill him dead?" I asked.

"Just get here!" she said before disconnecting.

I laughed as I set my phone down, then flopped down onto the bed while Christopher finished in the bathroom. If it was like yesterday, he'd be in there for a while. Of course, my dirty mind conjured up the activities that precluded a quick shower. The desire my mom and sister had squelched returned with a vengeance. I closed my eyes and brushed my fingers over my collarbone as I pictured Christopher stroking his cock. Those same digits headed south when I decided it wasn't fair for him to have all the fun. I got so caught up in the fantasy of what he was doing that I hadn't realized Christopher had shut off the tap until he opened the door. A plume of steam filtered into the bedroom, and Christopher stood there wearing nothing but a towel around his waist and a devilish smile on his face. Hello again, adorable dimples. Would I discover those sexy divots anywhere else on his body?

"Whatcha doing?" Christopher asked huskily.

I looked down the length of my torso to discover the tips of my fingers were tucked under the waistband of my briefs and almost grazing the head of my fully erect cock. I quickly retracted my hands and smiled up at him. "It's not what you're thinking."

"It's exactly what I'm thinking," Christopher said as he moved to the dresser drawer. I'd thought I'd known everything about this man, but he'd surprised me Thursday evening when he made the time to unpack his luggage.

Christopher removed a pair of underwear from the dresser before meeting my gaze in the mirror above it. Without warning, he loosened the towel and dropped it to the ground. His thick erection sprang forward. Everything in my core tightened, and a chorus of hallelujahs rang out. Then my eyes drifted to his glorious butt, so round and tight, and I discovered that, yes, Christopher had dimples in a different set of cheeks. A matching set was carved just above his taut globes, and I longed to lick them. And maybe bite the firm flesh below them.

Christopher bent forward and lifted his right leg into his underwear, giving me a glorious view of his sac. *Holy fuck. What was happening?* He repeated the action with his left foot giving me another peekaboo of his balls. They looked as firm and taut as his sweet ass. Christopher took his time pulling his underwear up his legs. By the time he snapped the waistband into place, I was so revved up by the show I was ready to capitulate to anything Christopher wanted if he'd just saunter across the room and—

My breath stuck in my throat when he did just that. He gripped my ankles and tugged me down to the foot of my bed until my legs dangled over the edge. I spread my thighs to make room for him as naturally as I drew my next breath. Christopher leaned over me, bracing his weight on one forearm. The difference in our heights meant my dick lined up with his slightly furry belly. The friction I needed to get off was right freaking there. Just a little lift in the hips and—

"You think I'm an honorable man, and up until this weekend, I would've agreed with you," Christopher said. His minty fresh breath reminded me I hadn't yet brushed my teeth. I wanted to recoil and run into the bathroom to correct the problem, but I couldn't look away from his intense gaze or budge from the proximity of his body. "I'm not going to keep telling you how much I want to explore these feelings with you. I'm going to show you. You've singularly awakened something deep inside me, and I don't think either of us is fully prepared for what happens when a Carnegie man falls for the first time. I've heard the lore and witnessed it with my parents, but this is unlike anything I've experienced."

"Falls?" I asked shakily.

"You heard me." Christopher leaned forward, pressed a sweet kiss to my lips, and pushed off the bed. "And you've been warned."

He retreated to the dresser and pulled out a shirt and shorts to wear until it was time to dress for the wedding. Now that there was a little distance between us, I could move again. I sat up so quickly it made me dizzy, then I bolted for the bathroom with Christopher's wicked laughter chasing me.

"Can I watch?" he asked.

"No."

I closed the door and locked it for good measure, not that Topher couldn't take it down with one hard thrust from his good shoulder. *Hard thrust.* My cock jerked in my underwear, reminding me how badly I needed release. While scrubbing my teeth, I tried to talk myself out of jerking off with him in the next room. A cold shower the previous morning had done the trick, but Christopher's stunt had me reeling, and I needed to regain my equilibrium and the upper hand. So I stood beneath the spray and welcomed the fact that Christopher was conscious of every stroke I made, even if he couldn't see it. Let him remember what my face looked like midorgasm and crave that connection.

I came so hard I had to lean against the tiled wall for support as my breath evened out and my sanity returned. I would've hidden in the bathroom for the rest of the morning if the water heater would've held out. I didn't have the foresight to grab a change of clothes, which meant I had to repeat Topher's earlier actions. When I stepped out of the bathroom with a matching towel around my waist, I discovered Topher stretched across the bed still in his underwear. A glance revealed the significant difference in his condition, though. His cock lay flaccid in his tight boxer briefs, and a few tissues were bunched on the bed beside him. And just like that, he'd regained the upper hand once more.

He stretched indulgently before sitting up. He rose to his feet, sauntered to where I stood gaping at him, and cupped my face. "We still found a way to come together."

I did the only smart thing that came to mind. I rose on my tiptoes and kissed Christopher like I would have if he'd joined me in the shower.

I straightened Jorja's train before circling back to the front. I took a few steps back and scrutinized the finished dress, looking for anything that didn't fit flawlessly. The corseted A-line gown with ivory knit lace overlay was perfection, and I allowed a few seconds to pat myself on the back before nodding my approval. Every part of the dress was repurposed or eco-friendly. I'd made the lace by hand using repurposed thread and salvaged the underlay from a dress I'd found at a consignment shop.

"Jorjie, you must be the most beautiful bride ever."

"Ha," she scoffed. "We've both seen our parents' wedding photos. Mom in her thrift-store hippie dress has me beat by a country mile." Jorja looked over at her reflection in the mirror and smoothed her palms over the skirt of her dress. "I do look damn good, though."

Persistent knocking interrupted our private moment. "You've hogged your sister long enough, Julian," my mother called through the door. "Open this door, or I'll get your boyfriend to kick it down for me."

Jorja and I shared a quick laugh before I crossed the room and opened the door to my parents. Mom let out an annoyed growl when I smiled at her, then stomped past me. Dad entered slower, a bemused expression on his face until he caught sight of his only daughter. He stopped suddenly and let out a soft gasp. Tears flooded his eyes, and he pulled a handkerchief from his pocket.

"Oh, Jorja," Mom said softly. "You take my breath away."

Dad sniffled several times, which caught Mom's attention. "I knew you would be the first to cry."

"And what do you call those water trails down your cheeks?" Dad asked as he stepped up to her. He leaned forward and kissed Mom's forehead tenderly. "Want to borrow my hankie?"

She giggled, accepted the cotton square, and gently dabbed at her eyes. Mom turned her full attention to me. "Julian, I've been honored to wear your creations before, but this is another realm of talent. Honey, I'm so in awe of you."

Dad placed his hand on my shoulder and squeezed. "Magnificent, son."

I swallowed the lump of emotion and said, "Thank you both."

"How did you have time to make this dress?" Mom asked. "I recognize handknitted lace when I see it, and Jorja and Otto have only been engaged for eight months."

Jorja and I looked at each other and shared a quick laugh before I explained. "Otto might've proposed eight months ago, but Jorja asked me to start making her wedding dress after their first date two years ago."

Mom and Dad turned their heads to study Jorja at the same time. My sister shrugged and said, "Daddy, you always taught us to shoot for the stars."

Our father smiled softly. "Yes, I did."

Jorja crooked her finger, and our parents stepped closer. She pointed to the stars I'd knitted into the lace overlay. "Those are for you, Daddy."

"My word," he said softly and teared up again.

"This moon is for you, Mama," Jorja said.

"Because I love you to the moon and back," she whispered thickly. She looked from Jorja to me. "Now I understand why you wanted us to wait." My parents jokingly played tug of war with the handkerchief for a minute before taking turns mopping their eyes.

"This is the happiest day of my life," Mom said. Then she looked at me and winked. "Your future wedding to Christopher will share the top spot someday."

"Whoa," I said, holding up my hands. "We're nowhere near that stage in our relationship."

Mom, Dad, and Jorja just laughed at me.

"Oh, honey," Mom said. "You should see the way Christopher looks at you."

"Same way I'm looking to tear into that wedding cake after months of low-carb dieting," Jorja added.

Mom laughed, snagged the hankie back, and dabbed her eyes again. There was a swift knock at the door, and Dad crossed the room to see who was out there. After a quick conversation, he returned to our sides. "It's showtime. Is everyone ready?"

We walked as a family toward the rear of the country club, where the rest of Jorja's wedding party waited for her. I kissed her cheek one more time, waited for the cue, then escorted my mom through the open French doors, down the broad stone steps, and across the perfectly manicured lawn. My gaze was immediately drawn to Christopher when we reached the seating sections. During the rehearsal, Mom had reshuffled the seating so Topher could sit with Aunt Tallulah in the front row. Lulu sat on the far end, and Christopher sat directly next to her. I smiled at him, and he flashed his dimples at me in return. I forced my gaze to the center aisle so I didn't stumble and drag my mom down with me.

I took the empty seat next to Christopher, and Mom sat beside me, leaving the final empty chair for Dad. Christopher leaned over and kissed my cheek.

"You look incredibly sexy," he whispered before pulling back.

I reached for his hand, and Christopher laced his fingers through mine. We remained entwined throughout the procession of bridesmaids and even when we stood up to watch Dad walk Jorja down the aisle. We didn't separate until the preacher pronounced Otto and Jorja husband and wife, but we reached for each other again as we trailed behind the bride and groom.

Family photos followed, and Christopher offered to step aside, but I tightened my grip on his hand. Maybe it was the atmosphere or my family's outlandish prediction that Christopher and I were destined for the altar, but I suddenly couldn't bear to have him missing from the memories of the day.

The reception was in the country club ballroom and went off without a hitch. The bride and groom wanted a down-home barbecue, and the caterer had come through. I'd always loved the way Christopher tucked into his food when he found something that pleased him, and he really enjoyed the baby back ribs and all the fixings.

He sat back in his chair several minutes later and tossed his cloth napkin onto the table. "I couldn't possibly eat another bite." And he stuck to his guns until the bride and groom cut the cake.

Jorja's dance with Dad made me cry, and Christopher put his arm around my shoulders.

When the DJ asked the guests to join the bride and groom on the dance floor, Christopher surprised me by standing up and offering his hand. He'd always avoided dancing during the various family events I'd attended, and there'd been plenty of opportunities to showcase his moves.

"Really?" I asked.

"Are you worried I'll embarrass you?"

I accepted his hand and stood up. "No way."

Dancing to fast music was a little awkward at first since he had his left arm in a sling again, but we found a rhythm that prevented me from bumping into his bad arm. The slow dances, though… Holy moly, having Christopher Carnegie's laserlike focus aimed at me was addictive. He made it too easy to forget we weren't alone, especially when he notched my chin up with his thumb and sang a sweet song to me or pressed his lips to mine like there was nothing he wanted more in the world.

I was breathless when the slow song ended and a raucous hip-hop song started. I pulled back and smiled up at him. "I need to use the restroom. Want to grab some drinks and meet me on the balcony?" I shouted over the music.

"I can't think of anything I'd like more." He kissed my forehead before heading to the bar.

I watched him for the longest time before heading toward the restrooms. The men's room was empty, so I was in and out in quick order and whistling to myself as I made my way back to Christopher. I'd started to recall the beautiful things he'd said to me over the weekend when a hand darted out from a dark alcove and snagged my wrist. I knew immediately who the cruel grip belonged to and wrenched my arm free. I took a few steps back, and my assailant stepped out of the shadows to follow me.

"What are you doing, Thad?"

"I was about to ask you the same thing," he slurred.

Great, he was drunk. I looked down the long corridor, hoping someone else was heading toward the restrooms, but we were all alone.

"Laying it on a little thick today, aren't you?" Thad asked. "All this lovey-dovey shit. The two of you aren't fooling anyone."

Fear gripped my heart. The last thing I wanted was for Thad to expose my sham relationship to my parents and ruin Jorja's wedding. *It's not a sham*, a little voice whispered. And it was enough for me to straighten my spine and turn my fear into fire. "You're drunk, Thad. Go home before you end up doing or saying something you regret."

He kept walking toward me, and I kept retreating until my back hit a wall.

Thad leaned in close, but I turned my head. "I did some checking on your *boyfriend*," he said snidely. "Want to know what I found out?"

I waved a hand in front of my face to dispel the alcohol fumes on his breath. Gross. It was hard to imagine I'd ever enjoyed kissing him. "I don't care what you *think* you discovered. I know everything I need to about Christopher Carnegie. He's the best man I know."

Thad snorted. "Maybe so, but he's not gay. He's not even bi."

I snapped my head around and stared at him. "What are you talking about?"

Thad rolled his eyes, and the gesture made him lose his balance. He staggered back a few steps, and I took advantage to put some distance between us, easing down the corridor to get closer to the party.

"You should've brought an escort who doesn't have a social media presence. I looked back through Christopher's accounts for years. He's dated a fuckton of beautiful women but not a single man."

"Christopher is not an escort. He's a police detective, Thad. And someone's social media posts rarely tell the whole story."

"Civil servants aren't paid squat. A guy who looks like him would rake in the money as a gigolo. Is he great in bed?"

I took a step backward for every one he took forward. I didn't care if it looked like I was retreating because I was. "I don't give a shit about what you think, but I care that you don't ruin my sister's night. And I sure as hell won't tolerate you casting aspersions on Christopher just because you're jealous."

He gripped my biceps and shook me a little. "I loved you, Julian, but you threw me aside."

I placed both hands on Thad's chest and shoved him away. "You didn't believe in me, Thad. I could never be with someone who mocked my dreams like you did. Christopher believes in me and has never once belittled my ambitions and goals."

"It's just the two of us here, Julian," Thad said leeringly. "You don't have to keep up the charade." He reached for me again, but I batted Thad's hands away and sidestepped him. He staggered forward but caught himself on the wall to keep from pitching face-first to the floor.

"Hey!" Christopher called out. His footsteps echoed on the polished marble, starting as a brisk walk and ending in a full-on run. "Baby, are you okay?" he asked when he reached me. I turned in his embrace, and he held me tight.

Thad snorted. "*Baby*. What a joke."

Ignoring my ex, Christopher pulled back and cupped my face. "What's going on here?"

"Thad thinks you're an escort," I told him.

"Or someone after Julian's inheritance," Thad called out.

"That's a brand-new accusation," I told Christopher.

"Jackass, I'm not an escort, and I'm certainly not after Julian's inheritance. You've insulted my character and Julian's intelligence, and I'm not going to stand for it." Tension coiled in Christopher's big body, turning his biceps into boulders of muscle. He was good and pissed, and the result could get ugly if I didn't deescalate the situation. Unbeknownst to Christopher, a small crowd had formed behind him, including my parents and Thad's. I wanted to ease the worry I saw in Mom's and Dad's expressions but didn't want to chance the confrontation between Christopher and Thad getting out of hand.

"Furthermore," Christopher snarled, "my dating history is none of your damn business. If Graeme and Naomi have concerns about my character or my intentions toward their son, I will happily sit down with them and answer any questions they have. All you need to know, *Thad*, is that I'm Julian-sexual. You need to spend time worrying about your relationship and keep your nose out of ours."

"I couldn't agree more," Tyler said, stepping forward to collect Thad.

"I'm not finished," Thad said, jerking his arm free.

Dad and Mark stepped forward. They each grabbed one of Thad's arms. "I believe you are finished, Thad," my father said. He looked at Christopher and said, "I'm very sorry about all this."

"You don't owe me an apology, sir," Christopher said.

Mom blew us both a kiss, then followed behind the dispersed crowd.

Christopher turned me in his embrace as soon as we were alone and ran his gaze over me from head to toe. "Are you okay?"

"Yeah," I replied. "I never felt in danger. I was more worried the drunk idiot would ruin my sister's wedding." I smiled up at him. "Julian-sexual, huh?"

"Yeah, you heard me. I'm crazy about you, Julian."

"I'm crazy about you too." I could cling to fears and uncertainties or shoot for the stars. "About that date…"

"Yeah?" Christopher asked hopefully.

"I'm free every night this week except Monday."

CHAPTER THIRTEEN

Christopher

PROPERLY ALIGNED ALL THE BUTTONS DOWN THE FRONT OF MY pale pink dress shirt on the first try and reached for my gray and pink striped tie hanging on my doorknob. All I needed to do was put the loop over my head and tighten the knot once I had it correctly positioned. But inspiration struck, and I hastily untied the knot, then reached for my cell phone on the nightstand. I found Julian's text thread and hastily typed out a message.

911. I need you.

Julian's response was immediate. *Oh, baby, I got your first aid kit right here.* His voice, full of innuendo and mischief, played in my head as I read the message.

Be right there.

I pocketed my phone, exited my room, and headed to the front door with a purposeful stride. I was hell-bent on finding out if Julian's body was still warm with sleep and didn't notice Harper in the kitchen until she cleared her throat. I halted suddenly and turned to face her.

She was in the middle of unloading the dishwasher. The coffee mug she'd retrieved from the rack swayed on the forefinger hooked around the handle. I recognized it as my lucky Georgia Bulldogs mug and knew she'd had company over the weekend because I'd washed it and put it away before I left for Atlanta with Julian. I was dying to ask who the hell had been drinking from my cup but remembered the advice Julian had given me when dealing with Harper and her mystery man.

"Where ya going?" Harper asked, though her smug smile said she knew precisely what my destination was.

"Julian is going to help me with my tie."

She set the coffee mug on the counter and walked toward me with an evil grin on her face. "Let me help you with that."

"Um, Julian is expecting me. I figured you'd left already. I might've even woken him up, so—" I tilted my head to the front door.

Harper laughed and shook her head. "You're fooling no one. Go on and git."

I narrowed my eyes. "You're not going to give me a lecture or warn me away from Julian?"

She shook her head slightly. "Nope. I'll leave all the ridiculous posturing to you. *I* trust *your* decisions. I know damn well you'll avoid hurting Julian at all costs." She smiled a little smugly. "Maybe I'll even admit a part of me saw this coming a mile away."

I quirked a brow. "Really?"

"Even the most open-minded straight guys would've been uncomfortable with the amount of flirting Julian leveled at you. And don't get me started on the cuddling you do on the couch."

"What's everyone else saying about us?" I asked.

Harper giggled. "No one is surprised, and everyone is happy."

"Oh," I said a little flatly.

My sister quirked a brow. "You sound disappointed."

"Only for not having this epiphany sooner." I winked, headed toward the front door, then stopped with my hand on the knob. "Make sure your boyfriend doesn't break my lucky mug, yeah?"

Harper crossed her heart and said, "I'll guard it with my life. Just make sure you take care with my best friend's heart."

"I plan to take care of every part of him," I replied with a wicked smile on my way out.

Julian flung open the door before I could knock. He wore a pair of dark purple briefs that looked amazing against his skin. "Where have you been?"

I wrapped my arm around Julian, backed him into his apartment, and kicked the door closed behind me. He was so warm and had obviously just crawled out of bed. Damn, I'd missed waking up without him blanketing my body. I lowered my head but stopped just shy of kissing him, and Julian vibrated with anticipation. "Harper stopped me before I could escape and teased me mercilessly. You know what else?"

"What?" he asked breathlessly.

"She let her boyfriend drink out of my lucky mug."

Julian's mouth quirked up on the right side. "The horror. Shall I bleach it while you're at work?"

I rubbed my nose against his neck, breathing him in. "You just get me, Julian."

"I've watched your every move and committed them to memory for three years."

I kissed him, long and lazily, as if neither of us had anywhere to be.

Julian broke our embrace and stared into my eyes. "You've got two choices: hand over the tie so I can help you finish getting ready or call in sick and let me strip you down."

I reached for my phone because there was no real choice to make there. I had plenty of sick time, and there was only so much I could accomplish from a desk.

"Wait!" Julian said before I could call the precinct. He blew out a breath and paced in front of me for a few seconds, then snagged the tie I'd looped around my left hand. "You're going to work. I'm going to work. We're not going to rush this."

"Rush it?" I asked. "We've had three years of foreplay."

"You'll live." Julian looped the tie over my neck, deftly knotted it, and smoothed his hands over my shirt. "I like you in pink. It brings out your tan and the natural golden highlights in your hair."

I wrapped my good arm around Julian's waist and hauled him to me before he could escape. "I know you like it, which is why I picked it out."

"Kiss me quickly and get out of here before I forget my good intentions."

I nipped his neck and made him yelp. "I don't want to do anything quickly regarding you." I captured his mouth and backed up my words with action. I didn't pull back until Julian whimpered in my arms. "I hope you have a wonderful day," I said.

"Right back atcha. Enjoy dinner with Diego and Levi."

My friend had called me Saturday while Jorja and Julian were revealing her stunning wedding dress to their parents. He'd invited me over for that night, but I'd told him I was out of town. When he pressed for more information, I'd reluctantly told him where I was and why. He'd laughed for several minutes, then said, "Burgers and beer at my place on Monday. No excuses," before hanging up.

"I'd rather be with you," I told Julian as I nuzzled his neck.

His breath caught in his throat, and he practically purred in my embrace. "Damn you," Julian groaned. There was no hostility in his tone, just pure unadulterated lust and need. "Time for you to go to work, and I need to shower and start my day."

I grinned because I knew what he was about to get up to in his shower. "Think of me," I called over my shoulder as I reached for the door.

"Why should today be any different?" he fired back.

I paused, wrestled with my conscience, then stepped out into the hallway. I already had my keys, wallet, and phone in my pockets, so I continued to my truck instead of returning to Harper's apartment. When I started the ignition, "Collide" by Howie Day was playing on the radio. My fingers itched to strum the acoustic chords in the air as I'd done on Julian's skin over the weekend. I turned up the radio and sang along with the first few lines of the opening verse. My heart swelled when I recalled how it felt to wake up tangled in Julian at dawn. Those weren't the only lines that suited us perfectly, but sitting in my vehicle and singing like a lovesick sap wouldn't pay the bills, so I shifted my truck into drive and pulled out of my parking spot.

When the song ended, my mind naturally shifted to a puzzle I needed to solve. Harper had never hesitated to introduce me to a boyfriend, so why now? I could press Julian, but putting him in the middle wouldn't be fair, and he'd never betray Harper's secret. Neither would Mom, Emma, Shelby, or Dad. The key to solving the riddle was to figure out why I was the last person to know. It had to be someone I wouldn't like, and I liked almost everyone. I considered the options as I pulled into the parking lot at the precinct. I got along with just about everyone, except Thad and—

The answer hit me like a freight train, or more accurately, it strolled across the parking lot. Coy fucking Beaufort. His recent attempts to be friendly and his presence at Harper's charity gala suddenly made sense. Of all the eligible bachelors in Savannah, why him? Coy was a player, and I wasn't referring to our football days. He went through girls like water and—

I slammed on the mental brakes and forced myself to view Coy objectively. I had to begrudgingly admit the Coy Beaufort who'd moved back to Savannah after college wasn't the same guy who'd left. He was a dedicated, reliable officer, and everyone besides me liked the man. It was possible, okay, it was very likely I hadn't given him a fair shake.

I killed the engine, unbuckled my seat belt, and shoved open the door. "Beaufort," I called out before he could head into the building. What I wanted to say needed to stay private between us. There was more gossip around the precinct than in ten beauty salons combined.

Coy froze and slowly turned around just as I caught up to him. "Hey, Carnegie. Did you have a nice weekend?"

"Yeah, the best," I said, though my dry tone directly contradicted the words. "I'd like you to keep your Crimson Tide lips off my Bulldog mug during your future visits to our apartment, though."

Alarm flashed in Coy's eyes briefly before his mouth lifted at one corner and laugh lines crinkled near his eyes. "Is that why the coffee tasted so bitter?"

"Nah," I said, shaking my head. "Harper just has a heavy hand with the coffee beans."

Coy chuckled. "Good to know. Thanks for the tip."

"I haven't completely let go of my grudges," I confessed.

"Yeah, well, I'm probably not done irritating you either."

We exchanged wry smiles, then Coy opened the door and gestured for me to go first. As far as truces went, it was okay.

My desk phone rang just as I was about to leave for lunch. The only action I'd seen that morning was my multiple trips to make a cup of coffee or refill my water bottle. I was eager to stretch my legs and get some fresh air. I also wanted to check in with Julian to see how his day was going, so I briefly considered letting the call roll over to my voice mail before my conscience got the best of me. What if it was a major break in a case and the caller lost their nerve and never tried me back?

"Detective Carnegie," I spoke into the handset.

"Oh good," Chief Mendoza said. "I was afraid you'd gone to lunch already."

"What can I do for you, Chief?"

"District Attorney Babineaux and Commissioner Rigby are here too, and we'd like to have a quick meeting with you if you're free."

"Of course, sir. I'm on my way." My heart was in my throat when I exited the Cold Case Unit and headed for the elevator. I pushed the call button and waited for what seemed like forever before giving up and taking the stairs two at a time to reach the main level.

Chief Mendoza's office was located inside the Major Crimes Unit, where I'd served my first stint as a detective. I opened the glass door to the bullpen but noticed Coy was the only detective there.

"Everyone out chasing leads?" I asked, trying to build on our nebulous truce. It still felt like one false step would land us back in hostile territory.

"Seems that way, but I just got back from lunch," Coy replied. "You looking for someone in particular?"

I gestured to Mendoza's closed door. "Chief asked me to join him, Babineaux, and Rigby for a meeting."

Coy smiled wryly. "I'd joke that you've landed in hot water, but we both know that's not true with all the positive press you've gained for the department lately. Good luck, but I'm confident you won't need it."

"Thanks."

"Hey, Toph," Coy called out as I reached Mendoza's door. "Want to grab lunch one day this week?"

"Yeah," I replied. "Sounds nice."

I knocked firmly on the chief's door, and he called out for me to enter. Mendoza, Babineaux, and Rigby all smiled when I strode into the room. I shook hands all around and sat down in the only empty chair.

"I have to admit I'm curious about the summons," I said.

"Not a summons," Babineaux countered. "It's a proposal."

I groaned dramatically. "Not you too, Ms. Babineaux."

Gillian Babineaux was a stunning Black woman whose beauty was only surpassed by her brilliance. I held nothing but the utmost respect for her and worried my sense of humor was about to get me in trouble. Her mouth trembled, then released an uncharacteristic snort that cracked up everyone in the room.

"I'd forgotten all about the fuss or would've chosen my words better," she said after we all settled down. "What was the hashtag? Dear Detective?"

"Darling Detective, I think," Mendoza said.

"Dashing Detective, maybe," Rigby suggested.

I groaned and buried my head in my hands. This was all my fault for bringing it up.

"About my...*pitch*," Babineaux said. "I'm sure by now you've heard the rumors about former ADA Adam Savant."

"Oh, yeah." Allegations of his predatory and malicious prosecutorial behavior were frequent topics on the *Sinister in Savannah* podcast. But I failed to understand what they had to do with me. Savant was gone before I became an officer.

"This line of work often comes with speculation and accusations of misconduct," Babineaux said, "especially from people who've been sent to prison for a long time. As the top elected legal officer in the county, I take these claims seriously, and I vigorously investigate each one. Misconduct in our office has been extremely rare." She took a deep breath. "Until now."

"I'm sorry to hear that, Ms. Babineaux," I said, though I was still confused about why they wanted to speak to me.

"To ignore such gross negligence goes against everything I stand for, and I had no choice but to file a motion to overturn one of Savant's convictions. The court docket is logjammed, so my hearing isn't for four weeks," she said. "If I'm not careful, every case Savant touched could get overturned. Therefore, I need to get ahead of the situation. I'm creating a temporary task force to review every case Savant prosecuted. That's where you come in."

"I'm flattered, ma'am, but I don't know anything about trying a case."

"My investigation goes beyond the prosecution," Babineaux said. "I need to break every case down, including the initial investigation performed by SPD or CCSD. I'm talking about everything from the initial interviews to the evidence collection and the arrest. An in-depth review from top to bottom."

"It's doubtful Savant acted alone, Detective," Commissioner Rigby said. "I want to know if anyone in the SPD helped facilitate wrongful convictions."

The picture was becoming clearer, but I was still confused. "Isn't that what Internal Affairs does?"

"Yes, but they'd need to know who to investigate first," Mendoza said.

"And I'm not just looking hard at SPD," Babineaux added. "My office has full-time investigators on staff who are often tasked with finding additional evidence after local law enforcement refers a case to us. I want to know if any of my investigators are compromised. No one is escaping scrutiny. My task force will include a local PI, two attorneys unaffiliated with my office, and two law enforcement representatives—one current and one retired. The five-member team will break down each investigation from beginning to end."

"And you want me to be the active-duty LEO representative?" I asked.

Mendoza leaned forward and captured my attention. "Your experience investigating cold cases has taught you how to look at the evidence with fresh eyes and from new angles, and that's what DA Babineaux needs. You know how to look for patterns and recognize when something just doesn't add up."

"Ma'am," I said, "I'm truly honored."

"But I can tell by your somber expression that you're hesitant to accept," Babineaux quipped. "What are your concerns?"

"I think what you're doing is important and honorable," I told her. "I think malicious prosecutors and dirty cops are an ugly blight on society. We should all be outraged by the possibility they even exist, but investigating my fellow officers puts me in dangerous territory and possibly paints a target on my back."

Mendoza cocked his head to the side and raised a dark brow. "I never pegged you as someone who cared what the cool kids thought or caved to peer pressure."

"With all due respect, sir," I said. "I think your comment is a tad flippant, and I'm insulted you'd think so little of me. I'm not worried about your perceived popularity contest, but I am worried officers won't promptly respond if I ever radio for backup in the field."

The chief narrowed his eyes. "They'd rue the day otherwise."

"Again, sir, I mean no disrespect, but I don't think my mama would find comfort in your sentiment when you're handing her a folded flag at my graveside service."

Babineaux's and Rigby's laserlike scrutiny was hot enough to burn a hole in my face, but I didn't tear my eyes away from the chief.

A slow smile spread across Mendoza's face, and he turned his head to Babineaux. "See why we picked him? Detective Carnegie is as honest as they come, and he's not afraid to speak his mind."

Had his remarks been a mere test? The idea infuriated me, and I worked hard to remain calm.

"Detective," Babineaux said, "if it helps, all public conversation about this task force will be worded as a referendum on my office and Adam Savant. I don't need your answer now, but I would appreciate a response by midweek."

"I understand what's at stake and the need for an expedient response. I promise not to keep you waiting, ma'am." I nodded at Mendoza and Rigby. "Is there anything else?"

"You're dismissed, Detective," Mendoza said. "I'd appreciate it if you'd keep me apprised of your decision once you make it."

I rose to my feet. "Of course, Chief. You'll be the first to know."

I wished them all a good day and exited as quickly as possible. I worried Coy would bombard me with questions or tease me about the meeting, but he was nowhere in sight. Instead of returning to my desk, I headed out to the parking lot and climbed into my truck. I'd planned to grab a bite to eat and check in with Julian, but I sat numbly in the park and wolfed down food I didn't taste.

I had an important decision to make and spent my lunch hour drafting a mental pros-and-cons list. My initial objections were loud, but they were soon drowned out by the righteousness of the decision, so I was at a dead tie when I returned to the precinct.

I set aside the mental gymnastics and buried myself in the cold cases assigned to me by working the phones and pursuing interviews. When it was time to leave, I was grateful to head over to Diego's place instead of going home to an empty apartment. I knew in my heart what the right decision was, but it wouldn't hurt to bounce it off my best friend who'd understand and appreciate my dilemma.

Diego opened the door to the townhouse as I jogged up the steps. His grin spread from ear to ear, and I knew there would be no shortage of ribbing. In fact, he lobbed the first grenade before I made it inside. "Guess I know why none of the marriage proposals appealed to you."

I just laughed and shook my head. I was just grateful he wasn't upset that I hadn't told him about my growing attraction to Julian. "Sorry it's taken me a few weeks to claim that rain check on the burgers and beers," I said. "Life has been a little crazy lately."

"I'll say," Diego said.

I looked around the townhouse, noting how much bigger it looked without boxes stacked everywhere. "Your new place looks great, D."

He smiled as he gazed around his home with pride. "Thanks. Wait until you see the backyard. I didn't get a chance to really show it off to you when you helped us move. Come hang out with me while I grill the burgers."

"Wait!" Levi said as he ran down the stairs, pulling a T-shirt down his torso. His hair was mussed, and his black-rimmed glasses sat crooked on his nose.

I looked at Diego and arched a brow. "Did I interrupt something?"

Levi stopped when he reached us and hugged me. "I just got home from work and changed clothes. I smelled like coffee and food."

"Two of my favorite things," I said.

"Not if you immersed yourself in it for ten hours a day." Levi owned a popular cybercafé called Bytes and Brew, which served amazing food and coffee all day long. He looked between his husband and me with big blue eyes. "Did you start the interrogation already? I told you I didn't want to miss a single second of it."

Diego rolled his eyes, and it became my turn to volley my gaze between my hosts.

"Interrogation?" I asked.

"There's no interrogation," Diego said, clapping me on my good shoulder. "Just some chitchat between buddies."

I wasn't buying it for a second but followed him out to the backyard. "Oh, wow," I said. "This is a great space." The yard was huge and surrounded by a privacy fence. It was the perfect spot for kids and a dog, both things I knew they wanted. There was a wide patio with plenty of room for a grill and outdoor dining area.

Levi pulled back two padded chairs, patted one for me, and sat down in the other. Diego chuckled and headed over to the grill, where he turned on the burners to preheat it. He faced me and crossed his arms over his chest, then preceded to do exactly what he said he wouldn't, lobbing one question after another about how and when the fake-boyfriend ploy had developed.

"Whoa," I said, holding up my hand. "Slow your roll, D."

"Yeah," Levi said. "And you didn't include the most important question."

I quirked my brow at him. "Which is?"

"What took you so long to realize you were crazy about Julian?" Levi asked.

Diego laughed as he checked the temperature on the grill. He turned back around and said, "I was getting to it, babe. You always start with softball questions so the person doesn't get defensive. The goal is to loosen lips, not seal them. We're not going to get the goods if you keep insulting our friend."

Levi stiffened in his chair. "I didn't insult Topher."

Diego sighed heavily. "You basically called him a moron without really calling him a moron."

Levi turned stricken eyes on me. "I would never."

Seeing he'd upset his husband, Diego crossed the patio and tilted his husband's chin up for a sweet kiss. My gut clenched because it made me miss Julian so much. As much as I enjoyed hanging out with these two, I would much rather be with the guy who held my heart in his talented hands. Julian had a full day at the tailor shop and needed to grade papers before his class on Wednesday afternoon. I would not do anything to hinder his success, but maybe I could steal a kiss or two to tide me over until our date.

The newlyweds pulled apart and smiled sheepishly at me.

"Sorry," Diego said. "I know we get carried away."

"Don't apologize to me. I love seeing you both so happy." I sighed deeply and looked over at Levi. "And maybe I was a little slow on the uptake, but at least I finally arrived at the destination."

He smiled gently. "And that's all that really matters. Does that mean you're dating for real now?"

"Yep. We're going on our official first date tomorrow night."

"So this is serious between you?" Levi asked.

"Very. I've never felt this way about anyone."

Diego looked over at his husband with a smug smile. "You owe me fifty bucks."

Levi laughed. "I don't have any cash on me. You'll either have to wait until I swing by an ATM or accept sexual favors in trade."

Diego waggled his brow. "Pretty sure you know my answer."

Now I knew how Harper felt recently. "Should I go?"

"No," the husbands said and turned their attention back to me.

"I want to hear the details of your weekend," Levi said.

"*All* the details," Diego amended.

I snorted. "I'm not telling you *all* the details."

Diego grinned like an idiot. "They're written all over your face. I knew you liked this guy because you talk about him all the time. But I don't think I realized the depth."

"I didn't realize I talked about Julian so much."

"Oh yeah," Levi said. "And you should see yourself right now. You're practically glowing."

My cheeks heated as they continued to stare at me with dopey grins on their faces. "Do you want to hear *some* of the details or not?"

"Yes!"

While they worked together making dinner, I regaled them with everything that had transpired since the Terrence Ramone bust. I kept the intimate details to myself, no matter how much prodding I got from Diego. After dinner, I insisted they let me help clean up. Levi packed the leftovers into a paper bag for me. When it was time to go home, I felt much more relaxed than when I'd arrived.

"Walk me out?" I asked Diego. "I'd like to talk a little cop shop for a minute."

"Of course."

I hugged Levi and thanked him for dinner and the leftovers before following Diego outside. He leaned against the side of my truck and crossed his arms over his chest.

"Everything okay?" he asked.

"Yeah. I'm just conflicted after attending an unexpected meeting with Mendoza, Rigby, and Babineaux."

Diego furrowed his brows. "Sounds serious."

"Yeah, it is." I repeated the conversation verbatim, including my concerns, and Diego remained quiet until I finished.

"You know what you need to do, Toph," he said. "If there's a dirty cop on the force, they need to go. They're a threat to the citizens and to good cops everywhere."

I nodded. "I agree."

"And I'll have your back no matter what. You know that."

"I do."

"Feel better?" Diego asked.

"Yeah, about everything we discussed."

Diego grinned. "I want to meet the guy who's finally won Topher Carnegie's heart."

I didn't bother trying to correct him. "Give me a week or two to lock this down before you scare him away."

"Deal." Diego hugged me tightly, then headed back inside.

Once inside my truck, I started the engine, then checked the rear-view mirror before backing out of the driveway. I caught a glimpse of my reflection when I did and recognized the glow Levi mentioned. That put a song in my heart during the trip home. I smiled when I saw Julian's little Prius in the parking lot of our apartment building. My grin grew when I stepped off the elevator and saw him standing in his doorway. He crooked his finger at me—as if I needed a summons—and met me with a hard kiss. I wanted to hoist him up and carry him inside his apartment, but I reminded myself how much work he still needed to complete.

Julian pulled back from our kiss and smiled up at me. "Want to come inside?"

I pressed my nose to his neck and breathed him in. "You know damn well I do." I wasn't just talking about entering his apartment, and neither was he. "But you need to grade papers, and I don't need to be a distraction."

"I could probably—" I cut him off with a quick kiss, then placed the bag of leftovers in his hand. "What's this?"

"Leftovers from dinner. I want to make sure you eat."

Julian inhaled deeply. "Then you should come in and make sure for yourself."

"You little minx." I took a few steps toward Harper's apartment so

I wouldn't be tempted. "Make sure you get plenty of rest. Tomorrow is our first date."

"I can't wait."

"Me either because I already know it's going to be the best of my life."

"Damn, you're good," Julian said breathlessly before he stepped inside and shut his door.

I just hoped it was the best date of his life too. *No pressure, Carnegie. No pressure.*

CHAPTER FOURTEEN

Julian

K NUCKLES RAPPED SOFTLY AGAINST MY APARTMENT DOOR AS MY heart knocked loudly against my ribs. Christopher hadn't wanted to meet in the hallway or at his truck. He'd insisted on picking me up at my door as he would with any other date. My clamoring heart told me this could be *the date* to end all others.

Christopher's warm chuckle filtered through the door. "I still have a key to your apartment. I won't hesitate to use it."

I'd asked him to water my plants while I was in Atlanta doing the final fitting for Jorja's dress. Harper had nearly killed my precious babies the last time I'd put her in charge, so I'd rolled the dice and hit it big with Christopher. I'd never asked for my key back and didn't want to think about why that was.

He tapped lightly again. "I know you're just on the other side of the door."

I lifted my forehead from the cool surface. "How?"

I'd been in position before he'd left Harper's apartment and watched his approach through the peephole. Okay, I'd been scoping out the hallway since I'd heard him arrive home from work, balancing a potted plant between his sling and chest. No one had ever brought me flowers or plants, and I was ridiculously charmed by the gesture. But then I freaked when Christopher, freshly showered and shaved, approached my door twenty minutes later with the pot in hand.

"Because I feel you," Christopher said.

I opened the door and smiled at him. "Hi," I said, dropping my gaze to the adorable succulent arrangement.

"Hi." Christopher's dimples were on full display when he extended the ceramic pot to me, and I cradled it to my chest like the treasure it was. "I had difficulty deciding between a floral bouquet or a potted arrangement. I chose the succulents because they'll last longer." His grin turned wry. "Unless you leave them in Harper's care."

The affectionate dig chased away my nerves, and I stepped aside so Christopher could enter. "You've got that right. Harper is so good at everything else, though. I guess her plant-killer tendencies keep her humble."

I shut the door and turned to find a new home for my latest green baby, but Christopher snaked a hand around my waist and hauled me up against him, my back to his chest.

He pressed his nose to the sensitive spot behind my ear and inhaled deeply. "I missed smelling you first thing in the morning. You're more addictive than coffee." Christopher lifted his hand and sifted through the curls I'd worn soft just for him. "Missed these too."

I took a deep breath and withdrew from his embrace when all I wanted to do was melt into him. I turned and looked at Christopher. A frown marred his lips and brow, and I realized he'd mistaken my action for rejection. I rose on my tiptoes and kissed him until his lips softened and the groove in his forehead disappeared. "If I hadn't put a little space between us, I would've pulled you into my bedroom. You're not the only one who hated waking up to an empty bed. I missed you strumming out a melody only you can hear on my skin. But if we stay, I won't get to experience the date you planned."

If this was my last first date, I didn't want to miss a single moment. Christopher held up his hand. "I'll behave…for now."

I chuckled on my way over to my multi-tiered plant stand in front of the only window in the living room. I rearranged a few pots to place Christopher's gift in the center of the display. It looked right at home among the others, and I was incredibly moved.

"Looks like you need a bigger plant stand," he said, coming to stand beside me.

I turned and smiled at him. "And a bigger window for more light." I placed a quick kiss on his lips, still not fully believing I could do that anytime I wanted. "Thank you so much for Suzie."

Christopher quirked a brow. "You name them?"

I nodded. "Still want to date me?"

Laughing, Christopher pulled me into a hug. "Even more. Maybe you'll share the names of the other plants with me."

"As soon as you tell me the song you play against my skin," I challenged.

Christopher cupped my face. "I'll sing it to you the next time I wake tangled up with you."

He sounded so sure that there would be a next time, and I found breathing impossible. Christopher chuckled and dropped a quick kiss on my forehead. "Don't overthink it."

"You're right," I agreed. "Shall we go?"

Christopher gestured for me to precede him to the door and placed his hand on the small of my back. He kept it there while I locked my apartment, then he reached for my hand.

I lifted our laced fingers once inside the elevator and said, "Technically, we're tangled right now."

Christopher backed me up against the wall and lowered his head until his lips nearly touched mine. "Huh-uh. I'm talking arms, legs, and dicks. No clothes between us this time. Just your bare flesh against mine. Then I'll sing it for you."

I placed my hand at Christopher's open shirt collar and trailed a finger lazily down the row of buttons. Awareness crackled in the air around us and pulsed through his big, muscular body. "Baby, you'll be singing for me long before dawn."

Christopher cupped the back of my head and kissed me. The elevator stopped on the lobby floor before he could deepen the embrace. The doors opened on a cheerful chime, and Christopher reluctantly stepped back so we could exit, but neither of us moved until a familiar snort came from outside the elevator. I peeked around Christopher and waved at Harper, who rolled her eyes and waved her hand in front of her nose.

"Gross," she said. "Reeks of pheromones and three years' worth of unresolved sexual tension in there."

Christopher laughed and smiled at me. "Should I tell her, or would you like to do the honors?"

There was no way in hell I'd discuss our physical relationship with his sister, but the little imp didn't know that. "Actually…" I began.

Harper threw her hand up to cut me off when the elevator doors started to close. She pushed her arm out to trigger the sensors in the door, and it reopened. "Are you lovesick fools going to exit, or are you just going to ride the elevator up and down all night long and suck face?"

"Suck face," I replied while Christopher said, "Exiting."

We swapped, Harper stepping inside the elevator and Christopher and I into the lobby.

"It's a worknight, so I want him home by eleven," Harper said and blew me a kiss.

"Gives you plenty of time to sneak your Romeo in and out," Christopher teased.

Harper rolled her eyes. "Just worry about your own love life."

I looked up at Christopher once the elevator doors closed. "Are you ever going to tell her you figured out who she's dating?"

"And ruin the fun for her?" he asked as he reached for my hand. "No way."

"I'm surprised Coy hasn't told her."

Christopher released my hand to open the lobby door for me. "He's probably afraid she's only seeing him to spite me."

"He has nothing to worry about on that front. Harper is crazy about Coy."

"And that's for them to figure out for themselves," Christopher said. He stopped suddenly and looked at me with an astonished expression on his face. "Not sure how I can be so wise when it comes to everyone else's relationships but dumb as hell when it comes to my own. It shouldn't have taken me so long to realize the affection I felt for you went much deeper than friendship."

I cupped his face and kissed him soundly on the mouth. "You're not the only one questioning why they hadn't recognized the signs sooner. Are we going to waste precious time ruminating on old memories or focus on making new ones?"

"Definitely new," Christopher replied.

Neither of us said anything else until we drove out of his parking spot.

"I hope you don't mind if I make a quick detour before our date officially kicks off," he said.

"Well, since I have no clue where we're going, I wouldn't know it's a detour." I looked over at his handsome profile. "If it's a trip to the pharmacy for condoms or lube, though, you don't need to worry. I've got us covered. Literally."

"Good to know, but I bought those things at lunchtime. I was a little overwhelmed by the lube options, so I snapped a pic and texted it to Diego. When he didn't answer, I figured he was working a case, so I texted his husband, Levi."

I was incredibly charmed by the idea of Christopher phoning his friends to get advice on the best kind of lube to buy. I'd heard him mention Diego and Levi dozens of times, but I'd never met them.

"What do they think about us going out?" Christopher laughed, and I playfully swatted his arm. "What?" I asked, suddenly nervous.

"You and I are the only ones who hadn't seen this coming."

I turned as far as my seat belt allowed. "Really?"

Christopher stopped at a red light and looked at me. "Yeah. I guess I talked about you all the time. I didn't even realize I was doing it. They're very excited to meet you."

"Oh, wow. You've already planned an introduction?"

"Between my favorite people? Of course." His left brow slowly lifted. "Too soon?"

The light changed, and Christopher forced his gaze back to the road. "Not at all."

Christopher chuckled. "Tell that to your heart. I can hear it pounding from over here."

It was racing as if we'd just crested a roller coaster hill. "Cannot."

"Can too."

I tried to discreetly even out my breathing, but Christopher's soft laughter said it hadn't worked. Instead, I turned on the radio to drown out my reactions.

"I get to choose the soundtrack for our date since you've picked the destinations."

"Fine by me," Christopher said. "I love all types of music, so go for it. I have a phone charger in the console, and you can hook up to Car Play if you want to access your own playlists."

I took him up on his suggestion and had just selected a song on my phone when I realized he'd turned onto Seiler Avenue. I hadn't expected his detour to take me down memory lane. My chest swelled with happiness as Christopher drove past the homes that were both familiar and foreign. Many of the properties had exchanged hands several times since Tallulah had sold her home and moved in with my parents. I'd only driven past it once since moving to Savannah. I'd gotten so upset that I'd run a stop sign and gotten pulled over by the sexiest cop in the world.

I was preparing to point out her old house when he slowed in front of it and turned into the driveway. The residence had been fully remodeled since the last time I was there. Instead of white siding with black trim, the little house was sage green with white trim. They'd painted the wide porch a warm, sandy brown color. I was too stunned to speak until Christopher turned off the truck. "What are we doing here?" I asked.

"My landlord called me this morning and said the renovations finished ahead of schedule, so I can move in whenever I'm ready. I also picked up the keys at lunchtime. I can't wait to show you around. There's a clause in my contract that gives me an opportunity to buy the house after the first year. I haven't even moved in yet, but I already know I'm going to exercise that option."

I looked at the porch where I'd spent countless hours daydreaming as a little boy. The longing I'd expected to feel was there, but it was surpassed by disbelief and more profound feelings I couldn't name. Sensing Christopher's gaze on me, I turned to him. "This is the house you rented?"

He narrowed his eyes like he couldn't get a read on my emotions. That made two of us. The feelings built until they burst out of me in a squeaky hiccup, which I followed with deranged laughter and tears of joy.

Christopher blinked rapidly, and I could practically hear his gears grinding as he tried to figure me out. Again, that made two of us. "Did I do something really right or really wrong?"

"This was Lulu's house," I said, still not believing it. Savannah wasn't a metropolis by any stretch, but of all the houses Christopher could've rented, he'd ended up there. "I spent most of my summers here as a kid, and this house means the world to me."

Christopher stared at me with a slack jaw, then looked back at the house. "Seriously?" he asked, meeting my gaze again.

"Yeah, but that's impossible, right?"

Christopher removed a keychain from his pocket and dangled the keys in the air. "This says otherwise." He lifted my palm and placed the keys in the center. "You do the honors." Christopher wrapped my fingers around the metal and gave me a quick kiss. "I knew this house was special the moment I crossed the threshold, and now I know why. Give me a tour. I want to see it through your eyes."

"Holy fuck, you really are going to ruin me for all other men."

Christopher winked and removed his seat belt. "Maybe that's my diabolical plan." He eased open the driver's side door and stepped out. I remained rooted in my seat as I tried to process what was happening. Christopher stood in front of his car and smiled at me through the windshield. When I still made no move to get out, he rounded the truck and opened my door for me.

"And then what?" I asked.

He pursed his lips and considered my question for a second. "I don't follow."

"After I'm hooked on you, then what?"

Christopher's smile was slow and fiendish. "If I told you, it would spoil the journey." He held out his hand palm up. "Do you trust me?"

There was no one I trusted more, so I placed my free hand in his, and we walked together toward the house. I stopped by the front door and looked up at him. "Please tell me the new owner hasn't painted all the original woodwork white or altered those big, beautiful archways between the rooms."

"Nope."

"Or that they gutted all the built-in art deco cubbies and bookshelves."

Christopher smiled. "Nope. Those were some of my favorite features. And before you ask, the wall of windows in the kitchen is intact. They're what sold me on the place."

I closed my eyes and pictured all the plants and herbs Lulu had grown in the kitchen. "Thank goodness."

I put the key in the lock and turned it. The door opened on silent hinges, and we stepped inside. My heart pounded as I cataloged all things old and new. The wood floors, trim, and exposed beams in the ceiling were left in pristine condition, though the finish looked new. Perhaps a hickory stain instead of cherry. The very first art deco feature in the house was the foyer. To the left was a built-in cubby with a row of hooks for coats and a bench to stow shoes beneath it. To the right was a half wall that opened into a bookshelf in the sunken living room.

The dining room featured a built-in buffet, china cabinet, and a corner knickknack cubby. I walked to the cubby and ran my finger over the edge of a shelf. "Lulu kept her bell collection here. People brought them to her from all over the world. She'd tell me about each one as she lovingly cleaned them."

I crossed the main hall and stepped down into the sunken living room. Christopher followed behind me at a slower pace. The long wall featured a fireplace in the center with bookshelves on both sides. "This would be a wonderful room to showcase your vintage guitars, and those shelves are deep enough for your vinyl record collection."

I felt Christopher's presence before he settled his hand on my hip. "I plan to hang my television over the fireplace. What do you think?"

"I like that idea. Lulu had one of those monstrous console things. It was opposite the windows, so you couldn't see the screen when the sun was on this side of the house. We popped popcorn and watched a movie every night." I stilled when a specific memory hit me.

"You okay?" Christopher asked softly.

I turned and smiled up at him. "Pretty sure Aunt Lulu knew I was gay before I did. I just remembered the summer she introduced me to Rock Hudson. I think I was ten."

Christopher chuckled and kissed my lips. "I'm dying to hear this."

"It wasn't as bawdy as you're thinking," I replied. "She had one of his movies on and told me it was a shame Rock couldn't be himself. I didn't understand and asked, 'Who is he really?'" I was thinking of a superhero or something, but Lulu told me that some boys prefer to kiss other boys instead of girls. She said Rock was one of those boys, but he had to lie about it to make movies. Lulu told me it was wrong to make people feel ashamed about who they loved. It was a few more years before I realized I was one of those boys who wanted to kiss other boys. Lulu was the first person I told. It was Christmastime, and she was at our house for the holiday. She held me tightly and said, 'I know, honey. Never let anyone tell you it's wrong.' That next summer, we watched as many Rock Hudson movies as she could find."

Christopher traced my jawline with his finger. "Damn, I love that woman. No wonder this place is so special to you." He leaned forward and rubbed his nose against mine. "Have you ever kissed a boy in this house?"

The tenderness in his eyes made it impossible to speak so I shook my head. Christopher tucked his fingers under my chin and lifted it. My eyes drifted shut as he pressed his lips to mine, softly at first, then more insistent when he slid his tongue between my lips. I opened for him, and he deepened the kiss until I forgot everything except the way he made me feel.

When we parted, Christopher stroked his thumb over my cheekbone and said, "Now you have."

"This is the best date ever."

Christopher chuckled. "It hasn't even started yet." He looked around the room. "Is this where she taught you how to sew?"

I nodded. "Yeah, Lulu taught me about fabrics and fibers and showed me how to sew, crochet, and knit. She had friends over several times a week. They referred to the gatherings as sewing clubs or book clubs, but they mostly drank wine and gossiped." I closed my eyes and memories of their laughter echoed in my mind. I met Christopher's gaze once more. "Lulu's lessons went beyond which patterns matched and which yarns made the best blankets. She's always encouraged me to think for myself and be my own person. You've seen what she's like."

Christopher pulled me into a one-armed hug, which I decided was way better than a two-armed embrace with any other man. Christopher's love language was touch, whether he knew it or not. With one hand on my lower back and the other in a sling, he still managed to caress my face with the intensity in his golden gaze. The warmth of his adoration ghosted over my cheeks as tenderly as his touch would. The gentle giant had the power to crush my soul in ways others never could, but as I stared into Christopher's eyes, I realized he never would. He saw me. I mean, he *really* saw me, and he was letting me know. Christopher placed a whisper-soft kiss on my lips.

"It must've been really hard for her to sell the place and move in with your folks," he said.

I nodded. "It was a royal battle between them. Lulu had been diagnosed with cancer, and Mom wanted her to have the best treatment money could buy in Atlanta. They locked wills but came to a compromise. Lulu agreed to stay with my parents while undergoing treatment and would return to Savannah once she was in remission. She really struggled during treatments, and I think it really scared her because she ended up staying in Atlanta permanently. She's a warrior in more ways than one, and I love her so much."

"Pride radiates from Lulu every time she looks at you, so I know the feeling is mutual."

I blinked, and a few rogue tears slid down my cheeks. "That is the nicest thing anyone has ever said to me."

Christopher dropped his hand from my back to wipe away my tears. "When I imagined our first date, making you cry wasn't in my plan."

I tilted my head to the side. "Not even tears of ecstasy?"

Christopher chuckled and pressed a quick kiss to my lips. "And he's back."

I settled my hand on his chest and fixed my gaze on his. "These tears feel good." I trailed my hand lower and stopped just shy of his belt. "The ones that come later will feel great."

His answering kiss was sweet and gentle, but the emotions they stirred in my core were naughty and savage. I pulled back before I commandeered his date. The longing expression in his gorgeous eyes said it wouldn't take much effort to convince him to forget his plans.

"I want to check on something," I said. "Then we can go."

I laced my fingers through Christopher's and led him into the kitchen. I paused when we entered the room because the wall of windows along the back of the house was just as breathtaking as I remembered. The new owner had replaced the old kitchen cabinets but had chosen ones with a similar look and feel as the original art deco design. White base cabinets lined the entire perimeter of the room except for the small eat-in nook off to the right. There were very few upper wall cabinets mounted in the kitchen, which was correct for the era. Their glass fronts weren't as ornate as the originals but still pretty. Another craftsman feature was the open shelves throughout the room. I crossed over to the ones by the kitchen windows and said, "Lulu filled these shelves with plants and herbs. And over there," I said, pointing to the stove, "she kept her dry spices, seasonings, and cooking wine."

"So that's where your green thumb comes from."

I nodded. "My mom has it too. She spends countless hours working in her flower beds and vegetable gardens." I looked into the backyard and noticed the owner had replaced the old metal fence with a nice wooden one. "Lulu had a small garden over there," I said, pointing to the right corner. "She grew mostly tomatoes, onions, peppers, and green beans."

"No okra?"

"Yuck," I said with a hard shiver.

"You just haven't had it prepared correctly," Christopher replied.

I snorted and shook my head. "Says every okra nut."

Christopher chuckled and tugged me closer. "Is this what you wanted to see?"

His proximity nearly made me forget my mission, so I stepped back and tugged him with me. I opened the door next to the stove and pulled him into the walk-in pantry.

"The landlord told me what was behind the door, but I didn't inspect the space. It's huge."

I heard him, but my eyes had started to mist over again when I saw the growth chart Lulu had made for me was still there. "I was sure someone had painted over it," I said, running my finger over the pencil marks and notations. The last one was from the summer I turned thirteen."

"Was that your last summer here?" Christopher asked softly.

"Yeah," I said wryly. "The next summer, I put kissing other boys into action."

Christopher's arm snaked around my waist, and he rested his head against mine. "Why don't we call Lulu and tell her our quirky news."

I brightened at the suggestion. "I have an even better idea. I can FaceTime my mom, and she can hand the phone to Lulu."

Mom was just as excited for Lulu to discover Christopher was moving into her old house. I turned the phone around and showed her the updates in each room. She, too, got tears in her eyes when I recounted my fondest memories with her.

"I regret that I didn't return for more summers with you," I said once I finished the tour in the backyard. Christopher had stayed in the house to give us some privacy.

"Oh, you have nothing to feel guilty about, my love. I wish I'd had the foresight to know you'd move to Savannah one day. I would've saved the house for you instead of selling it to strangers." She tilted her head to the side. "But maybe things turned out the way they were supposed to, yeah?"

I turned and looked through the kitchen windows. Christopher was opening cabinets and drawers. He looked so right standing in the space, like maybe him being there wasn't just a huge coincidence. "I think you're right," I agreed. We chatted for a few more minutes before she informed me that *Wheel of Fortune* was about to come on. "Lulu," I said before disconnecting, "thank you for everything."

"It is I who should thank you, dear," Lulu said. "You brought so much joy to my life every summer. I will cherish the memories beyond my last breath. I love you, Julian."

"I love you too, Aunt Tallulah."

I waited a few moments to pull myself together before I walked back inside.

Christopher shut the drawer and looked at me. "Everything okay?"

"Perfect," I said, crossing the distance and wrapping my arms around his waist. I looked up at him and said, "Though my next bout of joyful tears will occur when your big dick gets up close and personal with my prostate."

Christopher's mouth parted on a soft gasp as lust and need darkened his eyes. He blinked a few times and seemed to recover his thoughts. "I'm a sure bet, huh?"

I trailed my finger over his chest and was delighted when a shiver racked his body. "Aren't you?"

Christopher cupped the back of my head and said, "Hell yes," before locking his lips to mine. My brain went haywire, thinking of everything I wanted to do to and with him. I'd mentally stripped him down to his underwear when Christopher pulled back suddenly.

"Date first," he said.

I reluctantly agreed, and we locked the door behind us and headed to his truck. I didn't ask where we were going because it didn't matter as long as we went there together. I smiled when he stopped at Corleone Trattoria.

"This is my favorite restaurant," I said.

Christopher killed the engine and kissed me. "I know. I'll never forget the look on your face the first time I saw you eat takeout from here. I provoked a more rapturous response out of you when I brought you that eggplant parmesan than I ever did with anyone I took to bed."

I patted his cheek and gave him my best "oh sweetie" look. "You've put that expression on my face plenty of times. You just weren't there to see it."

"I will get to from now on," Christopher said as he shoved his door open. He volleyed his gaze between the restaurant and me, and a cute scowl formed on his face. It could've been my imagination, but I had a feeling Christopher didn't want anyone in the restaurant to see my reaction to the eggplant parmesan. But then he said, "Maybe we should get our dinner to go," and I knew I'd been right.

"I'll tamp down my euphoria," I promised. "I won't bang the table and cry out in ecstasy."

Christopher groaned softly but led me into the restaurant. I didn't want to tempt fate, so I ordered baked ziti instead. It was as good as the eggplant, but I kept my reactions G-rated. Christopher tucked into his spaghetti and meatballs with a gusto that made my heart happy. He caught me smiling at him and narrowed his eyes.

"Am I making a pig of myself?"

"No," I replied. "I love the way you enjoy food."

He sat back in his chair and patted his stomach. "If I'm not careful, I'll pack on weight while my shoulder heals."

"I'd still climb you at every opportunity."

Unfortunately for me, our server decided to check in with us at that precise moment. I worried it was too much for Christopher, but he laughed when the poor kid stumbled through his question and beat a hasty retreat when we assured him everything tasted wonderful.

"I'm serious," Christopher said once we were alone again. "I gain weight easily."

"And I seriously love a dad bod." I set my fork down and said, "I think you're incredibly sexy as you are, but I'd still feel the same way if you were bald or suddenly sprouted a bunch of back hair."

Christopher grimaced. "Hopefully not at the same time."

I chuckled but waved away his concern with my fork. "I'd just shave my initials in your back hair so everyone would know you're mine."

He tilted his head to the side. "I actually believe you."

"As you should," I replied. "As much as I appreciate your looks, I'm drawn more to your character."

He swallowed hard, and I could tell how much my words meant to him. "I feel the same about you, Julian."

I didn't know how long we stared at one another before the poor waiter returned to see if we wanted dessert.

"We'll take two boxes for our leftovers and the check, please," Christopher said. "Wait, do you want dessert?"

It was on the tip of my tongue to say no, but then I imagined feeding cannoli cake to Christopher in bed. I ordered a piece to go, and the waiter commended me on my choice before disappearing.

Once back in Christopher's truck, he started the engine and turned to me.

"I was going to drive out to Jesup so we could watch *Twister* at the drive-in theater. I'm still eager to share that experience with you, but—"

"I could go down on you in a more comfortable environment, like on my sofa or in my bed."

Christopher responded by pulling the gear shift down, but the truck lurched forward when he hit the gas instead of rolling backward. He engaged the brakes and smiled impishly. "You rattled me a little."

"Baby, I'm going to rattle you a whole lot."

Christopher took a deep breath and corrected his course.

"Tell me, have you ever played with your ass or asked one of your girlfriends to do it?" I asked. I took Christopher's strangled response as a no. "Is it something that interests you?"

Christopher fidgeted in his seat, and I dropped my gaze to his lap. He wasn't fully erect yet, but he was getting there quick. "Yes." His voice sounded choked and dry as if he'd been stranded in a desert for a week without water or he'd recently deep-throated a cactus.

I was having too much fun to show Christopher any mercy. "Would you prefer my finger, tongue, or dick?" I asked.

"I-I. Yes." He slowed at a four-way stop but rolled through it when he saw nothing was coming. "If I had my way, we wouldn't leave your apartment until you showed me everything."

"You know how I'm not a fan of binge-watching shows?" I asked.

He met my gaze briefly and nodded. "You prefer to savor each episode and let it settle before going onto the next one."

I reached over the console and trailed my forefinger over his denim-clad thigh. "I love anticipation." Christopher spread his legs, but I stopped shy of his groin. "Delayed gratification." I repeated my stroke, but this time brushed my pinky against his erection before retreating. Christopher sucked in a sharp breath, and I smiled. "Edging. Are you familiar with the concept?"

"Oh hell," Christopher said. "I'm not going to survive this, am I?"

I stroked upward again and squeezed Christopher's dick through his pants. "But you'll go with a happy smile on your face."

I let up on my teasing to ensure we made it back to the apartment complex in one piece, and I didn't taunt him during our brief elevator ride. I behaved until we were in my apartment with the door closed and locked and I'd stowed the leftovers in the refrigerator. Christopher was still by the front door watching me, so I crossed to him. I started to reach for his hand to lead him to my room but froze when I saw hesitation shimmering in his eyes.

"Is everything okay?" I asked.

He nodded vigorously, but I wasn't convinced. Was I moving too fast? Was he not ready for more?

"I don't think I'm very good at this."

My heart sank, but I refused to let my disappointment show. "This?" I asked.

Christopher squeezed his eyes shut. "I, uh, this is embarrassing," he said.

I stepped into his arms, and he reopened his eyes. "It doesn't need to be. Just tell me."

He swallowed hard, and I saw the struggle in his golden gaze. I almost backed off, but he said, "I've never pleased the women I took to bed. I don't think I'm good at sex." He took another shaky breath. "I think they saw my size and expected me to be, um…"

"Dominant?" I guessed.

He nodded. "I guess it's not in my nature, but I didn't realize it until I saw those assholes arguing if you were a power bottom or a…" He scrunched up his face, and I chewed on my lip so I wouldn't smile. God, could he be any cuter? "I can't remember the other term."

"A submissive bottom," I suggested.

"Yes, that's it." He tilted his head. "You read the comments on your channel?"

"No, but now I know you do." Christopher blushed, and I pressed a lingering kiss to his mouth. Joy was building inside me, and I was afraid it would bubble out of me in a giggle. I didn't want this beautiful man thinking I was laughing at him. "I'm just familiar with both the terms. This type of debate is pretty common."

"Um, which are you?"

"Definitely a bossy bottom," I said. Christopher scrunched up his nose adorably. "Same as a power bottom."

Because I was still pressed against him, I felt the tension fade from his body. I dropped my hand and ran the backs of my fingers along his erection. "Does that turn you on?"

His smoldering gaze was the only answer I needed, but I waited to hear the words. "So much." He licked his lips. "I've watched bossy bottom porn and imagined you ordering me to please you and…" A hard shudder rippled through him. "And now you know about my internet search history."

I grabbed his arm and tugged him toward my bedroom. Clothes, socks, and shoes came off between kisses and gentle caresses. My excitement amped up every time Christopher sucked in a breath or I felt need ripple through him.

"Sit on the edge of my bed and spread your legs," I said. "I want to choke on your dick."

Christopher looked momentarily horrified. "Just want to gag a little. Trust me, I love it and so will you."

He sat on the edge of my bed and spread his legs. I grabbed a pillow and dropped it on the floor between his feet. I knelt on the pillow and ran my hands up his hairy thighs and brushed them over his stomach. So strong and masculine and all mine. I leaned forward and nuzzled my face against his belly hair. "I love this so much."

"I wasn't sure if you liked it and almost shaved."

I jerked my gaze up to his. "Don't you dare."

Christopher swallowed hard and nodded. I rewarded him by sucking his left nipple into my mouth. He inhaled sharply, and I pulled back. "Not every guy likes this. Feel good?"

"So good."

I sucked it again but harder while rolling the other nipple between my thumb and forefinger. Christopher slid the hand of his injured arm into my hair and held my face against his chest. I sucked, nibbled, pinched, and rolled until he cried out my name. I pressed a kiss to his mouth and inched lower, kissing a path down his strong chest and stomach. I dipped my tongue into his belly button, then buried my nose in his trimmed pubes. His hand tightened in my hair, and I lifted my head to meet his gaze. I kept my eyes locked on his as I licked a path from his taut balls to the leaking head of his dick. I swirled my tongue once around the crown before wrapping my lips around his cock and taking him down to the root.

"Fuck!" he roared loud enough to wake the dead. I kept his cock buried deep and swallowed around the head, gagging just a little on his girth. The thick vein running the length of his dick pulsated against my tongue, and I figured he was already close to spilling down my throat. I pulled back slowly, easing his cock free one inch at a time. It smacked against his belly with a wet plop. I longed to give him a blow job while pegging his prostate but decided to wait until we got the first-time jitters out of the way.

"Lie down on your back," I said, then reached into the nightstand drawer to grab the supplies while he got into position.

I crawled up the length of his body, only pausing to drop a few kisses, until I straddled his hips. Christopher reached for me and pulled me down onto his chest for a long passionate kiss. "I can't wait until your shoulder heals enough so you can pin me down and take me."

Christopher wrapped his good arm around me and rolled to reverse our positions. He supported his weight on his good hand. "Like this?"

"Hell yes," I said, lifting my legs up and around his waist. "Now kiss me."

And he did, alternating between teasing, soft kisses and animalistic ones. The constantly changing tempo amped up my desire until I nearly forgot about being bossy.

I pulled back from the kiss and retrieved the lube. "Squeeze a little on your fingers and tease my pucker. Swirl it around the rim to wake up the nerve endings and ease the tip of your finger in to stretch it a little." Christopher's brow furrowed in concentration as he followed my guidance. I gasped and arched my back when he slipped just the tip inside my ass. "A little deeper. Slide your finger along the wall until you find my prostate."

"How will I know when I find it?" A moment later he let out a soft "Oh" when he found the spot. "There?" He pressed against my prostate and made my eyes roll back.

"Yes! Do it again."

Christopher pressed harder and chuckled when incoherent mumbling released from my lips. "You like that?"

"So damn much. I could come with the right pressure."

"Show me," Christopher said, rubbing the pad of his finger against the gland.

My cock jerked and leaked. "Fuck yeah. Just like that. Now give me two fingers."

Christopher slowly pulled back, added more lube, then eased two digits inside me, pegging my prostate like a pro.

"Three," I whispered hoarsely.

Christopher retreated, lubed, and sank three thick fingers inside my greedy hole. When he hit my gland, it felt like fireworks burst inside me. My balls drew tight, and my breath snagged in my throat as my cock jerked and splattered cum all over my stomach. I glanced up at Christopher and caught the wonderous, rapt expression on his face as he continued fingering my ass until the last drop fell.

"And now you roll a condom on your dick and fuck me."

Christopher deftly suited up and positioned his dick at my entrance. I drew my knees to my chest and wrapped my arms around my thighs to minimize the risk to his shoulder. It took him a second to line up just right, but then he pushed inside me. Usually, I didn't like anal sex after an orgasm, but I'd wanted to be claimed by this man from the moment I first set eyes on him. I craved the pressure and fullness of having him own me.

He stopped once the head of his dick stretched me wide. "This okay?"

"Perfect. Fuck me with that big dick. You won't hurt me."

Holding my gaze, Christopher snapped his hips forward, giving me just what I wanted, then continued to drive into me as his climax swelled. I kept my eyes locked on his face, memorizing every sign of euphoria—the snarled lips, blown pupils, and flushed cheeks. He dug his fingers into my ass cheeks and sped up, driving faster and harder until his big body stiffened and his dick pulsed as he filled the condom.

I released my legs and let them fall to the sides of Topher's hairy thighs, and he lurched forward, managing to catch himself with his good arm before he landed fully on top of me.

"Remember my ideal weight?" I asked.

Christopher eased down and buried his head in my neck. I ran my hands up and down his back and kissed his sweaty temple as he panted against my skin.

"Can I stay?" he asked.

I tightened my hold around his back. "Just try and leave."

Christopher chuckled, lifted his head, and smiled down at me. The exhausted joy in his golden gaze made my heart swoon because I'd put that expression there. "I don't think I could walk on these legs if I tried."

"You know full well what happens when you share a bed with me," I warned.

Christopher's smile turned naughty. "I'll be ready."

I lazily stroked his back and stared into his eyes. "I want to feed you cannoli cake in bed."

"Best date ever," Christopher said.

"And then you're going to tell me how long you've been watching my YouTube channel." He buried his head in my neck again.

"Do I have to?"

His pouty voice made me smile. "Yes. And while you're at it, you can finally admit you watched my season on *The Next Face in Fashion*."

Christopher lifted his head. "Fine, but you need to delete that Grindr app off your phone."

"Already did," I confessed. I raked my feet over the back of his legs. "I won't be needing it ever again."

CHAPTER FIFTEEN

Christopher

I WOKE TANGLED UP IN JULIAN THE NEXT MORNING. I'D NEVER BEEN a cuddler before meeting him, but now I struggled to sleep without him wrapped around me. Recalling my promise, I strummed the opening chords to "Collide" on Julian's warm skin. The first few lines of the song were my all-time favorite lyrics, and now they were even more special since I was living them.

Julian stretched and yawned as I played the intro, only lifting his head to look at me when I sang the first line in my sleep-roughened voice. He propped his chin on my chest and smiled. A dark curl fell over his forehead, and his green eyes shone brightly in the early morning light. By the time I reached the first chorus, the sleep had faded from my voice, and I sounded less froggy.

Julian stared at my mouth while absently drawing a heart against my skin as I sang. I paused to kiss him, needing to taste the smile curving his lips.

"Keep singing," he commanded once I pulled back.

"Making me sing for my breakfast?"

Julian's smile grew dirty. "Something like that." He swiped his tongue over my nipple, then placed a kiss over my sternum. "Keep singing," he repeated.

I sang the following line, and Julian inched lower and dropped another kiss. We continued the pattern until Julian's head hovered over my crotch. My words faltered when he ran a hand over my belly hair and growled, but Julian incentivized me to keep singing by nipping my inner thigh. At the top of the second chorus, Julian pressed his nose against my skin and inhaled deeply. I responded by pulling my feet closer to my ass and parting my thighs to give him better access to everything. My breath hitched and my brain froze when Julian swiped his tongue up the length of my erection and circled it around the leaking head. My tormentor licked his lips, leaving them shiny and oh-so tempting.

"Keep singing," Julian whispered huskily.

"I forget where I was."

"Then start at the beginning," he replied.

So I did, and Julian sucked my right nut into his mouth. He let it slide free to nuzzle his nose between them before cupping and lifting my sac. Julian kept his gaze locked on mine as he pressed his open mouth to my taint and sucked with the perfect amount of pressure.

"Damn, that feels good."

Julian lifted his head and grinned. "I know, but I don't recall that being part of the song." He shifted the rumpled covers around to find the bottle of lube we'd tossed aside and forgotten during our second round of sex after confessions and cake. "Keep singing."

I sang while Julian coated two fingers with lube. The next line came a little shaky when I felt the cool liquid against my pucker for the first time. Julian circled around and around the rim, awakening nerve endings I never knew existed. The tight ring of muscle seemed to have a heartbeat of its own, quivering and pulsing with the new yearnings

Julian brought out in me. I somehow managed to serenade him, though the words sounded breathless and out of rhythm.

Julian's finger, long and slender like a pianist's, pushed inside me. The burn was a little much at first, but the delicious friction against my nerve endings made me forget. Julian played me like a classically trained musician, and I fell deeper under his spell. He nudged me to sing a few times as he worked his finger back and forth. But when he pegged my prostate, I abandoned all attempts at singing to groan and grunt my pleasure.

"Christ, do that again," I begged.

Julian pulsed his finger against the gland, and I understood how he could come from that alone. Then he sucked the head of my dick into his mouth, sliding down the entire length until his nose nestled in my pubic hair, and nailed my prostate again. My orgasm ripped from me, flooding his mouth. I would've apologized for not warning him if I weren't too busy rubbing out my pleasure against his tongue. Julian groaned and swallowed everything I gave him and let my cock slide free from his mouth. Saliva and cum clung to the corners, so I swiped my thumb over his lips, then fed it back to him.

I crooked my finger, and Julian crawled up my body, stopping to straddle my waist. I fisted his cock with my right hand, using his pre-cum to work the length up and down. I was just about to urge Julian up higher so I could give him a blow job too, but he stiffened against me and painted my chest and chin with his spunk.

Laughing, Julian leaned forward and licked his essence off my face before kissing me deep and long as if we didn't have a care in the world or anywhere else we needed to be. Eventually, we separated to breathe, and Julian rested his head against my good shoulder. I thought of how far we'd come in just a few weeks.

"About last night," I said.

Julian lifted his head and arched a brow. "Yeah?"

"It was the best of my life."

Julian's bright smile threatened to burn my retinas. "For me too." He kissed me until we were breathless again. "And now I owe you breakfast. I have toast or instant oatmeal."

"I'd take you to breakfast, but I want to talk to Chief Mendoza before everyone arrives. I'll settle for coffee and toast. Maybe a quick shower together."

"Deal," Julian said as he eased out of my embrace.

I reluctantly followed, and we worked together to make a simple breakfast.

"This fancy cinnamon honey butter elevates the toast a little," Julian said after he chased a bite with a swig of coffee.

I set my empty mug in the sink, then kissed his lips. "I'd eat dry cardboard if it meant sharing more mornings like this with you."

Julian blinked for a few seconds before reaching out and pinching my bicep hard.

"Ouch!" I said, rubbing the afflicted spot.

"Just checking. Not dreaming."

Knowing time was of the essence, I didn't explore Julian's body the way I wanted to as we shared a shower, but I did snag the loofah from his hand and wash his back and sweet ass. Julian spun around and took it back.

"You'll be late," he said and urged me back under the spray to wet my hair. He knew about the significance of the meeting because I'd told him about the task force during confessions and cake. In my mind, whatever affected me also impacted Julian. I wouldn't make potentially life-changing, or even life-threatening, decisions without his input, and he made it very clear he supported my decision.

Less than ten minutes later, he walked me to his apartment door. Wearing my clothes from the previous day wasn't appealing, so I borrowed a towel and wrapped it tightly around my waist. With my balled-up clothes tucked under my sling, I used my good hand to cup Julian's head for one hell of a goodbye kiss.

"Go while you still can," he said breathlessly.

I pulled open the door and nearly ran into Mrs. Johnson and her dog, Phineas. She startled but smiled when she noticed Julian in a robe and me in a towel. "My, my, my. It's about time."

"See?" I told Julian. "Everyone got it before I did."

"Even my dog knew before you," Mrs. Johnson quipped.

Julian laughed and disappeared inside his apartment while I wished Mrs. Johnson and Phineas a good day. Harper's door opened just as I aimed the key at the lock. Coy Beaufort jolted, then grinned sheepishly. I would've tried to scowl menacingly if not for my state of undress.

"Better not have used my cup," I said as we passed each other.

Coy just laughed and headed down the hallway. I shut the door and found Harper watching the exchange with a raised brow.

"You're not going to lecture me or warn me away?" she asked.

"Would it work?"

"Nope," she said.

I smiled as I poured a second cup of coffee into my favorite mug. "Unless the two of you would get a real thrill out of it. I can catch up to Coy and threaten to beat his ass." Harper rolled her eyes, and I dropped a kiss onto her cheek on my way to get dressed. "I trust you."

She wiped away my gesture and rubbed her hand on her sleep shorts. "Yeah, well, I don't trust where your mouth has been. I borrowed your laptop last night, and your browser history was an eye-opener."

I didn't feel an ounce of remorse or embarrassment. "A man doesn't go into uncharted territory without doing some research first."

"And were you successful?" she called after me.

"I'm sure you'll be the first to know," I replied. I knew firsthand how much Harper and Julian loved to dish about their lives. I hoped Julian really laid it on thick and strung her along before telling her to mind her own damn business.

"Not if I can help it!" Harper yelled.

Yet I knew without looking that she was already texting Julian.

The MCU bullpen was empty, but Mendoza's door was open. As I approached his office, warm laughter came from within, and I realized the chief had an early morning visitor. I didn't want to interrupt, so I walked over to Coy's desk and left an immature but harmless note on his memo pad. Footsteps reverberated off the floor, and I jerked my head up in time to see Abe Beecham, Bryan County sheriff and Mendoza's best friend, step out of the chief's office. He wore a navy-blue polo shirt with the Explorer Academy logo on the chest. In addition to being a sheriff, Beecham oversaw the statewide program for future law enforcement officers. Since our academy was knew, his presence didn't come as a surprise, but he clearly hadn't expected to run into me at such an early hour.

"Morning, Sheriff," I said, extending my hand.

His big paw dwarfed mine. If I was built like a powerful lion, then Beecham resembled a Sherman tank. It wasn't often I ran into men that made me feel small.

"Good to see you, Carnegie."

After a few minutes of small talk, Mendoza appeared in his doorway. In contrast to his best friend, the chief was average height with a lean, sleek build. And it wasn't the only difference that morning. Where Beecham looked calm and cool, Mendoza looked hot and bothered. His hair was mussed in a way I'd never seen it and his mouth looked swollen and...well kissed? I volleyed my gaze between the two men. Was there something besides friendship going on here? Beecham lifted his hands and mimed straightening his hair. Mendoza narrowed his eyes at his friend and ducked back inside his office.

"Are we still on for lunch?" Beecham called out.

"Not after that stunt," came the surly reply from Mendoza's office.

Beecham chuckled and headed for the exit. "Be ready at noon," he called out.

I leaned my hip against Coy's desk to give Mendoza a few moments to tidy up. He didn't keep me waiting long. Informing Chief Mendoza of my decision to join the task force took less than a minute.

"You made the right decision, Carnegie," he said. "I'm proud of you."

"Thank you, sir."

"This goes without saying, but I'll remind you to maintain the utmost discretion." Mendoza lifted his right brow and added, "About all things."

"Of course, sir," I replied. "You can count on me."

Afterward, I headed downstairs to say so long to Sawyer and Holly before driving to the district attorney's office."

"I'm grateful you decided to join us, Detective Carnegie," Babineaux said, shaking my hand. "You'll be a wonderful asset to the team."

After our brief conversation, her assistant, a petite redhead named Daphne, provided me with a badge that would get me through secured areas of the building. Then she showed me to a small room where the other task force members waited. I recognized two of the faces, Rocky Jacobs, the private investigator and *Sinister in Savannah* podcaster, and Chet Dawson, a local defense attorney who frequently made headlines. I shook hands with Rocky, introduced myself to Chet, then met the rest of the team. Hilda Rochester was a former federal prosecutor from a neighboring district, and Joshua Berkley was a retired deputy from CCSD. The mood in the room was high, and I could tell everyone was pleased to participate.

After introductions, Daphne led our group to a secured conference room where rows of boxes stacked five or six high lined the entire room. My excitement fizzled a little when I realized the scope of our probe, and I wasn't the only one who looked like a deflating balloon.

"How many cases are we reviewing?" Chet asked, breaking the silence.

"One hundred and sixty-five," Daphne replied.

"Is it possible some of these people are no longer incarcerated?" Berkley asked.

"No, sir," Daphne replied. "I ran the list of names and confirmed the people represented in these files are still incarcerated." Daphne walked to the large conference table in the center of the room and picked up a stack of folders. "DA Babineaux has put together a checklist to help streamline the process. She wants Jacobs, Carnegie, and Berkley to focus on the initial investigation and Dawson and Rochester to scrutinize the legal cases. She wants your findings documented on these review forms," she said, pulling out a sample document from one of the folders and holding it up. "The docs need to be signed and initialed where she's indicated and placed in each case file. Our primary focus is to identify instances where there's evidence of malicious prosecution, including but not limited to coercion, witness tampering, Brady violations, and building litigation on unreliable witnesses like jailhouse snitches. But we're casting the net wider and looking at the initial investigations by SPD or CCSD and the follow-up performed by our in-house investigators once the case was handed off to us. In instances of wrongful conviction, it's likely the rot has seeped through the entire case, not just one side or the other. We also want to know if there's a consistent pattern of collusion between certain parties." Daphne took a deep breath. "You don't hear about a prosecutor's office going to these extremes very often, but Babineaux feels it's vitally important to maintain trust with the public."

"It could cost her during the next election," Rochester said.

"That's a gamble she's willing to take," Daphne replied firmly. "We're catering a special lunch today to thank you for joining the task force."

The promise of food was enough to perk me right up. Damn, I really was an oversized puppy. I clapped my hands and rubbed them together. "Oldest cases first?" I asked. "If there is evidence of malicious prosecution, the people who have been incarcerated the longest deserve their day in court sooner."

"I agree," Rocky said.

The rest of the team agreed, and Daphne looked on happily. "You're already off to a great start," she said. "I'll leave you to it. I've already shown you where to find the coffee, vending machines, and restrooms. Lunch will arrive at noon, and I'll set it up in the conference room where we met this morning. This door automatically locks behind you, so always keep your badges on you. If you need anything else, please don't hesitate to ask."

On the outside of each box was a sheet of paper listing the case files inside. They were already sorted and stacked in chronological order, making our jobs much easier.

"Babineaux is earnest about righting any wrongs," Chet said, sounding as impressed as I felt.

"I can't believe I'm going to say this, but I hope this task force is a colossal waste of our time," Berkley said.

"Agreed," Rochester replied. "The ramifications would have a staggering ripple effect and could taint the jury pool for years." She tilted her head and sighed, "But this is the right thing to do."

"When Adam Savant comes for Babineaux, and we all know it's only a matter of time, I will proudly stand in her corner," Chet said.

"How long before word gets out about the task force?" I asked.

Chet studied me closely. "You worried about backlash?"

"Worried? Nah, I have broad shoulders." I smiled and gestured to my sling. "Even if one of them is a little busted up right now. I'm just mentally bracing myself."

"A week?" Chet guessed.

"No way," Berkley said. "I'd say a day max. Someone inside this office building will talk to a buddy at one of the police precincts or the sheriff's department. Then that person will tell everyone they know."

"Gossip spreads through the cop shop faster than the speed of light," I agreed.

Berkley laughed and said, "Only occurs faster in church pews."

Rocky nodded. "Sounds about right. It's probably happening as we speak. I bet Daphne fields calls from the press before she even has time to set up our fancy lunch."

"I agree with Rocky," Rochester replied. "Means we better get to digging through those case files."

The five of us had different review styles, so it took a file or two before we were all in sync. Babineaux had put a lot of effort into choosing a team that would feed off one another's strengths and gel really well. I expected to be bored, but I was stunned when Berkley announced it was time for lunch. The Hummingbird Café had catered a delicious meal, and I didn't think the balance of protein, veggies, and carbs was an accident. The options would keep our brains functioning at optimum performance and prevent an afternoon sugar crash.

By six, we'd worked through a dozen of the oldest cases. The team had worried it was too slow a pace, but Babineaux had been pleased with our effort.

"Thoroughness over expediency," she said. "What's the verdict on day one?"

We hadn't found any overt evidence of tampering, coercion, or malicious prosecution in the first dozen files. I wasn't surprised because Savant probably had good intentions when he first started prosecuting cases. The struggle would come later after he'd had a taste of power and had his reputation on the line.

"Great work, everyone," she said. "Daphne took a few calls from local press late this morning, so word has already started to filter through the law enforcement community. I've declined to comment at this time and will continue to delay until I have relevant data to share or something forces my hand. I don't know if your names are connected to the rumored task force yet, but if so, I'd ask you to decline to comment until I've made my first public statement." She looked at me and said, "I think this will be toughest for you since you're an active-duty police officer."

"Don't worry about me," I assured her.

"He's got broad shoulders," Rocky said, patting my good one.

"Y'all get on out of here and enjoy your evening," Babineaux instructed. "Tomorrow morning will be here soon enough."

"Anyone care to get a drink?" Rochester asked once we exited the building.

"I'm in," Chet responded.

Rocky was also in, but Berkley and I both had prior commitments. The SPD softball team was taking on the Savannah Fire Department, our biggest rival. I didn't want to compare the game to something as significant as the Civil War, but it would pit husband against husband when Detective Blue Jackson took the field against fireman Zeke Jackson. I couldn't play, but I could support the rest of my team. I didn't bother changing before heading to the ballpark because I didn't want to miss a second of the jawing back-and-forth between the two departments during warm-ups. The teams didn't let me down, but there was a brief cease fire when Zeke and Blue shared a sweet kiss before parting for their respective dugouts.

I sat in the bleachers behind the SPD team and cheered them on, especially when Coy hit a grand slam in the bottom of the second inning to put us on top, four to nothing. I'd wanted to show Harper how hard I was trying to get over my grudge and had recorded him at the plate for her since she was still at work for another hour. I captured his hit, the jog around the bases, and the celebration with his teammates when he stepped on home plate. I texted it to her, and she quickly responded with a heart-eye emoji.

SFD came back and tied the game over the next two innings, and the game seemed to crawl by after that, which is how I noticed a subtle shift in behavior toward me from two detectives, Eads and Everly. I first saw it between innings when they were warming up at second base and shortstop. They engaged in a lengthy conversation behind their gloves and darted frequent glances in my direction. During their subsequent at-bats, they glared at me while on deck to hit. I didn't know either of them well but had only positively interacted with them at the precinct or on the field. The only thing that had changed since the last time I'd seen them was my participation in the task force.

If someone at the DA's office leaked the info to people at SPD, it wouldn't be at all surprising if an officer or two took it upon themselves to figure out who was participating. Nothing about my truck was notable. It was basic silver with a Bulldog sticker on the back window like so many of the thousands of trucks in Georgia. But the task force had exited the prosecutor's office together, making us easy to identify. It was also likely someone from the press had staked out the building. I'd known it was only a matter of time, so I squared my broad shoulders and waggled my fingers at the pissed-off patrolmen.

SPD pulled off a win at the bottom of the last inning when Blue dropped a base hit deep in centerfield, allowing Coy to score the winning run. By then, I was hungry and ready to see Julian, so I made a cursory round of congrats before heading to my truck.

"Yo, Carnegie," Eads called out before I got too far.

I stopped and turned to face Eads and Everly, who looked tense and ready to fight. "Do we have a problem, gentlemen?" I asked.

"Damn straight we do," Eads said.

"We hear you're working for that bitch in the DA's office who wants to overturn convictions and set child rapists and murderers free," Everly added.

I fought the urge to roll my eyes. Of course they'd use the types of offenders that would strike fear in the heart of the citizens and make the biggest splash in the press. "Well, you heard wrong, fellas."

Everly cocked a brow. "So you aren't working on the witch hunt that's masquerading as a task force?"

"Or are you disputing its purpose?" Eads asked.

"Take your concerns to Mendoza," I replied.

The two men moved closer, and their fists balled up as if ready to strike.

I detected movement on my left, but I didn't dare take my eyes off the threat in front of me. Coy put himself between me and the advancing detectives. "I know you two assholes aren't about to start a fight with Carnegie in front of all these witnesses."

Eads slapped Everly's chest and said, "He's right, buddy. We'll wait and have this chat at a more private time."

"I don't fucking think you will," Blue said, stepping up beside Coy. "My boo said you need to take your petty arguments up with the chief, and I suggest you listen."

Everly looked from Coy to Blue and shook his head in disgust. "You two are okay with him helping the DA release convicts onto the street?"

Blue crossed his arms over his chest and stepped closer to them. "If Mendoza let Babineaux borrow Carnegie, then he believes in her mission too. That's good enough for me."

"The question is," Coy said, "what's got your jock straps in a twist? Worried your policework won't look so good under a microscope?"

Eads stepped up until he was chest to chest with Coy. "You calling me dirty?"

"Are you?" Coy asked.

Blue stepped up so he was shoulder to shoulder with Coy. "And are you calling our boy a traitor?"

I'd had plenty of experience breaking up fights between my sisters, and I called on it now to defuse the situation. "Guys, look," I said, "I can't comment about the situation, but I'm insulted you think so little of me. I don't know who's gotten in your head, but they don't know shit about me or my character. If you won't take my word for it, then, again, I encourage you to talk to Mendoza."

Everly looked somewhat mollified, but Eads did not. Luckily, Everly seemed to be the leader in the duo. He clapped his friend on the shoulder and suggested they get a beer to celebrate their win. Eads reluctantly agreed, and the two walked away without an apology or even a directive to kiss their ass. Blue and Coy turned around to face me once they were sure the threat had passed.

"Thanks for having my back," I told them.

Blue smiled broadly. "Always, boo."

"If anyone is going to bust your chops, it's going to be me," Coy teased.

Chuckling, I clapped him on the shoulder. "Fair enough. I'd still like to buy you both a round of drinks. Maybe dinner too."

"Sounds great," Blue said, "but maybe we steer clear of Joe's tonight. I'm sure that's where Beavis and Butthead are headed."

I was still laughing at his reference when Zeke came over and joined us.

"Everything okay?" he asked, looking between Blue, Coy, and me.

"It's great. I was just offering to buy dinner and beer. How does Pearl's sound?" Just mentioning the saltwater grille's name made my stomach growl. I checked my watch and saw that both Harper and Julian should be done for the day. I looked at Coy and said, "Let's see if Harper and Julian want to join us. We'll make it a triple date."

"I love the sound of that," Coy said as he retrieved his cell phone from his bag. I suspected what he truly loved was any opportunity to spend time with my sister, especially now that I knew their big secret.

Julian answered on the first ring. "Hey, handsome," he said. "I'm almost home. Have you eaten yet?"

"No, that's why I was calling," I said and invited him to join the group. "Coy is checking to see if Harper wants to meet us too." Coy gave me a thumbs-up. "She's in. What about you?"

He didn't respond immediately, so I took a few steps away for a bit of privacy. "Julian, you still there?"

"Um, yeah," he said. "I'm here."

"What's wrong?"

"Nothing." I could tell by his tone that something was up, but before I could ask further, he said, "I'm just really happy."

"Because you love eating at Pearl's?" I teased.

176

He laughed. "Yeah, that's it. What time do you want to meet?"

"Now," I said.

His laughter sounded lighter this time. "Hungry?"

"Starved."

"I'm on my way. Oh, wait. Harper's calling on the other line. I bet she wants to ride together. I'll rendezvous with her, and we'll meet you there."

"Sounds good." We said goodbye and clicked off.

"They're going to meet us at Pearl's," I said. The four of us headed to the parking lot, where we went our separate ways.

The restaurant was busy even for a Wednesday night, but the hostess told us it wouldn't be long before a table was free. Julian and Harper had ordered a Lyft and arrived not long after us. I soaked in the gorgeous picture my boyfriend made in his slim-cut gray pants, pale gray dress shirt, and a purple-and-gray corset vest. Those colors made his green eyes pop even more. Julian smiled warmly when I introduced him to Blue and Zeke. He'd already met Coy, which didn't surprise me at all. His devotion to my sister wouldn't allow her to date someone he hadn't vetted first.

I put my arm around Julian's waist, pulled him against me, and kissed the top of his head. The smell of his shampoo and soap eased the tension leftover from the confrontation at the ballpark, and I relaxed into the embrace he returned.

The hostess showed us to our table, and our waitress promptly took our drink order.

"I missed you today," I said softly. I'd texted him briefly at lunch, but the grueling pace the team set hadn't allowed for anything else.

Julian looked up at me and smiled. "I missed you too. Did you have a good day?"

"Mixed bag, but I'll tell you about it later," I said as our drinks arrived. I lifted my beer in a toast. "Tonight, we're celebrating friendship and loyalty."

"And kicking SFD's ass on the baseball diamond," Blue said.

Zeke snorted and rolled his eyes. "You want to sleep on the couch tonight, big guy?"

"To friendship and loyalty," Blue said. We all clinked our glasses together and took a sip.

Our steaks and seafood were delicious, but I enjoyed the laughter and camaraderie the most, which was saying something. I loved seeing how comfortable Julian was engaging with my friends. He charmed everyone at the table but none more than me, and I couldn't stop touching him as the evening wore on.

Blue and Zeke were the first to part after a brief argument about me paying for dinner. "You can pick up the tab next time," I said.

"Fair enough," Blue replied, holding his fist up for me to bump. "Keep your head high and stay on alert, boo."

"I will." I shook Zeke's hand and wished him better luck next game.

I ended up having the same argument with Coy until Harper distracted him with a kiss. They stayed until I settled the check, and the four of us left the restaurant together. I knew damn well I was looking at the future. Coy Beaufort had grown up and was madly in love with my sister. I had finally woken up and claimed my Julian.

"Hey, Toph," Harper said before getting in Coy's car.

"Yeah?"

"Maybe you should pack an overnight bag before heading to Julian's apartment for the night. You'll incite a riot or give someone a heart attack if you keep parading up and down the hallway naked."

"Across," I countered. "It was two steps, and I was wearing a towel. Your boyfriend is my witness."

Coy threw up his hands in surrender before getting into the car. I laughed because he'd already stuck his neck out enough for me. Harper blew us a kiss before lowering into the passenger seat.

Julian climbed up beside me in the cab and grinned. "So you think I'm a sure thing just because you bought me a steak dinner, huh?"

"Um, no. I just thought—"

Julian laughed before leaning across the console to kiss me. He trailed his fingers over my inner thigh and let out a sexy little growl. "I am definitely a sure thing."

Once again, I shifted the truck into drive instead of reverse. "Don't let it go to your head," I said after we shared a good laugh.

"Too late. Take us home." The impish look in his eyes warned me I was in for a wild ride once we got there.

And while I couldn't wait to experience the journey, I kept picturing us in a completely different setting than his small apartment. My mind wandered to a quaint craftsman that offered rich history for Julian and endless possibilities for the two of us. I'd rented the house on a whim because I'd wanted more space and privacy than an apartment afforded, and I fell in love with the woodwork and the abundant natural light in every room. My plan hadn't extended to furnishing the house. The meager furniture I kept in storage were hand-me-downs from my dad's man cave after he got an upgrade. They'd been good enough for my first bachelor pad, but I'd put them in storage when I moved in with Abigail. There'd only been room for my bed and dresser in Harper's spare room, so I was still paying for storage until I found another place. And now that I had, there was no way I was putting the old junk in my new house.

"Is everything okay?" Julian asked. "I'd started detailing the wicked things I wanted to do to you, and your only response was a deep scowl."

I glanced over with a wry grin. "I call bullshit."

Julian sighed dramatically. "It's true. I was giving you my best dirty talk."

"Nope," I said emphatically. "That would've brought me back from the dead, and I assure you, I'm very much alive. But you have my full attention now."

Julian shook his head. "I'm too shy to repeat what I was saying."

That made me laugh. I'd seen him act more reserved in certain company, but he was never shy.

Julian crossed his arms over his chest and huffed. "Fine, you caught me. But you were scowling. Are you thinking about those cops who harassed you?" Blue, Coy, and I had told the others about the incident over dinner, though I didn't divulge any more details than I had with Beavis and Butthead. It just wasn't my story to tell. I'd leave that to Mendoza and Babineaux when the time was right. "What were their names?" Julian asked. "Ebony and Ivory?" He started humming the song.

"Everly and Eads," I replied with a snicker. "Maybe they come together in perfect harmony, but I doubt it. And I was thinking about furnishing my new house." I grimaced. "And maybe panicking a little."

"No panicking allowed," Julian said. "Tell me your concerns, and we'll find a solution. Is it that you lack a design or theme, or are you more worried about the expense and the logistics of moving?"

"Yes," I replied.

Julian laughed. "Knowing you as I do, you'll want comfort and function over form."

"Absolutely. I'm a big man and—"

"Baby, I know that all too well," Julian said with a leer that made me blush.

"Size queen."

"No lies detected," he replied without an ounce of shame. I saw him fanning his face from the corner of my eye. "Better get the conversation back to home furnishings before I launch into dirty talk for real."

"You started it," I accused playfully.

"And I'll end it." Julian's voice was husky and rich with promise, stirring a strong reaction that still caught me by surprise. "When do you want to do it?"

"As soon as I have you behind a closed door."

Julian chuckled. "Not that. When would you like to move?"

"I should be out of the sling in two more weeks. It will take longer to regain my full strength, but I can do more than just tell people where to put things."

"We've already established I'm the bossy one in this dynamic," Julian teased. "We'll hit up estate sales and consignment shops. You'll get more bang for your buck there. You can have the items delivered directly to the house. Then you call in all the favors people owe you to help sort it out. I guarantee those broad shoulders have helped a lot of people move."

"True," I said as I found an empty parking spot at the apartment complex. I killed the engine and sighed in relief.

"Better?" Julian asked.

I reached over and cupped his face. "I'm good now."

He shook his head sadly. "Our clothes are still on, and our dicks

180

aren't touching. You're just *better* right now." He pointed to the apartment building and said, "In there, I'll make you feel *good*."

Julian kept his promise that night and over the next two weeks. Oh, the things that man could do with his body and the way he could make mine sing. But the biggest surprises came when we hit up every estate sale and consignment shop in a fifty-mile radius. Watching Julian wheel and deal had become my favorite pastime as we found the perfect pieces to fill the house without putting too big a dent in my savings. During one of our outings, an antique sewing table from the 1920s caught his eye. He'd fussed and stroked his finger over the dull wood while he got a faraway look in his eyes. "I can't begin to imagine all the types of garments and household goods this old girl would've helped create over the years."

"Do you want to get it?" I'd asked. "We can load it up on my truck tonight."

He smiled wistfully and sighed. "I don't have room for it."

But I would, so I waited and snagged a salesman once Julian was deep into bartering over the dining room set I wanted to buy. We arranged to have the dining set delivered to my house and the other salesman slipped me the receipt and assured me the sewing table would be on the truck with the other furniture pieces. I couldn't wait to surprise Julian.

When we got back to the apartment complex, there was no discussion about where I was spending the night. If I had my way, I'd never wake up without Julian again.

CHAPTER SIXTEEN

Julian

OVER THE YEARS, I HAD DEVELOPED SEVERAL SUNDAY routines focused on self-care and recharging. I discovered my all-time favorite form the first morning we woke in Christopher's new house. We'd indulged in languid foreplay in the early morning sunlight that turned into a headboard-banging good time with me on my knees, my ass in the air, and Christopher plowing into me. The only thing he'd set up, and the most important in my opinion, was his bed, which we collapsed onto, panting and laughing after we climaxed.

"We probably shouldn't linger in bed," Christopher said. "We'll fall asleep."

Usually, that wouldn't be a big deal, but Christopher was owed several favors, so there would be a lot of people showing up to help us set up his house.

I slapped his bare ass. "I'll start the coffee, and you fire up the shower."

"Put something on," Christopher said as I slid from the bed. "The curtains aren't up yet."

I laughed as I pulled his T-shirt over my head and padded to the kitchen where I'd had the foresight to dig out the coffeemaker and supplies the previous night. I started moving a little faster when I heard Christopher shuffling around because I didn't want to miss a moment of his wet, naked skin bumping into mine in the shower.

We didn't dare dawdle because the Carnegie clan was known for their punctuality. By that, I meant they arrived at least thirty minutes early. We'd barely managed to get all our clothes on before the door-bell chimed.

"They're here," Christopher said, drawing out the last word like the little girl in *Poltergeist* before darting out of the bedroom.

I followed behind him at a more leisurely pace and had just reached the doorway when my cell phone vibrated with an incom-ing text, then another and another. Clearly, someone was eager to get in touch with me, though my nearest and dearest would ei-ther be present or knew I had a busy day ahead of me. When I saw two text messages from my sister and one from my mom, I assumed they just wanted to show their support for Christopher's big move. They started their messages with warm sentiments for a smooth day, but they also dropped a link to an article about Jorja's wedding. Mom added a little note, letting me know the article included a nice write-up about the dress I'd designed. Jorja's second text was all caps and shouted that the article had gone viral and all the comments were about the dress. At first, I thought she was pissed I'd stolen her thun-der, but her last sentence set me straight.

I'M SO PROUD OF YOU! THIS COULD BE THE BREAK YOU NEED!

"Julian!" Harper called out. "We brought donuts, and your

boyfriend won't let us eat them until you come out. He can only fend us off for so long."

I tapped out quick responses to my mom and Jorja, thanking them for sharing the article with me, and set my phone down. That's when I noticed the missed notifications from my various social media accounts. The sheer volume was staggering and overwhelming, and I chose to walk away from them rather than tumble down the rabbit hole.

Harper hadn't been joking. Christopher had placed himself between the donuts and his family. Our eyes met when I entered the kitchen, and he must've sensed something was up because he abandoned his station and crossed the room to me.

"Everything okay?"

"Yeah," I said, pressing a quick kiss to his lips. "Mom and Jorja just sent me a link to an article about the wedding. I guess it included a nice write-up about the dress, and it's getting a lot of attention."

Christopher's smile was broad, putting his dimples on full display. "Congratulations. I'm so happy for you."

"Thank you. I promised them I'd read the article later and text back."

Harper appeared beside us and extended a Boston crème donut toward me. "Saved the last one for you."

"Jerked it right out of my hand," Coy said with a cute pout in his voice.

I felt bad and offered to split it with him, but he shook his head and chomped into a jelly-filled pastry instead.

Reno, Emma's fiancé, lifted his own Boston crème to toast me. "Here's to fast hands and fierce women."

After devouring an embarrassing number of pastries, we divided up tasks. Since Shelby was pregnant, I handed her the clipboard containing my master plan, which included color charts and sketches showing where everything went.

"What about the spare bedroom?" she asked. "I don't see anything about it."

"Don't worry about it," Christopher said. "I'm planning a surprise for Julian."

Of course, that triggered catcalls and wild speculation about what he planned to get up to in there.

"It's not a leather room or sex dungeon," Christopher said.

"Damn," I replied, snapping my fingers. "When do I get to find out what it is?"

"After everyone goes home."

More catcalls and suggestions followed Christopher's response, and he just smirked and shook his head. "Get your minds out of the gutter and get back to work."

Dallas, Coy, Reno, and Christopher's friends did most of the heavy lifting while the rest of us unpacked. We'd labeled the boxes by room, which made it so much easier to sort and put things away. We'd made a lot of progress by the time I retrieved my phone to order pizza. There were additional social media notifications and direct messages, missed calls, voicemail messages, and more texts from my friends and extended family on my phone.

I knew the attention was supposed to be a good thing, but those dreams no longer belonged to me. Christopher was the future my soul yearned for, but tendrils of those old dreams rose unbidden, whispering luring things in my ear. I placed our pizza order, then turned off my phone before I could give in to the temptation to read what people were saying about me.

As always, mealtime with the Carnegies was a boisterous affair filled with laughter and love. They eased the heaviness in my chest, and the sweet kisses I stole from my man during quieter moments chased my anxieties away. Plus, I had Christopher's surprise to look forward to after everyone left. When Shelby decided to take a nap after lunch, I reclaimed the clipboard and lost myself in the process of making this a perfect home for Christopher.

"Where do you want to hang the vintage guitars?" Denver asked.

"In the living room," I said, showing him the sketch.

He patted me on the shoulder. "That's going to look nice. You have a keen eye for things." The compliment moved me, but I didn't have time to dwell on it because Audrey wanted help arranging the family china in the built-in cabinet in the dining room.

"This belonged to Denver's grandmother. She gave it to us after we were married with strict instructions to pass it on to our son and his love someday."

I swallowed the lump in my throat. "Shouldn't you hang on to it for a little while longer?"

She smiled gently and shook her head. "He's finally found the right person. Trust me. A mama knows these things."

I flung my arms around Audrey and hugged her tightly. "I was a shattered mess when I arrived in Savannah, but your family put the pieces back together again."

She pulled back and cupped my face. "We'd love to take some credit, but you're the one who put in the effort. We just gave you unconditional love and watched you flourish."

"We'll have to agree to disagree about that," I said.

We worked together carefully unpacking and stacking the dishes inside the display cabinet.

"Looks like they were made to be here," Audrey said once we finished. She kissed my cheek and asked what was next on my list.

By four o'clock, we had the house set up, and the only things left to put away were his clothes and toiletries, which we could tackle on our own. Christopher and I expressed our gratitude as everyone left, and we invited them back the following weekend for a cookout.

I turned to face Christopher once we were alone. "And now my surprise."

He took my hand and led me to the guest room. Christopher opened the door, and I saw the antique sewing table I'd fallen in love with while we were shopping for furniture. My eyes misted up as I ran my hand over the worn wood.

"I originally planned to sand and refinish the table, but I thought you might prefer its original condition."

I nodded through my tears because Christopher got me. I wrapped my arms around his waist and hugged him. "I love it so much. Thank you."

He tipped my chin up and said, "Move in with me. I know it might seem soon to most, but we've been circling each other for three years. I don't want to spend a single night without you."

I threw my arms around his neck and tucked myself under his chin. "I don't want to be without you either."

We kissed for a long time before breaking apart to tackle the final task on our list—setting up the bedroom. As happy as I was, I kept glancing at my phone. Christopher must've noticed because he picked it up off the table and brought it to me.

"You've been at it nonstop today. Sit down someplace quiet and soak in the adoration your stunning design deserves." He kissed my forehead and returned to hanging up suits in the closet.

I walked out onto the front porch, eased into one of the rocking chairs, and powered up my phone. I didn't know where to start, so I read the article Mom and Jorja sent me first. My craftsmanship had received glowing praise, and the writer included several close-up photos of the handknitted lace and the meaning behind it. There was even a video added to the magazine's social media presence. My eyes bulged when I saw it had been viewed a million times already. I skimmed over the hundreds of comments and was moved by the beautiful messages. My social media accounts had gained thousands of new followers, my YouTube views were off the charts, and I had hundreds of messages stretched over my accounts. I skimmed over them again because most just expressed how beautiful the dress was, but a few asked for custom dresses for upcoming weddings.

One message stopped me in my tracks, though. It was from Jonathon Henry, my favorite designer, whom I'd met briefly during my stint on *The Next Face in Fashion*. He congratulated me on a beautiful design and said his executive assistant, Emilia Sandoval, would be in touch soon. I started to reply that I looked forward to it but stopped.

"She'd be in touch for what?" I asked, scanning the messages but not seeing one from Emilia.

I shifted to my email next and found one from Rex Hyland, one of the executive producers from *The Next Face in Fashion*. According to Rex, he was developing a reality show and thought I would be the perfect star. But the email that shook me the most came from none other than Greer Spalding.

Darling, I may have acted too hastily. Let's talk.

xoxo

I mimed jerking off until I realized I was sitting on the front porch in broad daylight. I glanced around to see if I owed anyone an apology, but no one seemed to be looking in my direction. I felt overwhelmed and put my phone away without checking the texts or voicemail messages. I lost track of how long I sat there rocking until Christopher came out with a plate full of reheated pizza and two beers.

"Everything okay?" he asked as he dropped into the rocker next to me.

I leaned forward and kissed his lips. "I'm good."

He quirked a brow. "But our clothes are on, and our dicks aren't touching. How good could you be?"

I laughed and took a sip of beer. "Are you offering good?"

Christopher turned his head and sniffed his pits. "Maybe after a shower." He studied my face intently. "Judging by your expression, you might need something besides sex."

"Said no man ever."

Christopher chuckled but reached for my hand. "Did you get a lot of proposals today?"

For a minute, I misunderstood what he meant and said, "A few."

He leaned a little closer. "Are they better looking than me?"

I remembered the attention he'd received after his stint on *CrimeStoppers*. "Not that kind of proposal."

"What kind are they?"

"I'm not sure," I replied and recapped the messages for him.

"Sounds like some of them are sorry for the way they treated you." He reached over and brushed a lock of hair off my forehead. "You should at least listen to what they have to say. That way you don't have any regrets."

"About?"

"Us," he said.

"No way," I said emphatically. "You're the dream."

"I don't want to be the one to dim your sparkle."

Christopher repeating Lulu's sage advice on the porch she loved so much was my undoing. I plopped myself in his lap, and he enveloped me in his arms.

"You make me sparkle brighter," I said. "I never expected to be this happy, and I don't want to lose what we've found."

Christopher pressed a kiss against my temple. "I'm not going anywhere, and that's a promise you can take to the bank."

CHAPTER SEVENTEEN

Christopher

I STARED OUT THE KITCHEN WINDOW WHILE WAITING FOR JULIAN and Harper to finish getting ready for our double date. I'd left Coy in the living room to watch SportsCenter while I pretended to get a drink. The past two weeks had caught up to me, and I would much rather stay home with Julian than spend a night out on the town. My guy had been gone more than he'd been home lately, traveling to Milan, Paris, NYC, and Atlanta to meet with the designers who wanted his brilliance for their fashion houses. Even when he was here with me, Julian seemed a million miles away. Plus, I'd been working long hours combing through old case files with the task force. I'd turned into quite the workaholic with Julian away, pushing myself and the others to dig deeper and keep going.

The good news was that we'd finished going through all the files.

The bad news was that there were at least ten cases we flagged for possible misconduct from both the former DA, Adam Savant, and SPD. Considering the hostility Everly and Eads had shown me, I wasn't surprised to discover Eads had worked on seven of the ten investigations. But I took no joy in handing in my report to Mendoza. The chief accepted it with solemn gratitude for my work and reminded me that my discretion was of utmost importance while he worked with Internal Affairs going forward. It was an easy promise to make.

Julian and Harper's combined laughter filtered into the kitchen from the bathroom, and a genuine smile came to my face unlike the fake ones I'd been flashing around until my face hurt. God, it was good to have Julian home.

"Toph," Harper said softly from behind me.

I hadn't heard her enter the room, so I spun around and tried for my best fake smile. Harper sighed and rushed forward, wrapping her arms around my waist and resting her head against my chest.

"It's going to be okay," she whispered. "He won't leave us." She'd said this many times over the past few weeks, but her words had started to lack conviction.

"I won't begrudge Julian the amazing opportunities he's earned nor will I be just another person who claims to know what's best for him. That's how that idiot Thad lost Julian, and I won't repeat his mistakes."

"Attaboy," she said proudly.

"Where's my guy?"

She took a step back and looked up at me. "Taking a call. He said he won't be long. Does he seem off to you?"

"A little quiet, but I'm sure he has a lot on his mind."

Julian found us in the kitchen a few minutes later. The smile on his face was tired but so beautiful.

"Can you give us a minute?" I asked Harper.

"Of course." She pecked Julian on the cheek as she passed him. "Coy and I will meet you at the restaurant." The front door closed a few minutes later, leaving the two of us alone.

Julian shifted his gaze from me to the plants lining the shelves by the windows. "You've taken good care of our babies."

I tugged him into my arms. God, he smelled so good. Like sunshine and forever.

I gently caressed the shadows under his eyes. "You look tired."

"I'm exhausted. I don't like being away from you, and I don't sleep well."

My heart soared like it only did for Julian. "That makes two of us." I brushed the soft curls back from his forehead. "We don't have to go out tonight. I can call Harper and reschedule for another time."

Julian shook his head, and I saw his determination to carry out our plans.

"Let's head out, then."

Julian nodded and followed me out to the truck. We'd decided to eat at Pearl's again, then check out the Woodstock Lounge, the new bar that had become all the rage. Harper and Julian did most of the talking during dinner, but whenever Julian's travels came up in the conversation, he changed the subject. I wasn't sure what that meant. Had he made a decision he thought we wouldn't like, or did he just want a break from thinking? Worry flashed in Harper's eyes, and I winked to let her know it would be okay.

After dinner, Julian and I held hands as we walked to the lounge. The advertisement I saw online promised live music nightly and just the thought of it perked me up. Much of my life revolved around music. Mama taught me how to listen and feel music long before she taught me how to play it. I understood the role each instrument played and would pick one to follow all the way through a song. Then I picked another instrument and replayed the song to hear it all the way through too. I would keep doing that until I cycled through all the instruments on a particular track, then I moved to the next song on the album. Melodies stirred reactions deep in my soul before I was mature enough to put a name to the emotions. Later, when I was old enough to understand, I sought music for comfort or a way to escape. There wasn't room to wallow in an emotional upheaval when playing an instrument, especially when you were part of a band. If I had a bad night on drums, I threw everyone off. So I'd lost and found myself in music time and time again.

It was no different with Julian. He was happiest when working at his drafting table or sewing machine. I'd stand in the doorway and watch him sometimes, and he'd be completely oblivious to my presence. He'd mutter things like, "Measure twice and cut once, Julian." Instead of feeling left out, I felt lucky to witness his genius and would plan all the ways I'd demonstrate it when he returned to me. And he always did. Then we'd become the mutual appreciation society of roaming hands and mouths. Julian's body was my favorite instrument, and his cries of pleasure were my favorite song.

Harmonious voices drifted on the wind, but it didn't sound like a band.

"Karaoke?" Coy asked.

Then I saw the sign on the sidewalk and pointed to it. "Open mic night."

I loved the eclectic vibe of the Woodstock Lounge as soon as we walked through the door. I took a moment to appreciate the exposed brick walls, rich wood polished to a gleam, warm ambient light, and the variety of seating. There was the expected long bar with stools and tables with chairs, but the Woodstock Lounge included pockets of intimate conversation areas that looked like miniature living rooms peppered throughout the space. On one end was a simple stage just barely large enough to fit a small band, but the wall behind it featured album cover posters spanning several decades.

Harper leaned closer to me and said, "That stage is really something."

I nodded. "It's the closest I'll ever come to singing with Joplin and Hendrix."

The next performer, a young woman, walked up on the stage and introduced herself as Stella. Everyone in the lounge responded, "Hi, Stella."

"Hello," she replied.

Stella briefly closed her eyes and took a second before launching into a moving poem about love and loss so achingly poignant that I found it hard to breathe. Her words and voice fluctuated between lyrical and soft and raw and edgy. She changed the cadence from fast to slow, matching the mood and message so perfectly. Her words conveyed the highest highs and the lowest lows of the human experience—the heartbeat and pulse of humanity.

Julian squeezed my hand, and I glanced over in time to see a tear slide down his face. I reached over and brushed it away, and he turned to face me. I leaned down and kissed him, loving the way his lips softened beneath mine. We jerked apart when the room erupted with cheering and clapping after Stella finished her poem.

"You sign up to perform over there," Coy said, pointing to a table where an older guy stood clapping for Stella as she exited the stage.

The man sat back down, picked up a clipboard, and reached for his microphone. "Caleb Newkirk is up next," he said.

"Let's find a place to sit first," Harper said, scanning the room.

Julian pointed to a shadowed corner of the lounge. "A table is open over there."

We made our way to the table as the audience clapped for the skinny redhead who stepped onto the stage. Off to the side was an impressive assortment of instruments for performers to choose from. Caleb chose a set of bongo drums and carried them to center stage.

"Hi, Caleb," the audience said, and this time we joined in too.

"Good evening." He began tapping out a familiar reggae beat before singing Bob Marley's "One Love."

I would've been happy watching everyone else perform, but Coy and Julian were insistent Harper and I sing too. I hadn't played with the band since I'd gotten injured, and I was nowhere near ready to play drums, but I'd noticed a pretty Martin acoustic guitar among the other instruments.

"Come on," Harper said, nudging me with her elbow. We gave our drink order to Coy and Julian in case the server came by while we were gone.

There were at least a dozen performers ahead of us, which allowed me to think of a song I wanted to sing.

Harper hooked her arm through mine and leaned in. "What's your game plan?" she asked.

"For?"

"Keeping Julian in Savannah."

I tipped my head to the side. "I have no desire to hold him back if his dreams are leading him somewhere else."

Harper scowled. "You're just going to let him go without a fight?"

"Hell no. I'm going to amplify his sparkle."

She blinked at me for several seconds. "I have no idea what the hell that means, but it better not include my best friend being several thousand miles away. A part of my soul will shrivel up and die."

"Your heart might ache because you'll miss us, but it will soar to new heights when you see Julian flourish."

"*Us?* What do you mean?"

I winked and said, "I guess you'll find out." I continued toward our table while she growled my name in frustration.

I dropped into the seat next to Julian and looped my arm around his shoulders. He leaned into me, and I rested my cheek against the top of his head. The server brought our drinks, but neither of us reached for them. We stayed tangled up in each other until the emcee announced it was my turn to perform.

Julian sat up, but I cupped his face before he could get too far and dropped a kiss on his lips. "This one is just for you." Julian's mouth popped open, and I still heard his soft gasp over the audience clapping.

I tore myself away from him and headed to the stage. I selected the Martin and crossed to the microphone stand.

"Hi, Christopher," the crowd said.

"Hello, everyone. Tonight, I'm going to perform 'Crazy Love' for you. Many talented singers have recorded the song over the years, but my favorite version is by Van Morrison. My daddy played the album several times a week, and he'd sing the song to my mama as they slow danced. I hope you'll allow me some liberties to change the pronouns around a little because the person who holds my heart is the most beautiful man in the world."

There were a few catcalls and cheers, and I let them die down before I strummed the opening melody for the song. I kept my gaze locked with Julian's from the first word to the last, hoping to convey just how much he meant to me. The world around us faded into oblivion until it was just us, so the clapping afterward was jarring and caught me by surprise. I thanked the crowd for their warm reception, then replaced the guitar on the rack.

"Attaboy," Harper said when she passed me on her way to the stage.

Julian stood up when I approached, and I took him into my arms and kissed him hard. The people around us clapped and cheered, but I didn't know if they were applauding us or Harper. I pulled back when I felt his lips tremble under mine. His green eyes glistened with unshed tears, and I couldn't tell if he was upset, happy, or confused.

I gripped Julian's hand and tugged him after me. "We'll be back in a few," I tossed over my shoulder to Coy.

"Uh-huh. Forgive me if I don't hold my breath." I was really starting to like the asshole.

Outside on the sidewalk, I pulled Julian into the doorway of the closed barber shop next door.

I brushed my thumbs under his eyes to sweep away his tears. "I didn't mean to upset you."

He shook his head. "You didn't. I'm just…"

"Confused. Overwhelmed. Unsure how to let me down easily?"

Julian scrunched up his nose adorably. "What? No. Well, maybe I was a tad overwhelmed." He tilted his head to the side. "And confused. You've been giving me mixed signals lately."

"Mixed signals?" I racked my brain for a time when I was anything but supportive. "I don't understand."

"For the past few weeks, I've discussed opportunities that could take me hundreds or even thousands of miles away from you. Instead of being sad, you've been a sexy, lumberjack-sized cheerleader like you're excited for me to leave. But at night, you hold me in your arms like you're afraid to let go. And in the lounge, you sang like you wanted the whole world to know you love me."

I stroked my hand along the side of his face. "Baby, all those things are true. I'm so proud of the opportunities you've *earned.* I hold you the way I do because I won't let you go." I brushed my nose against his. "Not without me by your side anyway. And I do want the entire world to know I love you because I do."

Julian swallowed hard. "You are willing to come with me? But you love your life here."

"I love you more. There's that old adage about letting someone go if you love them, and if they love you in return, they'll come back." I smiled and said, "I say if you love someone, you follow them to the ends of the earth if that's what it takes."

"I love you too," Julian whispered. "You make me feel like I shot for the stars and landed on the moon."

I kissed his trembling lips. "I will not be the person who ruins your dreams. I'll do whatever it takes to see them come true. Need someone to haul your luggage around like a camel? I'm your man. Need security detail to keep the crazed fans away? I'm your man. Need someone to hold you together because you feel like you're flying apart? I am definitely your man."

Julian closed his eyes and took a deep breath. A playful smile toyed at his lips when our gazes met again. "When I arrived in Savannah, I was bruised and battered. I hadn't intended to stay permanently. I was going to lick my wounds and find a way to make my mark on the world again. I still dreamed of becoming the fashion house of the South, but the longer I stayed, the quieter that dream became until I replaced it with something new. *You*, Christopher. You are the dream. The life we're building is the dream." He exhaled a shaky breath, then said, "I admit the whispers of redemption and the lure of fame enticed the person I used to be, but not for long. I remembered how toxic the fashion industry is. Right now, designers like Jonathon Henry are desperate to have me on their teams, but they'd steal my glory for themselves at the first opportunity. I gave Greer the chance to atone for ruining my reputation. I even accepted her apology, but I can't forget it happened nor do I trust that she wouldn't blackball me again if another issue cropped up. I'd fallen out of love with the industry before I moved here, but my stubborn pride wouldn't allow me to admit it. Maybe fitting grooms and prom goers into tuxedos seems like a step down, but I enjoy it. Reed is a wonderful guy, and he gives me the flexibility I need to pursue my other ventures. I assuage my creative beast by making custom clothes and content for my YouTube channel. But teaching at the college has been the highlight of my professional career. I'm blown away by the new generation of artists who put as much emphasis on saving the planet as they do on creating beautiful clothes. That's the fashion future I want to be part of, which is why I'm so thrilled by the phone call I received before we left the house."

He practically vibrated with excitement, and my heart sped up in response. "Tell me."

"The dean offered me a full-time position on the faculty at SCAD. They are adding new courses to their BFA and MFA programs and want me to teach them."

I kissed him and said, "That's wonderful news. Congratulations."

"I won't get to teach full-time until next year, but I'm so excited."

I leaned my forehead against his. "I love you so much, and I'm so proud of you."

"I love you too." He pulled back and looked up at me. "You're not disappointed we won't be traveling abroad?"

"Oh, we will for vacations and things. I will still carry your luggage and act as your bodyguard."

Julian smiled slyly and took a few steps back, pulling me out of the alcove. "Why wait when we can role play that right now?"

I chuckled as he practically dragged me down the sidewalk. "Isn't it rude to ditch Harper and Coy?"

He turned around and walked backward, his green eyes glittering with wickedness. "Do you really care?"

I tugged Julian's hand to pull him up short, then lowered my good shoulder and hoisted him over it.

"Not in the least. Let's go home."

EPILOGUE

Julian

T HE FOLLOWING APRIL, MY FAMILY MADE THE TRIP FROM ATLANTA
to watch the Carnegies perform at the Savannah Music Festival.
There was a VIP section near the stage reserved for the special
guests of the bands performing each day, so we joined Coy, Dallas, and
Reno at the Carnegie's table and feasted on steak, shrimp, corn on the
cob, coleslaw, black-eyed peas, and garlic toast while waiting for the
performances to begin.

A lanky cowboy with a broad white hat jogged onto the stage to
kick off the night, then welcomed the Carnegies to the stage. The family
band was a local favorite and received raucous applause. My eyes zeroed
in on my man, who wore dark jeans and a white tank top that showed
off his sculpted arms and perfect chest.

I leaned toward my mom and said, "Don't start throwing undergarments or rush the stage when the shirt comes off."

Denver approached the microphone and thanked the audience for the warm welcome. He introduced the members of the band, then started right in on their first set of the night. I'd seen them play dozens of times, but they never failed to amaze me. The five of them were always so perfectly in sync. They covered songs from multiple eras and genres with Denver doing most of the singing. I knew they'd each get a rotation on the various instruments and a turn at the microphone, so I wasn't surprised when Christopher stood up and walked out from behind his drum kit.

"Ohhh," Lulu said. "I bet the shirt is coming off. Wooohoooo." She looked over at me and winked. "What? You didn't say anything about me behaving. Where do you think your mama learned it?"

Mom smiled sheepishly and winked. "I spent summers with Aunt Lulu as a kid too."

When Christopher accepted an electric guitar from Denver and walked to the microphone, I forgot all about my two favorite cougars. "This song is for Julian. It's called 'Just Say Yes.'"

The waterworks started before he even launched into the Snow Patrol song. I felt everyone at the table staring at me, but I couldn't look away from Christopher as he sang to me. The rest of the Carnegies added their voices to the chorus, and they harmonized perfectly. And I knew it wasn't just Christopher asking me to join their family. When the last note faded, Christopher hopped off the stage and walked to our table.

I threw my arms around his neck and kissed him while the crowd around us cheered and the Carnegies chanted, "Just say yes! Just say yes!" into their microphones.

I pulled back and stared into the amber eyes I loved so much. "Yes!"

The End!

On December 20, 2022, Emilio Mendoza and Abe Beecham will finally stop circling around their inevitability in *Just Say When*. You can preorder your copy here.
http://mybook.to/Just_Say_When

Want to be the first to know about my book releases and have access to extra content? You can sign up for my newsletter here:
http://eepurl.com/dlhPYj

My favorite place to hang out and chat with my readers is my Facebook group. Would you like to be a member of Aimee's Dye Hards? We'd love to have you! Click here:
www.facebook.com/groups/AimeesDyeHards

OTHER BOOKS BY AIMEE NICOLE WALKER

Curl Up and Dye Mysteries

Dyeing to be Loved
Something to Dye For
Dyed and Gone to Heaven
I Do, or Dye Trying
A Dye Hard Holiday
Ride or Dye
Curl Up and Dye Box Set

Road to Blissville Series

Unscripted Love
Someone to Call My Own
Nobody's Prince Charming
This Time Around
Smoke in the Mirror
Inside Out
Prescription for Love

Welcome to Blissville Collection (Both M/M Blissville series)

Volume One
Volume Two

The Lady is Mine Series

The Lady is a Thief
The Lady Stole My Heart

Queen City Rogue Series

Broken Halos
Wicked Games
Beautiful Trauma

Zero Hour Series

Ground Zero
Devil's Hour
Zero Divergence
Zero Hour Box Set

Sawyer and Royce: Matrimony and Mayhem

The Magnolia Murders
Marriage is Murder
Killer Honeymoon

Sinister in Savannah Series

Ride the Lightning
Mr. Perfect
Pretty Poison
Sinister in Savannah Box Set

Savannah Universe Standalone Books

Invisible Strings
Bad at Love

Standalone Novels

Second Wind

Fated Hearts Series

Chasing Mr. Wright
Rhythm of Us
Surrender Your Heart
Perfect Fit

Coauthored with Nicholas Bella

Undisputed
Circle of Darkness (Genesis Circle, Book 1)
Circle of Trust (Genesis Circle, Book 2)

ACKNOWLEDGMENTS

Many, many thanks to Susie Selva for her incredibly thorough edits and to Lori Parks for her keen eye during proofreading. These ladies are consummate professionals and are an absolute joy to work with. And much love to Jay Aheer and Wander Aguiar for this gorgeous cover and to Stacey Ryan Blake for her stunning interior designs. All of you make my books sparkle and shine so beautifully—inside and out. I thank my lucky stars that I get to work with such wonderfully talented people.

Many, many hugs to Melinda James Rueter and Racheal Yunk for bravely reading my rough drafts and providing priceless feedback. Love you, ladies!

xoxo
Aimee

ABOUT
AIMEE NICOLE WALKER

Ever since she was a little girl, Aimee Nicole Walker entertained herself with stories that popped into her head. Now she gets paid to tell those stories to other people. She wears many titles—wife, mom, and animal lover are just a few of them. Her absolute favorite title is champion of the happily ever after. Love inspires everything she does, music keeps her sane, and coffee is the magic elixir that fuels her day.

She'd love to hear from you.

Want to connect? All her links are in one nifty location. Click here: https://linktr.ee/AimeeNicoleWalker

Made in United States
North Haven, CT
12 October 2022

25336998R00129